JADED PRINCESS

CORRUPT EMPIRE DUET, BOOK II

KETLEY ALLISON

Mitchell Tobias Publishing LLC
Copyright 2018

Editing by Madison Seidler
madisonseidler.com

Sign up for Ketley's newsletter to receive a FREE full-length ebook:
https://ketleyallison.com/nl-sign-up

1 / POT SHOT

THE SCAR TISSUE HURT.

Puckered and pink, it webbed across my lower ribcage. The wound was small, the size of a bullet hole, but as it healed, it stretched and bubbled across my stomach the way lava slowly lurched out of a volcano—hot, burning—until it cooled into the permanent tar that forever altered the landscape it smothered.

The black couture dress I wore didn't help, its tight lace leaving little room for breath, never mind damaged skin. It chafed at every movement, but none of it showed on my face as I smoothed out the fabric, my fingers calmly running over the itching crater that was now part of me.

I took one last sip from my champagne glass, leaving a rim of blood red as I put it down beside the bottle of Dom I'd had sent up.

I eyed my purse, but decided it wasn't needed for where I was going. I left it lying across the California king bed, its straps tangled within unmade sheets, my t-shirt and denim shorts I'd worn earlier today also hidden somewhere within the folds.

I stepped out into the hallway, the door shutting behind me with a soft click, and smoothed invisible strands away from my face, though the French twist was so tight and helmeted down, it stretched my brain.

The elevator doors slipped open as I approached, a couple exiting arm-in-arm, the woman whispering something softly into her escort's ear. They were well dressed—probably leaving the same gala I was about to enter—the woman in a tight lavender number and the man in a tux. I barely glanced at them as I walked by, but every detail imprinted into my mind. Her wayward brown curl at the nape of her neck, his Patek Phillipe watch, her Jimmy Choos, his wedding ring.

As the doors closed, I lifted my chin, hands folded, all the way down from the thirtieth floor to the lobby. My heels sparked against the tile when I exited, and I pretended not to notice the extended stares cast my way while I headed down the opulent hallway leading to the ballroom. My footsteps passed pure gold, Italian marble, antique seating areas, clean lines, and exquisite taste.

The two uniformed men standing at the gigantic wooden double doors arced them open in unison once I approached. I nodded in thanks and entered into familiar surroundings.

More rich shimmers, clear crystal, and polished silver saturated my view. A small orchestra played in one corner with rounded, silk-covered tables in the center, some with half-eaten plates and others full. Most of the guests were mingling with a few seated patrons peppered throughout. With a price tag of $50,000 a head, I'd stand up only after I ate every single thing on my 50k plate.

I arrived late on purpose, dessert already melting on the painstakingly decorated tables with plumes of white bouquets in gold vases as the centerpieces, and there wasn't time to dawdle.

I cast a wide net, scanning and dismissing the handsome, the Botoxed, the naturally beautiful.

No piercing blue eyes linked to mine, and I dismissed the sorrow as soon as it came, getting back to the task at hand.

There, in the far corner, closest to the string quartet, stood the man I wanted.

Offers of a drink, or a dance, were politely declined as I rippled through the crowd. I hadn't thought about where I would've been seated had I arrived for dinner service. Possibly I'd have been in the middle, right in the thick of it, throwing back champagne in crystal goblets as I half-listened to the speeches and stabbed my heel at wayward Ferragamos running up my leg.

Eyes, opaque brown, lifted to mine when I arrived. His smile spoke of amused recognition and he lifted his tumbler of golden liquid in a polite hello.

"Scarlet," he said—purred, more like. "How lovely to see you."

The midnight blue of his expertly tailored suit somehow deepened his gaze.

"Dominic," I said.

Dom's companion, a stunning redhead in emerald—both in fabric and jewels—flicked her attention to me for about a second, then discreetly stepped aside and away, joining another crowd.

"I was about to write you off," Dom said as he slipped his arm through mine.

"You should know my habits by now," I replied, allowing him to escort me behind the orchestra. The skilled slide of horse hair against catgut was our percussion as we walked toward a carved wooden door hidden from view from the opulent guests behind us. I recognized "Clair de Lune."

"After you." Dom swept out an arm.

We were in another hallway, and soon a secret elevator, opening to a cavern I assumed was for VIPs hoping to escape cameras, fans, and one-night-mistakes they wanted to pretend never occurred.

Dom let me take the lead, and having done this before—in another state, another city, another hotel—I pretended to know which room to aim for. It wasn't smart to ever look stupid in front of these men, even doing the simplest of tasks.

Dom's footsteps slowed, and I pricked an ear at the change, coming to a smooth halt.

"Here we are," Dom said with a curve of his lips. He swiped his entry card and we were in.

The smoke hit first, the semi-sweet char of cigars and masculine exhales. It curled unseeingly against my bare arms and tantalized my nostrils. The clinks were next, large cubes in tumblers, glass and ice clashing. Then came the suits, the tuxes and loosened bow ties, the light dew on foreheads, and the thrown back, relaxed stance of some as they handled their chairs the way I was sure they handled their mistresses.

"A seat's waiting for you at table two," Dom said near my ear.

No music softened these walls, nor even a stray voice. Every sound, every tic, muted in this room, save for the satisfying *clack* of clay chips on felt tables.

I followed Dom's direction and took the last remaining empty chair at the second of five tables. Seven men sat around me, and somehow, they managed to make this section even quieter once I entered their crosshairs.

"Buy-in's twenty-thousand, honey," a man directly across from me said.

My suppressed eye-rolls were long overused, and so I offered him a wink, then deftly sank my fingers into my cleavage and pulled out a roll of hundreds. Running my tongue across my top lip, I unsnapped the elastic and let the Washingtons fan out before I laid them onto the stack in the center.

His swallow was his only tell of insult.

The dealer had already collected my buy-in and replaced the

cash with chips. I ran my finger across a stack of them before sitting back.

My mark was two men to the left. Mostly muscle, carved from the coal brought up from mines and an Italian heritage, he sat with confidence, providing a one-nostriled snuffle every time he had a bad hand. It wasn't obvious, a quick scrunch that, had I not been keeping him in my periphery, I wouldn't have noticed. Now that I had, I used it to my advantage with large calls and virtually zero checks.

Neri Sebastiani paid me no mind as he focused on his cards. He remained unflinching at my large bets and, when it ended up the two of us on a hand, he used the continued monotone he reserved for cocktail waitresses and dealers alike.

I wasn't doing well. In fact, I was sucking astronomically. This wasn't normal, but tics didn't dare mar my expression. Quirks of the lip were far from appearing as I continued down the river, becoming brash, utilizing my confidence, until all I had left was $500.

Out of $20,000.

Soon, that too was gone. I allowed myself to take a $5,000 credit from the house, and six hands later, I also blew through that. I gestured for another $5,000.

The dealer side-eyed me, and if the others could literally smile with their gazes, they would've. *Fresh meat*, they were thinking.

"I thought she was meant to be a challenge," I heard the man beside me say. A middle-aged white guy dressed in tailored precision, with his fly undone. "But she's just another of Dom's fish."

"You know who I am," I said loudly to the dealer. His thin beak of a nose turned up at me like he was a butler at Buckingham Palace. But he did as I asked and stacked two columns of chips in front of me after nodding to a man in the shadows with his laptop open.

Thirty minutes later and despite the two loans, I wasn't able to beat Neri or any other man at this table. This was a record for me.

After another hour, I found myself $40,000 in debt. If I continued to play, I'd only put myself further in the hole with the House, which was the last position I should be in. Dom collected money owed, and he did it hard. You did *not* want to be on the chum end of the loan sharking business.

The gut-swirl of disappointment was brutal, but I tipped my head and said, "It's been real, boys."

"There's no need to exit gracefully yet. You have two hundred left," Neri said in a low, buttery voice. The first time during this entire night he'd addressed me.

He had a light African accent. Rumor had it that, while his father was Italian, his mother was from Kenya, and she taught him the meaning of protecting family. If that meant using your bed post as a spear or your blanket as a garrote, you always made sure to stand in harm's way for those you loved.

I paused halfway between rising, understanding the note of warning. With $200 left in chips, I couldn't simply forfeit. There was an old saying in poker: *all you need is a chip and a chair*. I had less than the small blind left, but I was still forced to put it up and go into a hand, because in this next round, I was the small blind.

This made me look *very* stupid.

"Small blind is five hundred," I replied. I clearly couldn't afford it.

Neri lifted his chin. "Perhaps you have something else to offer in addition to the two hundred you have left."

I sat back in the velvet chair and crossed my legs, mimicking the move I so carefully perfected a few hours earlier in my hotel room. The slit of the dress fell open, showing a line of calf muscle. "What did you have in mind?"

I had no car in my name, and definitely no house or other assets. All I had was my denim shorts and knock-off Chanel purse thirty floors above. Any money I made was reinvested to protect my cover. This dress was a rental.

The rest of the table remained silent, some attention on my cleavage, some on my legs, but most were focused on Neri.

Neri puffed at his cigar, his full lips curling over the tobacco leaf. His silence left me enough time to notice that, while his bowtie had been undone about an hour ago, his clavicles sparkled with the sweat of mental effort.

He let out a smoke-filled exhale before he said, "You."

I lifted an eyebrow. "Pardon?"

"You can offer yourself into the pot."

I stifled a laugh. This long in the business, I should've shown surprise, but honestly, this was the least of what I'd been propositioned.

I'd heard about Neri's predilections, his weakness for young, blond women. He liked them so much, it usually didn't take more than $50,000 to get an unsuspecting woman to say yes. All cash. The balm to all our humanly woes.

"You're kidding," I said.

Neri tapped his cigar. "Do I strike you as a man who jokes?"

"You'd like me to whore myself out."

"If you want to say it that way, then fine. But if it means you stay in the game, that is your choice." He leaned forward, cigar tilted between two fingers. "I can see it in you."

The men around us weren't about to argue against Neri's wishes. What Neri said, he meant, and anyone contradicting him usually lost at least a nail bed.

"Play with all you've got," Neri said with a smile. His teeth flashed white.

"I believe I have." I gestured to the pot, now empty. "And I went into the red."

"So, then." Neri flicked ash into the ashtray. "Go into the black. The unknown."

My lips parted. Neri was closer to the truth than he could've imagined. I loved this room, these cards, the *money*. I wanted it all, and to stay in the game, I had to risk it all. At least, everything that remained.

Mumbles came from the tables around us, the clatter of drinks hitting trays numbing my ears as Neri's proposition snaked its way over my moral compass. My chair was jostled by someone walking by. A muffled apology by a familiar voice followed, but I ignored it.

"Only for one night," I said through the ringing in my ears. Then, to further add concrete to my words, I said, "I'll put myself into the pot."

"There we have it." Neri splayed out his hands, grinning wide. He settled his cigar on the ashtray.

The rest of the players weren't nearly as blasé. They sat, stunned, until Neri's gentle warning of "play, play," had them throwing their chips into the center.

I was given two tens—the ten of clubs and the ten of hearts.

The men placed their bets, and I did as well.

The flop came down: a ten of spades, ace of spades, and king of diamonds. I inwardly grinned—not daring to do anything outwardly. This made me ahead in the hand, since I now had three tens.

Another round of betting commenced, four men folding, and another turn came. The four of hearts, a meaningless card for this hand.

The remaining men folded, all except for Neri. I didn't have to put anything in the pot, since figuratively, I was in there. I didn't fold. A light sheen of sweat coated my brow, but I refused to draw any attention, instead remaining impassive, bored. I had a strong hand. My chances of taking the pot was high. I shouldn't be nervous. I had all of this handled.

The final card turned.

Five of spades.

My heart plummeted. The urge to brace against the table and vomit was strong, the desperation to heave even more so. But placidly, delicately, I showed my hand.

Calculations streamed through my mind, probabilities of the cards Neri could hold, the hand he could have.

Neri wasn't one to brag or smile. Ivory flashed between his lips, the quickest showcase from a winner I'd ever seen. He had the king and queen of spades.

A flush.

"So."

I looked up from my spread and into Neri's sharp gaze. My mouth was too dry to swallow.

He smiled. "It looks like you're mine."

I couldn't believe what I'd done. I'd just played myself. *Literally*.

"You may leave," Neri said, wagging his fingers my way. "I will call you when I would like to begin your services."

I stood on shaky legs, the heavy lace of my gown swinging against my ankles. There wasn't any point in giving this man more information as to where I could be found. Before I'd entered this room, he'd have known where I was staying, how much I had in my bank account, my passport number, and my social security information. He was in charge of this room, this hotel. This city.

"Yes," I said, demure, avoiding the piteous gazes of the men around him. They were probably thinking this little girl actually wanted to take on the don. And win. At the very least, he took my pride. At worst, my body.

But there was no taking involved. I gave it all to him.

I walked away, head high, though my fingers rubbed too hard at the scar beneath my bodice, and I almost flinched. But I made it out of that room and through the gala without a pitch in pace, and with blurred vision I rode the elevator to my floor and silently padded through the carpeted hallway, my heels spearing nothing but cotton.

Digging around my boobs, I found my room key, swiped my door open, and entered into the darkness.

"You are *fucking* out of your mind."

I startled. Might as well have clutched my figurative pearls when the voice spoke from my bed, his form in muted glow from the floor-length windows that allowed Los Angeles to enter the room.

I covered up my surprise by pulling off my heels. "Next time, don't elbow me in the neck when you pretend to trip over my chair."

"You refused to wear your earpiece." Kai flicked on the bedside light. "It was my last-ditch warning to get you to realize your moron bet and get out of there."

"Well, here I am instead." I peeled off my dress, clad only in my underwear as I strode to the bathroom to wash off my make-up. I left the door open because I assumed Kai would just break it down if I tried to lock it.

"What possessed you?" he asked, following me to the edge of the carpeting.

I made myself busy rifling through my cosmetics bag, daring a glance at the mirror. Kai's mouth was grim. "You truly think Trace is here. Sharing a bunk with the Italian-Kenyan mob boss, Neri Sebastiani."

I spun around, a bright pink makeup sponge in my hand. "Is that not why you came with me? Why you let me infiltrate one of the most popular underground games around?"

"To find Trace Saxon, I know. With your talent," he continued before I could argue, "we're nearer to scouting him than we've ever been, but putting yourself in danger, *allowing* yourself to go to that psycho-killer's house without any backup, was not part of our deal. So now we have to figure out how to get you out of it."

"There's no backing out," I said, returning to the mirror. "I lost all the money, put myself in debt, and wagered the only thing I had left. My body. My choice."

"Jesus Christ." I didn't have be looking at Kai to see that realization was dawning. "You did this all on purpose."

I let my silence speak for itself.

"I should've known." Kai smacked a palm against the doorframe. "You had our guys panicking first about the earpiece you so conveniently forgot, then at your wager, meanwhile none of us figured that your massive loss was deliberate. My boss is going to *kill* us, do you understand? He's gonna lynch me, then hog-tie you, then throw us off this balcony."

"No, he won't." I snapped my bag shut, then went after my toothbrush. "The FBI is in too deep now to pull me out."

"You think?" Kai stepped inside. "None of this is worth risking your life, Scarlet."

I turned to him, face bare. "Finding New York's largest gun importer isn't worth it? Stopping the river of laced heroine flowing into the city? Preventing child prostitution? I could go on, but I feel like I've made my point." I pretended Kai didn't just glance at my stomach. "I'm worth the sacrifice."

"If I knew those were the only reasons you were doing this..."

"What?" I challenged him. "Don't trail off now."

"I'm not continuing this plan, and you're not getting any more money from me." Kai let me pass once I threw down my toothbrush. And ignored him as I unclipped my bra and threw on an oversized t-shirt.

"It's not safe," he said. "I can no longer trust you with the cash, as you so epically proved tonight. These past two years, you've become this ... this suicide bomber."

"Oh yeah?" I peered at him over my shoulder. "And who do I have to thank for that?"

Kai pretended my verbal swipe didn't hurt, but knowing him as I did, it was easy to tell when he was faking it.

He said, "You don't give a shit anymore, Scar. That's terrifying me."

"It's my business how I cope with the deal the FBI threw my way while I was still recovering in a hospital bed," I said.

"Scarlet." His voice took on a breathless reasoning, like he was unsure who he was talking to anymore. Not his friend. Certainly not a simple cocktail waitress he'd recruited to learn a few poker hands in order to get closer to a mob boss's son. "You just sold your *body* to a man who collects saber-tooth tiger's fangs to turn into knives. I don't think you're understanding the consequences of what you've done."

"I understand perfectly." I arced back the covers of the tightly-made bed and shimmied in, tossing aside the little chocolate on the pillow. "You only need to recover from the shock that I premeditated the consequences of this night. It'll ebb, and you'll realize this was our only way into Neri's games at his house. You'll sleep on it, and then loan me the money to play even deeper underground where the real gossip happens ... I promise."

"I don't give a shit about that. I won't be able to *protect* you."

"How do you think we got here? The government has no idea how to play the cash—*I* do." I tapped my chest as I leaned back on the pillows. "I'm the one who's been learning and winning and earning us a seat into the big plays."

"You've become cocky in your jaded age."

"It's taken me years to come this far." I tucked deeper into the covers and reached over to the lamp. "I'm not about to stop. Either you accept that, Kai, or I'm asking for a new supervisor."

Kai shook his head. I caught the glitter of disappointment in his eyes before I clicked off the light.

"Good night." My voice was muffled from pulling the comforter to my chin.

"I love you, Scarlet."

My back was to him. Even cloaked in night, I hid my face in case any transparency managed to slip through the shadows.

"We'll talk more in the morning," he said, and once I heard the sound of the door shutting behind him, I buried my face in the pillow, squeezed my eyes shut, and screamed.

PRETTY GOOD FOR A CHICK.

It was an expression I heard routinely.

Pretty good.

Despite the hours I'd spent learning the craft, reading the books, eating mounds of M&Ms instead of dinner since they were the more appealing spheres to use as practice poker chips.

For a chick.

Regardless of my professionalism, of playing to win, of wiping out most of my competition once I'd gotten a knack for it.

Admittedly, I used my feminine wiles to my advantage. A flash of leg here, a bat of fake eyelashes there ... it helped. But my salon-perfected hair and spin classes didn't assist in spotting the right card in the river or playing the odds when they weren't in my favor and winning anyway. The rush of success and the thundercrack of losing, the thousands of dollars more often than not slipping out of my fingers until I'd figure out how to rake them back. Nothing came without sacrifice. Not the fast way or with luck.

And this time, I'd lost. Terribly and irrevocably, both at cards and in life. But I'd fought, and finally sat in a suite at a luxury hotel in the center of Los Angeles. Yet, to the FBI and players alike, I was still *pretty good for a chick.*

Well, this chick had breakfast sent up to eat in her room.

There was little cash to spare, but I figured the FBI could fork over a few more dollars for an omelet and some home fries.

Yeesh. I cringed upon looking at the room service menu. Or maybe more like $45.

Didn't matter. I'd spent the better part of this year taking their ten grand sums and turning it to fifty. Eventually, I flipped that fifty into hundreds of thousands. On and on the wheel of fortune went as I took my seat at clandestine tables with no room for the tourists of casinos and hoteliers.

My talent for cards had flourished. I was no longer the cocktail waitress with rainbow hair playing her first round. Once Kai had spotted me, he'd sensed my cravings for something more. And once I'd discovered he was an undercover FBI agent, he'd pushed me to become as good as he was in order to lure his most coveted prey: Theo Saxon, dark prince to New York's eminent mob boss, who preferred to supervise illegal poker games rather than traffic weapons and young girls the way his older brother was wont to do.

Unfortunately for Kai, within a year I'd surpassed his skill. Perhaps my determination to become better was because of my past, but more likely, it was due to the burn of losing the man I'd loved and the fact that he hadn't said a word to me after he disappeared.

Not. One. Entire. Syllable.

Most of the time, I ignored the idea that Theo had long moved on. He wouldn't—not with the kind of love we'd left on the table. Theo had to come back at some point. Whether it was to try to save, chastise, or just plain yell at me for refusing to exit sticky situations, well ... that was up to him, because he'd have to fucking *appear* first.

So, two years ago, when the FBI had proposed I become part of the tactical plan to chase down and eventually capture the fugitives, Theo and Trace Saxon, there'd been no room for hesitation.

In other words, I didn't have a choice.

According to them, I was Theo's weak spot. Using me, putting me into plays where I could be in danger and he'd be forced to swoop in and rescue the damsel. Somewhere in the midst of that, the FBI was convinced Theo would reveal where his older, more threatening brother, Trace, was—

Ha.

In the beginning, I'd followed the FBI's rules and played into their idea that Theo wanted to be a hero, but underneath my guise, I'd planned. I'd learned and crafted, and instead of becoming a victim, I turned infamous.

A young female in her mid-twenties playing strong and winning big in the New York City backrooms wasn't the norm. Within a year, I'd received invitations to the biggest sharks around and eventually, was able to stretch my talents outside the city limits.

Pretty good for a girl.

Theo had to hear of me. Unless he truly was a fugitive hiding under a rock. I'd made certain of it, winning big, taking on powerful men, earning notoriety.

Yet, there was no sign of him.

Two years of honing my skills with the government during the day and throwing chips in with the big boys at night, and I had yet to catch a single flash of his face.

I searched for clues. With law enforcement bearing down so heavily, Theo wouldn't pop in front of me in a line at Starbucks. He'd send me hints, hidden in napkins in restaurants or written in the steam of mirrors after I stepped out from hotel showers. It was such a hopeless wish that I scoffed every time I checked my medicine cabinet, but I had to *believe* that he'd get into contact with me somehow, to at least let me know he was all right.

If Theo loved me, that was what he'd do.

That thought bucketed me like rain.

My home fries were cold by the time I got to them. I pushed them aside and tugged the plush white robe tighter as I curled up in the standard sofa chair of hotel rooms and gazed out the window.

LA provided blue skies today, its cityscape so different from New York. They had the tall, concrete towers in common, the multi-level stacks of buildings playing out like a giant's version of Tetris on his cell phone. But LA had wider roadways. It was flatter, greener, and, I thought as I made a face at my half-eaten egg white omelet filled with more spinach than goat cheese, a helluva lot more health conscious. I missed my street bagel piled with pasteurized dairy.

A *ding* came from my purse, and despite the lurch in my stomach, I uncurled from my position and retrieved my phone. I half expected to see a summons from Neri.

I'm stopping by in ten was Kai's message.

"Great," I mumbled and stripped off my robe. I hadn't yet showered, but Kai wouldn't care. Instead, I threw my bleached blond hair into a messy bun and donned my denim shorts and white tee I'd slept in. My toes had nasty blisters from the shoes last night, so I kept them bare, curling them into the plush carpet surrounding the bed, enjoying the sting the friction brought. If all went according to plan, this would be my last night in the five-star hotel.

Kai was staying in a motel down the street. While Kai was a patron of the fine poker establishment I'd been to last night, he wasn't as known as I'd come to be. He didn't have to keep up appearances once he exited the room, and the FBI wasn't about to fund it.

I'll miss you, I mouthed to the extra-fluffy down pillows, when Kai knocked.

I padded over as his pounding became more insistent.

"Change your mind yet?" he asked in greeting as he strode past me. He brought with him the scent of fresh air and his leather jacket. His cheeks were tinged pink from either the light chill outside, the exertion from his walk, or his incredible rage at me.

"No." I gestured to the settee where I'd been sitting. "Coffee?"

"No—dammit, yes." He poured himself a cup out of the sterling carafe. "Haven't slept a wink, thanks to you."

I resumed my seat, picked up my mug, and sipped.

"You're fucking calm considering you just gave yourself over to a middle-aged mafia owner," he said.

I took a larger sip to settle my nerves as I continued vigilance out the window, watching a plane silently cut through the sky.

"Did you even plan out the terms with him? Like, I dunno, for how long?" Kai gestured with his ceramic cup. "Or when? How? *What* is required of you?"

I set my drink down on the glass table with a rattling *clink*. "I figure we'll get to the details once I go over there."

"Scarlet." A hand came down on my own. His was startlingly cold to my warm. "This is me you're talking to. No one else is here, I'm not wired, Chenko isn't listening," he said, referring to his supervisor. "So, tell me, truly, what is going on with you."

"I've tried everything." The words came out mainly as breath as I stared at the table between us. "I excel at this game so well that I'm requested at all the high stakes tables and whored out by the FBI and—and all for what?" I met Kai's stare, and to my chagrin he was blurry. "Theo doesn't see me, Kai."

Kai leaned forward. "I see you, honey, and it's not looking good. What you're doing...we discussed this. Said that if it became too much for you, if searching for Trace and Theo took its toll and had you turning back into that girl who throws herself in front of flying bullets, we'd stop."

I squeezed his hand then let go. "You're sweet to think that."

I hadn't told him what Peter Chenko had said to me while I was still recovering in the hospital bed after being shot, the moment he came in and shut the door. And I didn't plan to tell Kai. To Kai, the FBI was a living, breathing Superman. He still believed they were the good guys.

"Oh, no?" Kai cocked his head. "From my perspective it's looking like we were done weeks ago. This isn't flushing any Saxon out. You should've stopped playing, Scar."

"You're wrong. We've finally gotten our lead. Trace has been staying with Neri. I overheard it at a game a week ago, and he may still be there."

"We've been down this road before. It's probably another of Trace's plants, to put us off the scent. I'll call Chenko right now." He pulled out his phone from his jacket pocket. "We can—"

"*No*, Kai. I'm going through with this. Tell Chenko I'll speak with him directly."

Kai lifted his phone out of my reach when I went for it. "This department will wring you out until there's nothing left but a husk. You know it, yet you continue to let them ask more of you."

"My choice," I repeated from last night.

"You're right. You're good at this. Too good. You could leave us behind and run your own empire. But instead you're here, pining after a fugitive who we may never catch. We've lost resources, attention, we're basically all down to you, Scar. You're the only one bringing in the funds to continue this espionage."

"Exactly. We can't stop now."

"You're not hearing me. I'm ending this. We've relied too much on you and in return you've become..."

He didn't have to say it. Cold. Unfeeling. Simply imitating humanity. A sociopath.

"Theo did it to you first," he continued. "But I'm part of this creation, too."

"I'm not a monster."

Kai sighed while keeping me, unblinkingly, in his sights. "Not yet."

I lifted out of my seat, massaging my neck as I padded to the bathroom. "You should leave. I don't know what kind of surveillance Neri's guys have put me under."

"I made sure I wasn't followed."

"Doesn't matter. We have to be safe."

"Scarlet..."

"What?" I swung around. "This discussion is over. We're continuing the play—actually, no, *I'm* continuing, whether or not I have you or Chenko behind me."

Kai stood. "If this is your version of a last stand—"

"Theo's come for nothing else."

I blurted it out. Unthinking, the words uncurled and arced out of my throat like a viper darting at a threat. I'd inadvertently exposed a weakness and instantly hated myself for it.

Kai waited a beat, while I got my breaths under control, until he said, "Theo is not a bear you can draw out of hibernation. The only person you're trapping is you."

"I have it under control," I said and entered the bathroom.

"That's what worries me," I heard him mutter before I twisted on the tap.

Kai wouldn't be there when I got out of the shower. If these past two years had taught Kai anything, it was that I did what I wanted. And because it got results, he let me. But I was responsible for those new lines in his forehead, the fading tint to his brown eyes. He met me, and his world began losing color.

I scrubbed any lingering guilt away by using the complimentary brown sugar scented soap. The included lemon shampoo helped massage some hope into my scalp. I'd carefully planned my moves last night. I'd been practicing, honing, ever since receiving news that Trace had been spotted at one of Neri's games. Or maybe Theo. They looked so much alike, it was hard to tell sometimes.

The FBI wanted Trace, but there was no question who I was aiming for. The police could continue to focus their efforts on the older brother, and by all accounts I'd been helping them do so, but in the shadows, I searched for my own escape. Despite what it was doing to Kai—and I hated carving a wedge between the only friend who remained—I had to find Theo.

As I combed my wet hair, I realized this was the most danger I'd ever put myself in.

And the closest I'd ever come.

NERI SABASTIANI's summons was as I expected.

Slid under my door at the random afternoon hour of 4 PM, an embossed ivory envelope rested on the luxurious white carpet with the innocence and appeal of a wedding invitation.

But forever vows, it was not.

I bounded over from my usual seat by the window where I pretended I wasn't nervous by chewing on my cuticles. Without pause, I ripped it open where I stood.

Your presence is requested at 19:00 this evening.
Be ready in the lobby.
A car will be waiting.
Neri

Holy shit. It was actually happening. I held the card to my chest and took a few deep, penetrating breaths.

You can do this.

I'd come this far. It would be a mistake to stop.

My hair was already done. To pass the time I'd wandered

the city streets and found a blow-out salon in between sampling the juice bars and gluten-free pastries at the coffee shops. My strands now rested in romantic waves slightly past my collarbone with a deep side-part. I planned to pair it with the second dress I'd rented, a deep cobalt off-the-shoulder designer gown. The envelope didn't say black tie, but it didn't have to. Neri was fancy enough to demand "dress to the nines" through silence.

The getting ready part was easy. I took my time with my make-up, adding black cat-eyes to my lids and a sweep of sparkling, luscious lip gloss. Highlighter shone against my cheeks and collarbone, and my skin was supple-soft from the hotel's lotion.

I didn't want to leave all of myself behind, so I sprayed my signature peony scent that my former best friend, Verily, had bought me years ago and I still restocked regularly. I spritzed it into the air and walked through the cloud, clad in my dress but barefoot, the scent bringing with it images of Theo grazing his nose against my neck, sweeping up until his tongue hit the lobe of my ear.

I closed my eyes against the stinging after-bite of that remembrance.

The dreaded shoes were next. Gorgeous black heels with glittering threads, they clicked with high-class authority but clamped like a pit bull's jaws.

No matter. The pain would keep me grounded.

Neri and his people probably wouldn't let me bring a purse, or if I did, it would be searched so specifically even the lining wouldn't survive, so I decided to use a very small clutch instead. I did, however, sift through my purse until I found what I needed and slipped two dissolvable capsules between my cleavage.

If my military math was correct, there was still forty-five minutes until I was meant to be ferried away by a car, and I intended to utilize that time by ordering a nice, cold, stiff drink at the lobby bar. Maybe two.

Kai wasn't anywhere to be seen once I reached the ground floor, and I'd had my eyes peeled to spot any sign of him from the elevator to the entrance.

I took up an unhurried position at the bar, still watchful, and ordered scotch on the rocks. A smattering of men and women had the same intentions I did, but most kept to themselves and their vice of choice. I wasn't sure if five-star hotel lobbies still housed escorts and their clients, but glancing about casually, there were a few other gorgeously dressed women speaking low in their partner's ears.

The scotch hit like fire in the back of my throat, but it was a needed burn. I sipped, alone, swirling my drink and staring into it like I could read my future.

"Could I buy you another one?"

I glanced up, a polite *fuck off* ready to roll off my lips, when an expression was caught in my periphery. No, a face.

Theo.

I slipped off my stool, still clutching my scotch, peering furiously at the spot on the other side of the bar.

"You all right, honey?"

The same voice as before, a Texas drawl, was owned by a weathered cowboy face older than my father's.

"No, thank you," I said, speaking to him but staring off in an entirely different direction. "I mean yes, I'm fine, but I don't need another drink."

"Your loss," he said, then made his way to the corner where another woman in a nice dress sat on her own.

Where was he?

My shoulders slumped. It was my subconscious, the part of my mind forever craving Theo and crafting him out of the reflections of mirrors, bottles, and wood varnish.

Fighting back frustrated tears, I finished my drink in one gulp. The ice clanked against my front teeth.

How much longer can you go on this way, Letty?

I signaled to the bartender. "One shot of chilled Patron."

He nodded, and I waited for the liquid that would drown out any further questions.

"Miss Rhodes?" A gentle hand landed on my elbow. "I'm the night concierge. I believe your vehicle is here."

My hands involuntarily clenched. "Thank you. I'll be just a minute."

He nodded, dapper and clean in his uniform suit. Who knew what kind of clientele would sully his guest-compliant veneer this evening, but I refused to be the first. There was no use in telling him everything, pleading with him to help me before I enter into the waiting car of LA's preeminent arms dealer.

A fogged-over shot glass slid over to me and I downed it before it came to a stop. "Put it on my room, thirty-twelve," I said in a rough voice, then straightened my gown and walked toward my chosen fate.

The car was a liquid black sedan, classically made by Aston Martin. I wouldn't expect anything else from Neri, and when the suit-clad chauffeur opened the rear passenger door, I slid in with a smile, my lips still cold from the tequila.

More liquor awaited me in the side-door compartments, but I chose a bottle of ice water instead. I'd had enough alcohol to give me courage and I'd need a level head for the rest.

The ride was quiet, the chauffeur mute. I busied myself calculating whether this trip would've taken longer in NYC because of traffic lights at every block, or here in LA due to the long, flat roads and heavy traffic. It was a calming, boring thought that I held onto, sipping my water every now and again until forty minutes later, we drove into a circular driveway in Malibu.

The mansion was white, with Roman columns framing the

wide double doors that would take two of me to lay a hand at the top. A Greek goddess fountain gushed water. As soon as the door was opened and I stepped out of the vehicle, the waterfall sound created a spa-like quality unheard of in the East Village of New York.

There was no wind this evening, and my perfected waves stayed in place as I thanked the driver and sashayed toward the door. It opened with a silent sweep as I approached, a man dressed in an all-black suit gesturing to come inside.

"Miss Rhodes," he said as I stepped into the entryway. I recognized him from last night, one of Neri's bodyguards.

I tipped my chin in greeting, but my gaze ping-ponged across the black and white marble flooring, the sweeping ivory staircase that unfolded in an upside-down U in front of me, and the touches of red velvet interspersed in red cushions of the loveseat nestled in the middle of the U. Drawn-back curtains showcased original paintings that were probably more expensive than the mansion that housed them.

"This way," the bodyguard said.

I followed, choosing to study my surroundings rather than what awaited. Black, white, and red were the continued patterns as we curved behind the staircase and into one of the many white-painted doors lining the back of the house.

Was this where Neri hosted his high-stakes poker games? Illegal gambling didn't always have to happen in clandestine basements. The higher I managed to climb in this game, the more luxurious the rooms got, the richer the clientele, the riskier the wagers. There was the feeling like this was it, as soon as I stepped into the car at the hotel. I'd reached the top.

Now there was only room to fall.

"Boss is waiting for you in there." The bodyguard indicated the second door on the left.

With a deep breath, I turned the knob.

"At last."

Neri sat supine behind an incredibly large Cherrywood desk, clean of debris such as papers, pens, or anything else that would suggest he ran a legitimate business. I wondered what he needed with an office like this—a whole library of books behind him in dark wooden shelves.

I squinted and read that a lot of them were law textbooks.

Ah. Irony.

"Hello," I said, then cleared my throat. I sounded too croaky.

"Regretting your wager last night?"

Neri stood. The dark interior matched his dark skin. It was impossible to tell his expression, but experience told me to always treat him as I would a shark.

"Not at all," I said. "I half-hoped you were running a game this evening."

"So you could further pick the pockets of my business partners? I think not."

Ah. Sarcasm.

Neri came around the corner of his desk. "Your reputation has proceeded you, but you know that. Last night ... that wasn't your usual self."

I remained stoic, standing out like a bright sapphire in the low shades of this room.

"My father designed this office," Neri said. He was eerily keen on others' thoughts, and I made note to keep even the slightest tic under control. "My mother, the rest. I believe, once coming to America, the movie *Clueless* inspired her."

I nodded like I agreed and mentally commanded my hands to relax.

"Do you like it?" he asked.

"It feels very law professor," I said. At his answering uptick of his lips, I knew he appreciated the honesty.

"Boring, stale, reeking of old cigar smoke, yes," Neri said. "Though my father is long dead, his memory in here remains strong. And why I will not change a thing. But we won't be staying. Come." He held out his elbow.

After a brief hesitation, I took it.

We exited the office and there were many more bodyguards than the one I started out with. I counted six as we passed, and like dominos, they fell into step behind us. I staunched my curiosity from cricking my neck and staring behind me, keeping my attention straight ahead. My heart fluttered so hard it might as well be a canary trapped in much too small of a cage, but my steps were smooth, despite the blisters.

"I won't insult your intelligence," Neri said, but it was in such a low voice that combined with his accent, I had to strain to hear. "I am not leading you to a bedroom to have my way with you."

My fingers tightened on his arm, then loosened. It was my only tell.

We turned into the deserted kitchen, where his hired chefs and staff prepared his meals, farther back in the mansion. I wondered how deep this house went.

Only the bare minimum of lights were turned on in order to

find our way, and my curiosity piqued when we bypassed the dining room and wet bar, and approached patio doors.

"I do not rape my women," Neri continued.

I nodded like he was giving me a courtesy, though inside I burned with adrenaline. I was ready for anything, constantly on alert. Neri had me bet one entire night with him, and it wouldn't be for nothing. I was simply waiting for the axe to fall.

We headed outside to the back terrace, my arm still in his. It took every atom I possessed to prevent him from feeling what I was thinking as we stepped over the stone tiles with carefully trimmed bright green grass bordering the squares, and down another set of stairs with thick gray banisters. When I touched it for balance, it was freezing.

A roar of sound broke through the cloudless night and I jerked, instinctively drawing closer to Neri, then, realizing my mistake, boomeranging away.

"Not to worry," he said over the noise. "Come this way."

I was in heels, wearing a couture gown, tramping through lawn with sounds that suspiciously sounded like some mode of transport next to a man that could snap my neck with his bare hands, and like a rabbit, I curled into myself, ready to bound, eyes so wide I'm sure they were mainly white.

Lights flashed, then kept flashing, ahead of us. Blades sluiced through the air, creating artificial wind that ripped through my hair in an instant.

A helicopter.

"After you," he said, holding out his hand. Then, to be heard, he yelled, "Come. It won't bite."

Thoughts whirling, I lifted my hand to his. This wasn't supposed to happen. I was supposed to remain in this mansion. Kai was meant to be somewhere close by, ready to initiate action if needed. The FBI was supposed to burst through the doors at a moment's notice.

When I made a bet that I deliberately lost to spend a night with a young, hungry, ruthless don by the name of Neri Sebastiani, Kai was pissed but he'd follow. I knew he would.

And now I wouldn't have him. Wherever I went, I'd be on my own.

Isn't that what you aimed for? Always wanting to be alone, the sole survivor, the only one in pain. You asked for it, Letty. I love you, but your death wish is granted.

I bit the inside of my cheek to keep from screaming. Neri helped me up into the helicopter. My inner twin was right. Cassie always was. I signed up for this, and whatever happened, it would be my own fault.

"Champagne?" Neri asked once he'd settled the headsets on both his and my ears. "Or perhaps something stronger?"

"Champ—bubbly is fine," I said, then repeated myself when Neri gestured he couldn't hear. He reached under his seat and pulled out Cristal.

"You'll need it," he said ominously before he popped the cork and palmed it. The sound didn't reach my ears through the humming of the soda can I was crouched in.

No bodyguards except one shared our space and the door was promptly slammed shut. I pictured the rest outside, and if any of them studied my face through the window, it probably appeared as a stricken ghost through the glass.

We lifted off the ground as Neri handed me a glass. I pressed my other hand to the window like Kai could see me do it.

Neri leaned back. "You're in for a treat, my dear."

I gulped down the golden carbonation, resting against the seat, but my back was ramrod straight.

Yes, the men, the players, the House, was right. I followed through with any hand I held, I bet with purpose and never overplayed my cards. I knew when to call and the best opportunity to check. I played against oil guys, finance men, trust fund kids and celebrities. I faced off with mobsters and their sons and daughters. I was part of the underground and flourished in a way I never would if I stayed legitimate, went to college, and became the administrative assistant my resume wrote me out to be. I watched drugs trade hands, lines of coke be snorted on the table, handguns be passed under. Not much made me flinch, not anymore. Until now. Prior to this moment, I was pretty good at this game. Damn good.

For a chick.

And now I was trapped like one.

THE HELICOPTER WENT from land to ocean in what felt like a millisecond. My legs ached fiercely from tensing them ever since the machine left the ground—and it wasn't from fear of flying. I enjoyed flights, once I was in my seat and through the dreary battle that was the TSA. I ordered coffee or wine, stuffed headphones in, sat back, and listened to music in the seat's arm.

Now, I clutched a crystal goblet of champagne like it could maybe help me chisel out of this flying tin can.

Neri remained unperturbed. He sipped casually at his drink, but not enough to actually drain the liquid. He, like me, was using it as a prop. But unlike myself, I had no idea why he was continuing his sobriety as we chopped through ocean air. He could have so many things in store for Scarlet Rhodes, idiot extraordinaire. I could be auctioned off to the highest sex bidder or turned into a foreign slave in a country with no extradition requirements. Cutting a quick glance to Neri's bodyguard sitting next to him, I thought, hell, they could toss me out the door right now and have me smacking into the water before Neri lifted his glass for a third sip.

Neri didn't bother to make conversation, which, under usual

circumstances, I appreciated. But I did *so* want to know if he planned to bring me back to Los Angeles by the end of this.

"We agreed to only one night," I found myself saying through the little microphone curved in front of my face. Two giant Princess Leia-type gray headphones protected my ears.

Neri glanced at me, the whites of his eyes like ivory tusks. He adjusted his headset, then spoke. "Yes, you bet as such."

"So..." I lifted my glass, gesturing outside, "Where are we going?"

Neri might have smiled, but I couldn't tell. "That will be up to you, my dear."

I paused. As in, what? If I behave myself accordingly? If I choose all the right moves?

Oh, if only Neri knew.

The chopper tipped, and I braced myself on the seat though I was belted in, champagne sloshing.

"Ah," Neri said, peering out. "We've arrived."

I followed his gaze, half expecting Alcatraz. Instead, what greeted me was a slash of white carved out of the blackened saltwater, lights of our helicopter circling blurry spotlights around its target.

"A ... boat?" I asked, more to myself.

"Indeed. Stay still for this," Neri said, and leaned back himself.

As far as landing a helicopter went, which I knew nothing of, it was bumpy, but tame. Most of my drink landed on my forearm and not the gown. This boat had a fucking helipad, so it couldn't be titled a boat in my head any longer. A yacht. A luxury, million-dollar yacht that only sheiks and billionaires possessed, and celebrities used as rentals.

The bodyguard went first, while the blades were still spinning, and hopped out. Once the door was open, the headsets were useless so Neri simply waved me on to go next.

I crouched out of my seat, stepping tentatively but avoiding Neri's helping hand. My hair lifted in an instant as soon as my forehead hit fresh air, the strands tangling into a visor that obscured my vision. A hand clamped on my arm, too sweaty and hammy to be Neri's, and I leaned into it anyway, taking the steps out of the chopper with the carefulness of a toddler wearing her mom's heels for the first time.

He rushed me out of the blades' arc immediately, and we came to a stop along the edges of the painted helipad target while we waited for Neri. My head tilted up, unbelieving of the fact that this boat—sorry, *yacht*—had at least three stories to it. And that wasn't counting what could be under my feet.

As soon as Neri cleared, the helicopter lifted, curved slightly, then flew back whence it came.

There went my ride.

Neri lifted his eyebrows as he passed, "Welcome to the *Hatari*. Follow me, my dear."

"Are we—is there a game going on?" I asked as I came up beside him. This wasn't unheard of. A lot of high-priced poker games were played on the host's yachts, most especially when they could cross into Mexico and enter international waters to avoid tariffs.

Was that where we were? Mexico? I grimaced. *Shit*.

International waters also meant Kai would never find me. Or my body, if it came to it.

We entered through sliding glass doors where the interior was well lit and I blinked against the unexpected brightness. I suddenly felt exposed in such a tight gown and quiet place. Like I'd missed the ferry to the Governor's Ball and landed on a mafia king's instead.

Plush. It was the only way to describe the main room where we stood. White leather couches, but the cushions were so pillowy it would be like sitting on clouds. Real fur rugs were splayed under coffee tables and side tables.

Red accents outfitted the walls. A ruby-painted skull of what maybe was an elk or some other creature with horns adorned the space above the couch. A rifle was mounted on the mantel above the fireplace.

Hunting-chic, if that were a style, would be how I'd describe Neri's watery lair.

"Perhaps you'd like another drink before we move on?" Neri asked. He must have seen my graceless moves in the helicopter. My arm felt sticky from the spilled champagne.

I spotted the bar ahead, with a lot of brass adding to the white marble. "Um. Sure."

Neri's man moved toward the bar, but I stopped him. "No, it's okay. I'll do it."

The man ignored me and kept moving.

"Henry, it's fine," Neri said. Then, he turned to me. "We're not dealing with our usual kind of poppet. This one has a few more preemptive moves than what we're used to."

I offered a tentative smile before passing Henry and taking up position behind the bar.

"Afraid I'll do something to your drink?" Neri asked, his voice containing the velvet of a tempting threat.

"I'm afraid anyone will, given the opportunity," I responded.

Glasses, glasses, where were the glasses ... I bent down to search the lower cupboards. My heartbeat had to be as loud and audacious as the helicopter blades that had just departed. Subtly, I reached into my cleavage.

"I have no such fear. Pour me one as well, my dear."

I straightened, propping two lowball glasses laser cut from crystal on the bartop. Turning, I found a fourteen-year-old scotch that should do nicely, and despite the circumstances, the glug and slosh of the copper liquid were comforting sounds in this otherwise silent room. Not even the waves dared to splash against the yacht's hull.

"Wait."

Henry held up an arm when I made to carry the drinks to Neri, who had sat himself on the couch below the—Elk? Antelope? Impala?—red-painted skeleton horns. I didn't realize Henry had taken up such close residence near the bar.

"I'll try it first," he said.

"Neri has a poison-taster?" I asked before thinking to shut up.

Henry didn't bother to respond. He grabbed a small straw from the bar, sipped, plugged the mouth hole to prevent any backwash, then discarded the plastic.

A *professional* poison taster.

Henry held up a finger when I went to take the glass, I guess waiting for any effects. Sighing, I said, "Should I make you one, too?"

Seemingly satisfied, Henry handed the glass back. "I'll take this one. Make the boss a fresh one."

I didn't waste time, bending down to grab another glass and poured. Henry was close, but easily distracted by my ass. When I straightened, I made sure to adjust my breasts, an added bonus. I then went to Neri, who unfurled from his laid-back stance and nodded his thanks.

After tasting, he said, "You chose one of the good ones."

"I know good scotch when I see it," I said.

"Excellent. Then you won't mind drinking some of mine."

He patted the cushion next to him, and after brief hesitation, I took it. Every synapse in me wanted to scream out, but I met his stare with placid calm.

I smiled, took his glass, and drank deep. I made sure my swallow was audible when I handed it back.

"Good girl," he said calmly. He turned the glass until he

found my lipsticked rim, tilted it so his lips met my stain, and drank. His eyes didn't linger on anything but me.

"As wonderful as it would be to sit here and pick your brain," Neri said, lowering his glass and resting against the pillows with no cares, no fear. "You only have so many hours at my disposal."

If it was a question, I didn't want to answer it. He discussed this night like it had allotted hours, like a transaction, but his attitude contradicted his words. I'd been involved in a lot of fucked-up moments and avoided plenty, but this was not a time I was here for. The deepest part of me, the part of my mind I'd inherited millions of years ago from my ancestors, told me that there was another plan in place, something sinister.

Neri set down his drink and rose, and I automatically mimicked him.

"Stay here, Henry."

Henry remained at the bar, arms crossed, but his eyes followed us all the way out of the room and I had to avoid the instinct to look back several times.

We took a very narrow spiral staircase farther into the hull. As we descended, I imagined the water crushing the ship from all sides, and me, willingly entering its depths.

Ten feet below water level, we stopped. My shoes made no sound on the carpeted hallway. While also narrow—and with a lot more ivory and mahogany than upstairs—it still exuded first class, but with no windows. That could be a good thing, considering if I were to look out, the only thing I'd see would be my underwater grave.

We circled the staircase until we were near the bow of the boat, and Neri stopped at a door that was carved in a way that made me think it was the master quarters.

I didn't want those quarters. I didn't want to see a bed.

"This is where I leave you," Neri said.

Against my better judgment, my brows furrowed.

"Enter at your own risk, my dear." Neri stepped away, the carpet absorbing the sounds of his footsteps as he departed.

I stared after him.

If this night could get any weirder ... to think, a few hours ago I'd had visions of my life being perilously close to the end. Instead, I was helicoptered in to some gun tycoon's luxury cruise ship without any explanation as to why I was standing by myself in the galley.

My next move was obvious: turn the knob. I'd come this far and there was no swimming away from it.

Silently, I did. There was no break in carpet from the hallway to the room, so my footfalls remained undetectable as I moved forward.

The lights were off, and I didn't dare grope for a switch. It would lead to seconds of distraction that I couldn't afford. I waited for my vision to adjust and remained very still, waiting for whoever might be in here to make the first move.

I wasn't disappointed.

"Does this help?"

The voice was a whisper, a growl, a deep, resonant sound in the midst of silence. And I knew, before hearing the *flick* of the lighter and seeing the flame of the candle grow and flicker beside him, that my heart was about to plummet.

Theo.

THE PLANES of his face glowed through the flickering flame. It was altogether possible the small light travelled far enough that he could see the glisten of my tears.

"They say it's unsafe to light candles on a boat," I said. It came out crackling, like I was recovering from a throat infection.

The man I'd been pining after for twenty-four months stood five feet away, regarding me like he hadn't broken me open, then salted the wound by popping up right at the moment I'd given up.

The firelight carving of him changed as he shifted. "That's the first thing you want to say to me?"

Theo might as well have used those words to flip a switch.

I strode forward and slapped him. Before he could recover—or so much as lift a hand to touch the stubble I'd just scraped my palm across—"How *dare* you? Do you have any idea—" I hitched, my breaths suffocating. "You left me. I haven't seen you in years because you decided to walk off without any kind of—"

"Scarlet."

"I was in a *hospital*—" My pitch rose, my chest heaved, and his profile became as watery as the ocean surrounding us.

His hands fell onto my shoulders. "Scarlet—"

"Your brother shot me, I nearly got my best friend killed, and all I had to hang onto was you. Do you know what that was like? To be feeling your hand one minute and dozing off thinking I was safe, then waking up to an empty chair? An empty hospital room?"

Theo's grip slid to my elbows, but I yanked out of his hold. "Don't touch me."

He held on tighter.

"Don't *touch* me!"

"Listen—"

"*I loved you!*" I heaved the statement out as if it were actual, bloody tissue loosening from my lungs.

Theo pulled me closer, though I still fought. "I know."

I smacked at his chest, then curled my hands into fists and punched at his torso. "I fell in love with you and you didn't care. You left. You *left*."

"I had to."

I kept pummeling. My expression was twisted into all kinds of grief, rage, sheer adrenaline. Having him near, a tangible person to hit—like I could reach into his chest and hurt his heart the way he'd sucker-punched mine—was something I'd been hoping to do but never actually believed he'd allow me the pleasure.

"Calm down."

His voice remained low. Theo didn't dodge from any of my scattered, hurling fists.

"Don't you tell me to *calm down*," I hissed between swipes. "As far as I'm concerned, I can do whatever the fuck I want because you've given me two years to think about it."

"This is what you pictured?" He ducked against a well-aimed swing at his temple.

"It's what I *dreamed*."

He straightened. Gestured to his chest. "Then come on. Hit me all you want. Hurt me until you feel better."

I choked, sobbed, the hand I held in the air falling to my side. Theo let me shudder, allowed these moments to contain a background percussion of grief.

"Let me touch you," he said softly.

I shook my head, crossing my arms. God knew what I'd do if he pulled me against him, if I were able to bury my face in his neck the way I'd ached to do in the middle of the night, under cold sheets that weren't mine. When the nightmares came.

"You walked away, and it was like you died," I said. My back was bowed. I was in pieces, Theo's image so shattered in my mind that it was hard to fathom he stood before me. Whole.

Theo's alive. Thank God he's alive.

"You didn't come back," I said. "You didn't give me any sort of sign that you were okay or do anything to make me believe what we had was real or important. You might as well have been buried before my eyes."

Theo made a move to step closer, but after a low warning from me, stayed where he was. "What I did ... it was difficult for me, too."

"No," I said, much louder than I intended. "You didn't *have* to leave me at the hospital without a goodbye. You didn't *have* to cut off all contact with me for years, you didn't *love*—"

"I left you in the hospital so you wouldn't die there, by my brother or any other of my family's hands. I stopped speaking to you for the same reason, because we'd gotten too close, you were too involved, and despite doing everything in my power to keep you safe, you got shot. Right in front of me. You were nearly killed, Scarlet, and not because of anything you did, but because I became part of your life."

While listening, I forgot to close my mouth. I had to swallow, bring back my saliva, before saying, "I've heard that excuse before. I believe it was when you were stroking my face telling me everything was going to be okay. It was my choice to stay with you."

"You're saying that a lot lately, aren't you? Your choice."

I froze, my mouth falling open again.

"Another argument of yours I should point to—my leaving you for years. You really think that's true? I've watched you, Scarlet, since the first time you were wheeled out of the hospital and brought to your parents in Westchester. From the time you recovered enough to move back to the city. The moment you took your first seat back with the cards. The second you realized you could make it a prolific—albeit dangerous—career. The deeper you sank, the harder I swam. I saw it all, Scarlet. And if I couldn't be there, then someone I trusted was."

"So you had me followed?" I swept my arms out. "Where now we've ended up on a luxury yacht with a crazy gun trader and this is the time you decide to reveal yourself?"

"Don't pretend like you didn't know what you were doing, basically diving off cliffs—"

"—I didn't need you lurking behind the scenes!" I shouted. "I wanted you here, beside me! And you're telling me you were with me the entire time, witnessing me *beg* for you. Did you have cameras installed in my home, too? My friends followed? What else, *Sax*?" I asked, using the name his mafia family preferred to call him. "How else did you make me into your pawn? Did I do everything you wanted? Is that why you're here? Mission accomplished?"

"No cameras. But I saw you break." Theo continued, nonplussed, "I knew the moment you accepted I wasn't coming back and can pinpoint the exact time you plunged yourself into this deadly game of spinning knives you keep asking to be a part of."

"Just because you're here doesn't mean everything's fixed and I'll stop."

His eyes closed, Theo's first sign of exhaustion. "I'm here to try."

"So, I finally put myself in enough peril to get you to show your face, huh?"

"Yes, your plan succeeded." His tone wasn't dry, or flat. It was simply him. Theo. And he was telling me in no uncertain terms that I was being an idiot.

As if I didn't know that.

"You've gone too far, Scarlet."

"Which means I'm close."

"Stop looking for him."

I bared my teeth. "Never."

"You have no one at your disposal, do you understand that? The police, the FBI, they can't be around you anymore because you're too unruly. Your friends, Verily and that boy Noah, they're not in your life anymore because you walk too dangerous of a line. You're estranged from your parents for the same reason. You're doing this alone, Scarlet, and you are creating a situation where I might not be able to get you out of it."

"Until this moment, I assumed you weren't anywhere near me. You think I stepped into Neri's helicopter thinking you were going to be on the other end? *No,* Sax. I did it because I'm getting closer to Trace."

"And what did you think Neri Sebastiani could give you?"

"Information," I spat.

"And then what? What will you do once you've confronted Trace?"

"Kill him."

At last, I startled him enough that he stiffened. "No. That's not in your blood."

"He ruined my *life!*" I screamed. "What little there was left of it, he ruined. I've been turned upside down, twisted and deformed, and I lost the one remaining thing that mattered—you —because of *him*. Then he shot me. He wanted me dead. So it's only fair I return the favor."

"What have these years done to you?" he rasped.

"Prepared me. Put fight in me."

Though it hurt—oh, it *wounded*—I shoved past Theo toward the door.

"Scarlet, get back here."

I didn't bother refusing. The distance I was putting between us was sending enough of a message.

"Scarlet! Where do you think you're going? On a boat with limited space?"

I tripped, nearly clanging my chin on one of the steps of the spiral staircase. Damn it, Theo had stuck his hand through one of the railing's gaps on the stairs and hooked my ankle.

"Do you forget where you are? Neri's my co-conspirator, not yours." Theo glared at me through the same gap.

I gave him an ice-pick gaze right back. "Neri and his good buddy Henry aren't a problem right now."

Theo's eyes narrowed, suspicion at its finest. He said carefully, "And how do you know that?"

"Easy." I kicked out, dislodging his grip before lifting my skirt and resuming my steps. "I drugged them."

The glitter of his eyes caught fire before being shoved into the darkness as I broke contact and continued up.

"You—*what*?"

"I feel it needs to be said one more time," I called out, knowing he followed behind. "I didn't board this boat thinking you'd be here to conduct an epic rescue. I had my own cards to play, so if you don't mind, don't get in the way." I gave myself enough time to turn back and say, "I'd given up on you, Sax."

"Don't do this," he said.

We'd hit the parlor, the same area where Neri and Henry were still hanging out—or, now splaying out. Neri was sprawled on the white leather couch and Henry had hit the floor behind the bar. Both were completely passed out, and all glasses were drained of scotch.

Theo took in the scene. "You gave them some potent mother-fuckers."

"Slow-acting roofies," I said, while rolling Neri onto his back. "Newly on the market. Poker isn't the only underground connection I've made."

"And the FBI didn't question this?"

I leveled Theo with a look. "I'll give you enough time to answer your own question."

"Neri will kill you for this," Theo said, but didn't bother trying to stop me. I'd piqued his curiosity, and he was watching me with interest. Or maybe morbid fascination. Where did his rainbow-haired beauty go?

"Hardly. I'm not stealing anything he'll know about."

I pulled out my phone and a cord from the purse I'd left on the couch, searched through Neri's pockets and found his. I plugged the two together and began downloading all the information on Neri's cell.

"You think you're going to find Trace through Neri's contacts?" Theo asked.

"I received credible information that Neri's been in contact with him, information that's since been confirmed."

"And how's that?"

I glanced up long enough to nail him with a look. "Clearly, he's been in contact with the Saxons."

"I only asked him to have me here so I could get to you. He did it as a favor. You have *no* idea what he was planning on doing with you, do you?"

"Had you not intervened?" I asked dryly.

"This ride is going to the Tijuana, Scarlet. Where you were going to be auctioned."

"Huh." I settled a hand on my hip. "And to think Neri was so impressed with my poker abilities."

If Theo had the capability of expression, this would've been the moment. "That fact doesn't concern you?"

"As you can see, I had it covered."

"And how were you going to get off this yacht?"

"There are two lifeboats, one on either side, out of the eye of the captain, who is likely still driving this mansion thinking there's nary a problem."

"I don't know what's more concerning, the fact that you used 'nary' in a sentence, or that you've studied the blueprints of this boat. What if there was a storm? Or Neri decided not to take you to his ship?"

"Stay one step ahead at all times, that's what you taught me."

The *ding* on my phone let me know the transfer was complete. I unhooked and shoved Neri's phone back in his blazer pocket.

"He'll look for you. Track you down."

"Neri won't find me. At least while he wants me. Then, when I reappear, he'll be on to other matters and won't care about the girl who escaped his clutches by drugging him and stealing one of his blow-up rafts. Not exactly something he'll want to advertise."

"You don't think so? He can kill you without giving anybody a reason."

"He doesn't want me dead."

"I just informed you he was going to auction you off as a sex slave to the highest bidder."

"Probably what he told most of his big honcho friends. In reality, he covets respect. He wants to recruit me to play in games, take cuts—or most—of my winnings. I sense he was taking me to Mexico so he could strong-arm me into opening an account and making a deal."

Theo paused, likely realizing his scare tactics weren't working. "Would you have agreed to it?"

I pondered. "I didn't think it would come to that point. And it hasn't. So." I dropped my cell into my clutch and snapped it shut. "I guess this is the end of the line for us."

Theo stared me down like his glare alone could stop me in my tracks. "I've underestimated you."

"Chase me all you want, Sax. Attempt to run me down, do all of those things that you've now deemed necessary to come out of hiding. But I'm not the girl you knew anymore."

"No," he agreed. "You're not."

I wondered if he'd really let me go.

Scarlet Rhodes and Theo Saxon were no longer. And my end game had to occur whether or not Theo wanted it to. Whether or not he'd be ... hurt.

Theo had been keeping to the shadows, creeping along edges of light like he was always apt to do. That part of him hadn't evolved. Even now, he stood near the bar, away from the halogen lamps, Henry's supine toes nearly touching Theo's shoes. The rebel in him hadn't changed, either—while we all took off our shoes before entering the interior of the *Hatari*, Theo stayed in his.

There was a metaphor in that, I was sure.

"But neither am I the same man."

Theo stepped forward, the recessed lights above the bar gliding across his features, highlighting them. Spotlighting his face to the extent that I gasped.

"Oh my ... *Theo*."

The words escaped me, the pain behind them leaking first, before I could bury it beneath my hardened shell.

A scar, beginning at the top of his right eyebrow and cutting across the bridge of his nose before ending in the middle of his left cheek. It was thin—as thin as an expensive black-market blade—and light pink, almost white. A few years old.

Theo always had a darkness in him, one I'd recklessly tried to unearth when I was young and stupid. But now, it was forbidden to me. I couldn't ask him how he'd gotten the lurid evidence of the badness in his life, because I no longer had the right.

"When?" I asked once I'd schooled my features.

"I'd rather not explain while standing in front of a knocked-out weapons lord and his sidekick."

There wouldn't be any other time, I wanted to say. But it didn't matter. Theo had his plans, I had mine.

"I'm sorry," I said, though I didn't know why.

I showed him my back, this new image of Theo etching into permanence, the long-term of him never receding from my mind even after the time that stood between us. But despite the mark, Theo wasn't made grotesque. Children wouldn't scream at the sight of him. Even flawed, he was much too beautiful. If anything, his presence was more commanding, his angles sharpened, the eerie history of his scar casting an additional allure. A mark of Cain, a warrior for the devil.

I'd dream of him tonight, of softening his sins with my lips.

"So am I, Scarlet."

I paused at his voice, and that was my mistake.

Someone crept into my blind spot, and my shock followed too late after the prick in my neck.

The floor wobbled, my knees unable to keep the balance. I was caught, my face flopping into the hard lines of the man who steadied me.

Neri? One of his henchmen I didn't count? But I'd studied everything ... I made sure there was an out before stepping into the Asten Martin...

Though hazy, I forced my gaze up, and grimaced.

"When I wake up," I forced out to say to Kai, "I'm throwing you overboard."

Or maybe I garbled it. The crease between his brows could've been because he didn't understand, or maybe that he understood too well.

"You're safe," he promised me.

There was no safety in this game. Every person was out for themselves, every tic a sign of a plan, malevolent smiles hidden behind the fan of cards. Every gamble took on the chance of ruin.

Which was why I made no friends. I'd even kept Kai at a distance, though I couldn't help my growing affection for him. We'd worked closely for a long time, and I'd thought I'd caught every clue to his feelings, in the way he moved his brows or chewed on the inside of his cheek, the scent of his fear and the sound of his laugh.

But I'd forgotten. There was a time when I was his student.

Two years later, despite his vow to become a civil servant, his sworn oath into the FBI, Kai decided to cash in on duplicity instead.

God*damn* him for fucking me over first.

I woke up with no tongue.

There couldn't be one, since the entirety of my mouth felt like it'd been stuccoed together.

"She's waking up."

There it was, the Betrayer's voice.

Kai put his hands on me, but I shoved them aside, eyes still closed. "Go away."

"There's not many places to go around here, hun," Kai said. Despite my continued *thwacks* against his arms, he helped me upright.

I blinked, slowly at first. The stucco had traveled from my mouth to my eyelids. Everything was grit.

"Here." Kai held a bottle of water in my eyeline, which I accepted and shoved to my mouth before I registered it as a suspicious act of kindness.

Choking mid-swallow, I spat it out.

"Ah—Christ, Scar!" Kai wiped at his face.

I'd be remiss if I didn't "accidentally" aim the spray at his face. While he was still wiping with the back of his hand, I shoved the bottle at his chest. "Thanks, but I'm maxed out on drugs today."

"It's not ... *spuh*." He rubbed his mouth, spitting out my detritus. "It's just water."

But I wasn't attuned to Kai anymore. I took in my surroundings, somewhere small and wooden, my palms pressing into a thin, cot-like mattress. A circular hole was to my left, a window of sorts, and there was a sway, unrelated to my cotton-cloud mind, that had my body gently swinging.

Damn. I was still on a boat.

Chuckling came from my right, and I noted the crossed suit-legs of the person in the chair, the rest of his form hidden from view, but I didn't need to see the rest of this man to know.

The last scene I remember was facing Theo on the *Hatari*, the man of my dreams who crept his seduction into my nightmares, the way I'd been forced to remember him for so long. He wasn't one for photos or social media. There was nothing I could look to in reminder during times of deep loneliness. All I had was memories, snippets, flashback pain. To have Theo close by again caused the worst kind of love, the pull of him nearly driving me to forget the nights I only had his ghost for company.

Then, so clearly, reality crashed down, and his scarred face forced the reckoning that his time away may not have been too peachy, either.

I cleared my throat and said to him, "You stalk me, corner me, turn Kai against me, then drug me in order to toss my unconscious body onto another ship. You might as well face me."

Theo leaned forward, elbows on his thighs. I expected it, but he still took my breath away. Not simply because of his new flaw. He was the same beautiful demon I'd engraved onto my heart. The sheer sight of him smacked me awake in a way that made it seem these past few years without him were just a dream. Scar tissue served only to frame the old wound and create a tangible pain while looking at him.

"There was only one way to get you off Neri's property safely," Theo said.

Funny, his lips were moving, but all I heard was *blah blah you're a girl who I had to step in to save blabby blah*.

"I had my own exit," I bit out. Then, glancing at Kai who still stood at my elbow, I yanked the water out of his hand and glugged.

"You're welcome," he said.

"I haven't even started with you yet," I said after swallowing. "Marcus is getting a call as soon as I get my hands on a phone."

Kai's eyes formed into slits. "You wouldn't dare."

"I'm going to tattle to your boyfriend that you're a terrible person who drugged his best friend and there's nothing you can do about it."

Theo ignored the two of us, saying instead, "Yes, we both know you were going to *Titanic* your way out of there and float away on a lifeboat."

He said it with such a wry tone, like it was a crime caper I'd never succeed in.

Bastard.

"I would've gotten away just fine," I said. "The bad guys were down for the count."

"And likely waking up pissed off right about now." Theo straightened. "Tell me, what were you going to do once out on the open ocean with a blow-up raft?"

I clamped down on my lower lip to stop the sneer. Theo caught it anyway, and said, "I'm honestly curious. You've thought in quite a lot of detail thus far."

I sighed, figuring telling him wouldn't bust anything else up that hadn't already been busted. "I'd hired a sailboat, gave the captain the coordinates on where to wait for me, and was going to get to land from there."

"That's putting a lot of hope in a stranger."

"Welcome to the modern world," I said, "Where women get into strange cars alone under the protection of an app, rent rooms owned by unknowns in foreign countries, and hire boats in the middle of the night from a website."

Theo cocked his head.

"It would've been there. The sailboat, I mean," I said. "There was good money in it for the captain."

"Tell me, what was this vessel called?"

"*Heaven Sent.*"

Theo smiled.

"Goddamnit." I threw myself back against the pillows.

He spread his hands. "Welcome to the *Heaven Sent.*"

"Is there no moment in this night where you decided *not* to screw me over?" I asked the ceiling.

"I call it protecting."

"Why, though?" I turned to look at him. "You had so many chances before. I gave you—"

"I'm aware."

"And this was the tipping point for you? Right at the second I was getting *good*, predicting all the right moves, remaining one step ahead, *now* is the time you decide to throw everything I've done, all I've crafted, into this damned ocean we're floating across?"

"You needed to be stopped."

"Took your fucking time," I mumbled. Then, like a child, I crossed my arms and stared at the wall.

"And leaving Kai behind in Los Angeles was a part of your strategy, not a mistake," Theo surmised.

"I couldn't let him be here, in case it turned—" I stopped myself. Glared at Kai. "I couldn't have any FBI intervention. I—" *I was too close to the end game.*

"Yet here you are," Kai said, breaking his silence. His lips flatlined as he hit me with a stare. "I intervened."

"Just not in the way you thought," Theo said.

"No," I agreed, and ended it at that. I was not about to admit to these men that they'd been one step ahead of me during the entire showcase of this night, even when I thought I'd been so genius-tricky when I discovered Neri had hired a helicopter to fly to his yacht the very night I was to be "commissioned" to him.

"Please don't think of it as a betrayal," Kai said near my side. "I only agreed to Theo's plans to protect you."

"When did Sax contact you?" I asked without looking at him.

When he didn't answer, and Theo didn't elaborate, I persisted. "I'm going to find out anyway, whether it be because I ask incessant questions or crawl out of that circle window and hold my breath underwater until you give in, so you might as well tell me."

"A few months back," Kai admitted.

"Uh-huh," I said, lifting into a sit again. "Could that have been around October?"

Kai chewed on the inside of his cheek.

"Right around the time I gained entry into Neri's games?" I asked.

"Does it matter?" Theo interjected. "I'm here, you're here, Kai's here."

"And you've appeared out of thin air with a new proposal," I said. "That you took to Kai first."

What I wanted to say was, *you chose to contact an FBI agent over your ex-girlfriend. A girl you said you'd choose over all else.*

"Yes." Theo stood. "Go home."

I gave half a head-shake. "Nope. Next suggestion, please."

"This is not for you, Scarlet." He stepped closer, and in automatic defense, I scooted away. I didn't need to feel his heat, as well as his voice, against my skin. "Look at what it's done to you already."

"Made me stronger?"

"No." He bent down to my level, but I didn't want him to spot even a glimmer of tears. "The woman I've seen in the game rooms, decorated in lace, hidden in couture with a smile of stone, pocketing scores of ceramic chips to the chagrin of many powerful men, this isn't what I wanted. You were supposed to go back to your old life—"

"How?" I asked, defiant. "How was I supposed to do that when you tore me out of it the instant we met?"

Theo, a man of few words, had run out. He backed off.

"I don't trust either of you," I said. "So let's get this boat to land."

"Play me for it."

I cut a glance to Theo, rigid, as usual, in a dimly lit section of the room. For an instant—less than a second—I wondered if he strayed to dark interiors not to increase his predatory effect on people, but because he was ... ashamed ... of his new face.

Pressure increased in the back of my jaw, and I released my molars. I could not fall victim to wanting to heal him. Not again.

"Excuse me?" I said.

"Yeah, excuse you?" Kai asked Theo.

Theo reached into his pocket and pulled out a deck of cards. "You and me. One on one."

"Besides the fact that you wander around in a suit with a pack of cards in your pocket," Kai said, "we had a deal. I agree to cooperate with your intervention only so I can get my girl, then get her home." Kai glanced sideways at me. "I don't betray the FBI for just anyone."

"Don't make me feel guilty for your choices," I said to Kai, feeling strong enough to stand. I had to do *something* to equal the playing field. "And as for you, *Sax*, that's a hard no."

Theo cocked a brow. "You tell me how good you are and your ability to run these games and the men within them just fine, and you don't want to sit down with me over a simple run of Head's Up?"

I licked my lips.

"Scarlet," Kai said. "Don't you dare say yes."

"What are the stakes?" I asked.

"I win, you go with Kai onto a plane to New York without so much as an arm-swing or a peep," Theo said.

"And if I'm the winner?"

"That's up to you."

"No. Nuh-*uh*, you two crazy kamikazes," Kai said. "You know what she's gonna say, Sax, why the *hell* would you—"

"If I win, I stay with you," I said over Kai's sputtering.

Theo was too cloaked for me to see his expression, but my imagination interpreted it just fine. A flinch, a flicker of hesitation, before he said, "Deal."

"*What?*" Kai screeched. "This is—damn the two of you. Actually, shame on *me* for thinking I could broker a deal with either one of you and come out clean. This is ridiculous. I'm leaving."

"Kai," I said. "There's nowhere to go."

"Nowhere to go *yet*," he retorted, hands on his hips.

I walked over to him, hiding my stumble over the shock of no longer wearing stilettos.

"I need you," I said to Kai. "We've been in this from the beginning."

"And we've spent a grand total of twenty-four months chasing down false leads as well as enduring minor brushes with death. Granted, we traveled the country and made a ton of money—of which you lost *all* of last night—but I am not continuing this, Scar." Kai took a deep, cleansing breath. "God, I exhaust even myself just thinking of it."

I said, low, so only Kai and I could hear. "We're so close. Now we have Sax. He's right in front of us. He could lead us to Trace."

"It's not worth it anymore," Kai said. "I want to go back to the city, sleep in my bed instead of a hotel for once, be with Marcus. All the things I've been denied since hooking up with your ass."

"You want to give up, after all this?"

"Scarlet, I'm going to level with you. We're on a sailboat hired by a known FBI fugitive which we're chilling on only because we had to escape a luxury yacht owned by a notorious African arm's dealer, a violent man whom you *drugged*, only to enter into a one-on-one poker game with the man whose brother tried to kill you. A guy who ripped out your heart and forever changed you as a person." Kai continued, after a huge inhale, "This has become fucking absurd and I'm out."

"I didn't do all of that, work on connections for years, just to run when things got tough."

"*Tough?* This is James Bond type shit—"

"We've never gotten—"

"And I'm talking about the modern version, not the sixties *oh, let me just have my martini before I pull out my pocket pistol, pew pew pew*—"

"Kai, listen to me—"

"We are dealing with *automatic weapons*—"

"You're a trained FBI agent for chrissakes—"

"I want to find him, too."

Kai and I both paused, mouths open, pointer fingers outstretched, and turned to Theo's voice.

"It's why I left you," Theo continued. "Why my family turned against me. To confront my brother and force him to pay for what he's done."

"See?" Kai said, throwing up his hands. "If Trace's own flesh and blood can't locate him after all these years, what chances have we got?"

"I know where he is," Theo said.

"Fucking dammit." Kai plopped into the corner chair.

Slowly, carefully, I faced Theo. "You're lying."

"Believe what you want." Theo crossed the room, coming so close that the electric static of him hit the small hairs of my arm. "But you can play for answers instead. Your choice. I'll be on deck."

Silence descended after Theo exited.

"That is totally like him," Kai said, waving at the shut door. "Call me all mysteriously on the phone, come in here, be all dark and brooding, throw a bunch of juicy secrets at you then depart ominously." Kai rested his chin in his hand. "I did not miss that guy."

I did.

"I'm going to play him," I said, then turned the knob.

"Fine." Kai sighed. "This ability I have to supervise you like a father is incredibly taxing."

"Don't give up on me," I said before leaving, and caught the softening of his expression before I stepped out.

Carefully, I navigated the narrow, dark wood hallway, using my hands for balance against the walls as the boat gently lolled. Specks of dizziness kept appearing in my vision, after-effects of whatever drug Theo had used to knock me out. It wouldn't be enough to derail me in cards, of that I was sure. My mind felt clear—or, as crystal as it could be, considering the heartbreak of my life had just appeared out of nowhere—but I wouldn't let that get in the way, either. My ability to cut out the white noise while playing was remarkable, a talent Kai often harped on because I used it on him when he was in the throes of a lecture.

Facing off with Theo would be a true test. Not only would I be playing against my ex, I'd also be seated across from a champion. There existed players much better at cards than me. Theo was one of them. After all, he was the one who held his hand out from the underground in a reluctant beckoning to descend, and I clasped it willingly. Just like Kai had said...

A coating of allure...

I wouldn't let temptation wrap me in its satin bondage again. I caught my reflection in one of the nautical themed mirrors, white as bleached bone, before ascending the small staircase.

"This time," I said to my hardened, marble eyes, "I'm the one with the ace."

THEO STOOD AT THE BOW, just in front of the first mast that held a giant, white, billowing sail, his hands resting on the railing.

The captain was behind me as I appeared from below deck, and he paid attention long enough to offer a flat smile before getting back to navigation.

No need to mention that his *original* client just popped out in front of him. Theo probably paid him triple my offer, therefore I was nothing but plankton to him now.

The stars were so bright as to be pinholes in a huge, black velvet blanket, offering a peek to the world on the other side. Living in the city, it was easy to forget what a true night sky looked like, a gorgeous, glittering, all-encompassing distraction.

"Sax," I said upon approach, and he lifted, highlighting his profile.

People weren't supposed to be beautiful in the dark. Forms were only outlines, blurs of shadow, indistinct. Yet I saw every detail of Theo. The crevices below his cheekbones, the slash of his jawline. How his bold blue eyes shaded when his emotions consumed him. The straight carving of his nose, the stubble against the pads of my fingers. The dip of his lower lip when I slid my finger down, opening his mouth, waiting for the fire of him to meet mine.

I remembered him completely.

"Your decision?" he asked once I stood beside him. The metal rail was freezing, inching its ice into my fingers the instant I took hold of it.

I looked out instead of at him, soothed by the city sparkle spread like scattered glitter along the horizon. "Game on."

He pushed off and motioned something undecipherable to the captain. He said to me, "As soon as we hit land."

"Fine by me," I said.

The boat sliced through the rolling waves. The night started out calm, but the wind was picking up, giving white peaks to the ripples, appearing as skeleton hands clawing up from the depths.

Shivering, I spun away from the view. Theo stripped off his blazer and draped it over my shoulders.

Every rational fiber I possessed demanded I rip off the coat and throw it at his chest, but it was still warm from his body. My icicle fingers latched onto it, pulling it tighter, before my brain could slap some sense into my skull.

And it smelled like him. The intense vintage scent of earthy oak. On Theo's body, he could make it timeless. I resisted burying my nose deep in the lapel and staying there.

When he reached out a hand, I stiffened.

"I need to..." Theo gestured to his jacket. "My phone."

He pulled one side away from my décolletage with care. My eyes wouldn't leave his as he reached in, his knuckles scraping across the thin skin just above my breasts, sending electricity to my nipples, already piqued from the cold.

I kept my stare and frozen expression, despite the urge to tremble, masking that his touch had such a bold effect.

Theo's attention moved to my lips, spotting the tremor before I could control it. In response, his mouth parted, but I forced mine shut and hardened my gaze. I hoped it shined like the sharp edges of diamonds.

He found his cell and pulled it out. Did he linger, just slightly? I thought so.

Theo tapped on the display before putting it to his ear. With the hum of the boat and the slap of the waves against the hull, I couldn't understand the muttering, but he kept my attention, the way his jaw moved and how he shoved his free hand into his slacks pocket. His white button-down stretched across his pecs and showcased that yes, indeed, while Theo had been gone he'd still found the time to work out.

His gaze slid to the right and I blinked, pretended something was in my eye.

A sharp sound to my left drew my attention. We'd reached the docks, land being deceptively closer than it appeared on the horizon. A crew waited to catch the ropes thrown by the captain's staff, who suddenly appeared from the cracks and crannies of this vessel.

Theo offered his hand, but I shook my head. I couldn't keep *sensing* him like this, and besides, I was barefoot and could navigate over the decks and docks just fine.

I hoped Kai had the foresight to grab my Louboutins on his way off this ship.

The men anchoring the boat paid little attention to us as we stepped onto the dock and kept striding. I hid my sea-legs pretty well as I kept up with Theo, the cartilage in my knees squishing like jelly.

Theo paused, and I nearly bobbled into his back. At his half-turn, I peered over his shoulder and noticed, in the midst of ships, yachts, sailboats, and speedboats lined on each side of the pier, was a table.

A felt one.

It wasn't my expectation that we'd show down in the ballroom of a grand hotel or the game room of a millionaire's mansion, but I also didn't consider that we'd be flipping cards outdoors on a dock.

Theo had already made his way to one of the chairs, which he pulled out.

"Um."

"You bet yourself in last night's game," Theo said. The dock had become eerily silent, save for the gentle bobbing of boats, and his voice carried easily. "If that's not deciding to be all in, then I don't know what is. So, going against me shouldn't make you hesitate."

My right eye twitched. "I pause only because we don't have a dealer."

"Head's Up doesn't need one."

"In this game? With you? Yeah, we do."

"Guess that's where I come in," Kai said behind me, two gorgeous black shoes hooked in his hand. Excellent.

"Fine," Theo said. "We'll get another chair."

Kai waved that off. There was no time to linger. I took my seat, Kai standing between us. He'd found the deck of cards, cracked open the cellophane, and we were on.

Everyone else had either disappeared or taken refuge on a boat. It seemed to be only the three of us. Theo's brows were lowered, casting black crescents across his cheeks and hiding his thoughts. One hand was casually splayed on the table, waiting for his two cards.

You're back in his game room, Letty.

I set my shoulders, envisioning this as just another round of kicking ass and teaching lessons, and not a moment where I sat across from the man who changed my entire world as soon as I laid eyes on him two years ago.

"So we're clear," I said as Kai shuffled, doing his fancy tricks that neither Theo or I would appreciate, "If I win, I don't go anywhere. We find Trace and bring him to justice together."

Theo gave a slight nod. "And if you lose, you let Kai take you home, safe, and away from this."

Away from me, he meant.

I'd never see Theo again if he won. I doubt he ever wanted to reappear in my life until I'd forced his hand, and now here he was, a Triton calling to me. Enticing me to tumble back into what I'd so sorely missed and disappear into the ocean together. Forever.

At times, it seemed impossible I was looking at him. In other moments, all I wanted to do was shoot him. Theo represented all that remained sad, broken, unfixable.

Yet, I did not want to go home.

"Okay, put in your blinds," Kai said. "Who would like to begin the totally pointless process of using chips?"

"To the left of the dealer," I said, leaning back in my chair and crossing my legs.

Theo acknowledged his start with a brow arc.

With deft flicks, Kai passed us our two cards. I flipped up only the corners of my hand. A King and a Jack of hearts. How appropriate. Casually, I glanced at Theo in an effort to gain any clues to his, but this was more out of habit than believing I could spot a tell. Theo had none.

But then again, neither did I.

"I'll raise," Theo said with the inflection of ordering another bourbon on the rocks.

I paid attention to the column of chips he pushed to the center. $2,000, when the little blind was $500. Theo was being cautious.

"Call," I said. I could be cautious, too.

Kai laid down the flop. A Jack, a nine, and a five, of mixed suits. "Check," Theo said. "$3,000," I announced, pushing chips in the middle and trying to remain as expressionless as possible. Theo called without a word.

Kai laid down a fourth card—the turn. Another five.

I tapped my index finger on my cards, still face-down. I had a mediocre hand, yet I could wait for the fifth card, see if I could catch it on the river, but it was a risk. Normally, in a poker room, I'd fold and wait for the next round. However, Theo was putting my goals on the line with this game. Wagered my sole purpose in life, now that it had so sorely changed since I'd—

Something brushed against my ankle.

My cheek spasmed at the contact. Studying Theo, I decided it couldn't be him, due to the sheer fact that he was doing everything he could to get away from me. Nor could it be Kai, since he was standing at the edge of the table.

A dock rat, perhaps? Did those exist?

It happened again. A light caress that sent the chiffon of my gown brushing against my bare calf, blooming goosebumps over my skin like the blossoming petals of a rose.

"Check." Theo interrupted my inner monologue.

Rodents should not be adept at sexual come-ons. I glanced down.

Nothing, except for the black lacquer of Theo's shoe.

"Scarlet?" Kai prompted.

I straightened while sending a threatening throat-clearing in Theo's direction. For appearance's sake, I studied the corners of my cards again. Fine, whatever. I pushed in $2,000. We'd each been given $15,000 in chips, so the first hand would not choose my fate.

"Call," Theo responded.

Kai dealt the river, a three of spades. Meaningless.

"Do you fold?" Theo asked.

We had no chips, nothing to bet but ourselves. I flashed back to Neri's game, but intended manipulation wouldn't work here, not with Theo. I could pretend to be a damsel all I wanted, even throw in a lower lip tremble. He'd tip me off this dock and ask for the real Scarlet.

"No," I responded. Simply.

"I missed you."

I responded to Theo without missing a beat, "No, you didn't."

He put his elbows on the table. "You can't know that."

"But I do," I said, glancing up from my cards. "Considering the last thing I remember is seeing your back leaving my hospital room in the dead of night."

The tip of his shoe hit my leg again, and I sucked in a breath, because it stayed there, touching me. Even though leather separated us, the thick make of the shoe preventing Theo from feeling anything at the proximity, the contact conducted an electric shock. Theo's eyelids lowered.

"Perhaps I should give you two a moment ... or another five," Kai said from above. "Are you two ready to ride the river?" Kai flipped over the last card.

"Check," Theo uttered, once again leaving the decision to me.

"Check." I wasn't going to push my luck.

"Show your cards."

"Show me yours first."

I flipped them over with a jerk of my thumb.

Without breaking eye contact, Theo turned his. A ten and a Jack.

I won, but that meant nothing. "Your playing was piss-poor," I said.

"You won the hand, and you're unhappy?"

"Considering the Sax I remember from before, you went easy on me."

"You're now that much closer to getting what you want."

"Screw you."

"You're welcome."

I shoved my cards at him, toppling the small piles of chips in the center. "I do not appreciate the graciousness."

"Clearly."

"I'm gonna go," Kai said, backing up. "For a while. That ship still available?"

Theo angled his head at me.

"Go ahead," I conceded to Kai, though my stare stayed on Theo. "But if you could bring back a few drinks, I'd appreciate it."

"I am not your—"

"Please," I said, cutting Kai off. I needed the assurance that he'd be back within minutes. "Vodka. With a twist, on the rocks."

Kai mumbled something, but as he passed behind Theo, he asked, "And you, sire? What would your palette appreciate on this gorgeous night?"

"Bourbon. Rocks," I said.

The skin under Theo's eyes formed little upside-down crescents. Almost a smile.

"You're interrupting the game with this pointless distraction," I said to Theo once Kai departed.

The tip of Theo's shoe grazed up my shin. I shot my leg back, away from him.

"Stop," I whispered.

"That's the problem," he said, coming closer. "I can't."

"You've been able to for the past—"

"Don't you get it, Scarlet?" His eyes flashed. "Resisting you is the hardest thing I've ever done. Being away from you, that made it better, but not easier. And having you in front of me now? It's a cruel kind of torture."

"To have me this close?" I challenged. "This is no cake-walk for me, either, but at least I have enough self-control not to caress you under tables and bring back memories better left at the bottom of the—"

He flew over the table, cupped my jaw, and seared me with his mouth.

Hands raised, eyes wide open, I let my lips warm under his, until eventually, inevitably, my fingers dug into his hair and my eyelids shuttered.

Theo wasn't kind, but I didn't want him to be. His lips were hard, his tongue demanding I let him in, but I could join in on the sword-fight, too.

Teeth nicked, blood was drawn, and a growl sounded low, deep in his throat. The sound had those rose petals traveling to my nether regions pretty damned fast.

In an instant, cold smacked into my face. I steadied myself against the table, since somehow I'd come to stand, while Theo paced away, wiping his mouth.

"Fuck, Scarlet," he said.

"Fuck *you*," I snapped back. But licked at my lips.

"You need to go. We can't do this."

"You mean, you can't," I said, covering the tremble in my voice by crossing my arms. "I was doing just fine in this game."

He turned, meeting my eyes. "Being with me hurt you. Staying with me, that will surely kill you."

"I'm in charge of my fate, not you," I said. "And my motivations are vastly different than from what you remember, so let me decide what's going to end my life and what won't."

"This is your last warning."

My arms dropped to my sides. "Are you so worried that I'll win?"

His jaw clenched in the way that carves out the cheekbone and sharpens the jaw. Sexy conflict.

I shook myself out of it and gestured to his seat, toppled over onto the wood. "Fair is fair."

Theo stalked over, lifting the chair upright in a single arc and sitting down, resting his ankle on his other knee. "I'm not concerned that you'll win. I'm concerned over what will happen when you lose."

"Game on," I said, and plopped down in my seat.

By the time Kai arrived, we were both seething at each other over the green felt table, bringing a chill to the air previously unnoticed.

"Ah. I see I've missed nothing," Kai said as he approached, two highball crystal glasses in each hand.

He set the vodka at my elbow, and the bourbon at Theo's. "Let's do us all a favor and bite this bullet, throw the baby out with the bathwater, swallow the pill, you get where I'm going here."

"I couldn't agree more," I said to Kai. "Let's up the stakes."

"One game," Theo agreed. "Sudden death."

"Thank the stars," Kai said. He frowned at the mess of the table, but with a few sweeps of his hand, tidied it enough to begin again. He threw us our cards and laid three down face-up.

I took a look at my cards, then slammed my palm on top of them.

Theo's eyes were deeply shadowed by his brows when he checked his, and he kept them that way.

"I'll raise," I snapped, and spilled all of my chips into the center.

"Uh, I haven't even laid down the riv—" Kai started.

"I'll see your raise," Theo said, low in his throat, and had his chips meet mine. He kept one, weaving it in between his fingers in a pattern that was as if he were playing music into the air.

It was exactly like how I'd met him. The way he played with his chips was how he played my body.

I swallowed through the remembrance.

Sighing, Kai flipped the last two cards. I scanned them, calculated my odds in the time it took to bite into an apple, and revealed my hand.

"*Fuck.*" Theo shoved away from the table. Kai parroted the sentiment.

I smiled, then said to Theo, "When did you say our plane departed again?"

Kai pointed at Theo, though his back was turned. "You were supposed to be better than her."

"I *am* the best at what I do," Theo said.

I shrugged. "For a man."

"Sudden death was stupid," Kai spat. Theo still hadn't faced us.

"But efficient." I stood, brushing imaginary lint off my thighs as I rose. "Before we leave, I need to go back to the hotel, get my stuff."

At last, Theo spun on his heel. "It's already in the car."

Good—I nearly said. My hands paused in their smoothing.

Kai met me on the same wavelength. "Did you deliberately lose to her?"

Theo stalked toward us, then easily past us. "If you're coming, Scarlet, you'd better hurry."

"But—but—" Kai looked to me, like I could somehow possess all the answers to Theo's motivations.

"Dude, I don't know," I said. Theo's form was slowly blending into the black of the night. "But I need to go before he disappears again."

"Scar, wait." Kai caught my elbow. "I have such a bad feeling about this."

"Then why did you agree to work with him in the first place?"

"I didn't—*argh!*" If Kai had fangs, I would've seen them. He released my arm in a dead drop. "Everything I do, all I've done, is to try to do right by the law, yes, but also to keep you *safe*, Scar.

When we first started this, we totally knew it was dangerous. Probably stupid—definitely insane. But you were the only link remaining to the Saxons we had. A family growing in riches at an alarming rate, and off the backs of criminals and bodies. Even if the FBI no longer believed in using an uninformed, uneducated, barely experienced cocktail waitress—"

"Is this supposed to make me like you again?"

He palmed his chest. "I believed in you. In *us*. But now we've crossed that line from danger to definitely dead. You can't go with him," he repeated. "And you absolutely cannot do this alone."

"I won't be alone." I pointed in the direction Theo departed. "I have him. He's lethal."

"Exactly my worry."

"Sax won't hurt me," I said softly. "Not physically."

"Even he admits he can't *keep* you from getting hurt."

I paused for a long exhale. A boat sounded its horn in the distance.

Kai stepped closer. "You know what this means if you go with him."

I didn't answer.

"He's a fugitive," Kai said anyway. "And you'll be one, too."

An itch began at my shoulder blade. Absently, I scratched it, and the *zing* of pain as I broke skin was both surprising and pleasing. "It's our last chance to get Trace. Sax probably *does* know something, and Trace will be in the wind by the time we figure it out for ourselves."

"I don't think you fully understand," Kai said. "The FBI will consider you a traitor, they'll come after you, too. I didn't tell them Theo contacted me months ago. I definitely didn't disclose that I agreed to work with him in order to try and get you out of this."

"I don't give a shit about that."

"Oh, yeah? Well, aren't you the brave one. How about this,

then? I'm calling Chenko right now. Telling him we have Theo. Admitting all my wrongs."

I reeled. "Kai, don't—"

He lifted his phone out of my reach. "I'm not letting him get away, Scar. Not this time. And especially not with you. I didn't agree to any of this. He broke his promise. I'm bringing him in."

"*Don't!*" I grappled for Kai's hands, and he twisted, smacked, elbowed me out of the way as he tried to press Chenko's contact button. "You're making a mistake, we don't have enough—"

"We have a Saxon!" Kai shouted, arms spread wide. "And I have you. So what more am I waiting for?"

I leapt for his phone again. Missed. When his screen flashed in front of me, I saw the ominous green call button.

"You can't!" I cried.

Kai's thumb hovered, then paused. His face showed genuine concern. "Scarlet, you can't possibly still love him."

"I don't," I replied.

"You're about to push me off a dock so I don't get him arrested."

I thought fast. "Because this isn't right. We don't know where Sax has been, who he's been interacting with, if he's been hanging out with his brother or his father." The last part, I knew to be a lie. Theo couldn't stand his father. But, Kai may not have the full dossier on that, and an iota of loyalty festered at the bottom point of my heart where maybe, it was nobody's business how Theo was abused, sold, and tortured by his sire. Not after the man he'd become.

Stop it, Letty.

I shook out of the reverie. "We don't have enough, Kai. Two years of work can't culminate into a lucky shot."

"Sometimes it can."

"You called him here, planned something with him to take me out of this game," I said. "That makes you an accessory."

Kai glowered. "First of all, Theo contacted *me*."

He glanced back at his phone, but I recognized hesitation when I saw it.

"We need more," I said. "Think about it."

"You can't..." He shook his head. Then, in a way of instinctual warning, I watched his forehead smooth out. "Maybe you can. Theo's the best lead to Trace, you're right. It's why we wanted you to work for the FBI in the first place. Here's an idea. What if you let Theo lead you to Trace, and then..."

"Spit it out."

"You turn both of them in."

A humming had begun in my ears the moment Kai had a change of heart. Now, all was quiet, including my mind. "What?"

"Theo and Trace Saxon, Scarlet. You're the only one who could do it."

My bare heel caught a splinter as I backed away. The *thwick* of the way it slid into calloused skin brought tangible pain to the moment. "I ... Kai, I can't."

"You have to."

The only other time I'd seen Kai sport such determination and calm stubbornness was when he'd revealed to me he was an undercover agent. And I knew, the same way I was aware that Theo Saxon was different from any other person in his family, that Kai wouldn't settle for anything less than both brothers on their knees in handcuffs in front of him.

"This would make your career." I said it before thinking—as I was thinking—a swirl of thoughts and warnings swirling like moths in my head. "Not to mention, erase any charges that could be laid against you for double-crossing the FBI by communicating with Theo these past few months."

"Don't you *even*," Kai said, pointing ferociously at me. "That man has brought nothing but death and destruction to me, to *you*. He needs to be out of our lives, you need to become the person you were supposed to be before meeting him. There are so many reasons why he needs to go. And you fucking know it."

I swallowed.

"You're doing this," he said, and held out his phone. "Or I'm calling Chenko right now. Your choice."

Chenko's face flashed in my mind's eye, the way he'd leered over my hospital bed, the smile he'd held over me. If I didn't do this, buy enough time, he would come through on his threats, and all my work would be wasted.

The direction Theo had walked was empty, but I pictured him there, hands in his pockets, his broad back, the confident stride and measured control he possessed.

He once was mine.

"I have nothing in my life except for this," I said to Kai. "Finding Trace, making him pay for the damage he's caused..." I absently rubbed at the raised bump underneath my right breast.

"You still have your freedom," Kai said. "If you leave right now, you'll no longer have the FBI backing you. I'll be the only one who knows your motives. Or, I can finish this. Bring Theo in the minute you give me the go ahead."

"Is this what liberty is supposed to look like?" I tipped my chin up to seem taller, even if my eyes sheened over. "I don't have Sax, I don't have my *sister*"—my voice broke—"Verily can't stand to be around me anymore, I have no career, no future."

"You have parents that love you. Me," he pointed in the middle of his chest, "who loves you."

"My parents can barely look at me without..." My breaths were ragged, but I mustered enough strength to say, "I'll do it."

"Even if you're forced to betray the man you love?"

I nodded but kept my stare. Theo wasn't mine anymore. "Even that."

Kai shoved a hand into his hair and rubbed, sending it into ruffled spikes. "All right. Then we're doing this."

My shoulders drooped, unsure if winning was supposed to feel like losing so badly.

"On one condition."

I grimaced. "Of course."

He dug into his pocket, pulling out something that sparkled like sunlight even though there was none to speak of. "Wear this."

Unconsciously, I reached for it. "What is it?"

"A necklace. Used to be my mother's." He shrugged.

"Kai, I couldn't."

"Wasn't finished. Used to be my mom's, until the techies at the FBI turned it into a tracer."

I squinted at him in confusion.

"Back when you were in the plans, I mean, back when there was a task force and every effort to arrest Trace and bring him back to the U.S., this was made for you. In case you were ever sent into something that the rest of us couldn't tail you into. We just—everything ended so fast, the whole mission was scrapped, so there was never a need for it. But I kept it, for obvious reasons."

"And it still works?"

"On my laptop, yes."

"But why..." I shook my head. "Have you been carrying it around, waiting to collar me like your pet, since we first decided to do this?"

"Maybe," he conceded. "But you're slippery."

I curled my fingers over the jewelry, the metal now warm from my skin. "Am I going to put this on and have the FBI's air force surround the plane I'm on with Sax? They'll take us down before I even have a chance to find the other brother."

"First of all, the FBI doesn't have an air force." At my sneer, he continued, "Secondly, they reduced spending on this task force a long time ago. I'm not about to show them my hand when we haven't even seen the river." He winked.

I brought the necklace closer to my face.

"Besides, it won't be on constantly. As soon as you have—*if* you have Trace, press this small button on the back. See?" He turned over the medallion, and just barely through the detail, I spotted a pinhole.

"You're gonna need a pen or a safety pin to push it," Kai said.

"I'll be sure to do that," I said. "In the midst of a tense confrontation with Trace, I'll ask him if he has a ballpoint handy."

"It's a failsafe. Don't scoff at the only thing that is allowing you to continue on without me."

"Fine," I said. "So I push the button and then what?"

"A tiny light in the front will light up green. My phone will receive an alert, and I can track you, or send any cavalry you need to contain him. Ideally..." Kai eyed me warily. "Both of them."

"All right." I sighed. "I really should go."

"I'll put this on you first." Kai spun me around, hooking the necklace at my nape. He then held my shoulders, pivoted me back toward him, and pulled me into a tight hug.

"I'll wear it because I trust you," I said into his neck. My arms wrapped around him just as firmly.

"I mean it. I love you." He kissed my cheek as he let go. "And call me. For anything. Ever."

I nodded, and after one final hand squeeze, turned and strode after Theo.

"I still think this is a shit-for-brains idea!" Kai called out.

"I'll wait for you to repeat that when I see you again!" I replied over my shoulder.

"You better." Then, as his voice was trailing off, I heard, "Hey, who's going to clean all this poker paraphernalia up?"

I tossed a smile his way as I kept walking, but he didn't see that it fell as soon as I turned around and entered into the shadows.

A LOW, sexy rumble sounded to my left as soon as I stepped off the wooden dock and onto the concrete of the deserted parking lot.

A sound that could only be the purr of Theo's very expensive, very seductive car.

I paused, putting on my heels. Although grit was still caught on the underside of my foot, I thought my steps were just as alluring and powerful as I hip-swayed over to the car.

A blur of movement within the interior and the passenger door was pushed open. I slid in, gritting my teeth at a pebble nestling between my pinky-toe and the tight leather of my shoe. As soon as I was comfortable, I subtly coaxed them back off.

"Last chance," Theo said as the engine roared. He stared straight ahead.

I mimicked his body language and replied, "I'll take the gamble."

A flick of his wrist, a spin of the wheel, and we burned rubber out of the lot and into the unknown.

We were silent for most of the drive, because we didn't know what to say to each other.

What words should be spoken to the lost love that was somehow found again, damaged and incomplete? I supposed we weren't going to talk about the kiss.

I chewed on my lower lip, staring out the passenger window and pretending like these questions didn't matter.

When we slowed at a stop light, the only car on the road, Theo said, "We're almost there."

"Where?" I asked.

"We're taking a plane. Private. It's ready to go as soon as we arrive."

I fiddled with the air conditioning controls, but to be honest, I had no idea if it controlled the air or the gas in this techno-monster-mobile we were in. "Automobiles, planes ... all I need is trains, then I'll be complete."

"That will come," he said. Cryptically.

Giving up on the pilot controls, I fell back in my seat.

"Cold?" he asked.

Since my arms were more snakeskin than human, I was forced to nod. It took him a full one second to cut off the air blasting at me and replace it with heat instead.

"Your bag is in the backseat."

I loosened the seatbelt and folded toward the back, finding my bag in the dark and unzipping it one-handed. Right on top, where I laid it this afternoon (which already seemed like it was three weeks ago) was my ratty old heather gray hoodie. Actually, not mine originally, as I had no plans to go to NYU. It belonged to my sister, one of the last remaining vestiges of her that I possessed. It no longer smelled like Cassie, but it fell across my shoulders exactly as it had over hers, and was so stretched out, the sleeves caressed my knuckles, just like they did on her. The drawstring was missing, the U was becoming unstitched, but it was my most prized possession.

When I had it settled over my body, I caught Theo staring. He immediately went back to keeping us alive by directing his attention to the road, but I couldn't help but sizzle under the attention.

"Not many people smile so sadly when they put on sweat-shirts," he said in a low voice.

Fizzle.

"I told you I was chilly."

"Mmm," was his reply, then made a wide left turn through an open metal gate.

We motored down a long roadway into an airstrip where a charter plane awaited.

Planes had the most powerful presence out of all man-made machines. Their sheer girth and ability to block out a horizon, the fact that they could cut through and float on air despite weighing a thousand tons. This "small" aircraft was no different, painted all white with a navy blue belly. Its wingspan still made up at least eight of me.

A man stood by the stairs leading up to the aircraft, hands gently folded.

Theo parked our car with the wheels opposite to the plane, and after turning off the engine, he put it in park.

"Afraid of this thing rolling into the plane?" I asked, smirking and slipping on my shoes.

"You'd be surprised," was all he said before he unclipped his seatbelt and stepped out.

Touché. Theo would have more past experience with private jet snafus than I would.

I unfurled out of the vehicle and made moves to grab my bag from the back, but the man who had previously been in front of the plane, was now in front of me.

"Jeez, you move fast," I said. He offered a small up-tick of one side of his mouth in return.

"Allow me, Miss," he said while reaching for my bag. "Feel free to join your escort and board."

"It would be my pleasure," I muttered as I stared over his bent form to the imposing machine.

I wasn't a nervous flyer—not exactly, anyway. But ever since my sister's death, ridiculous ways of my life ending seemed to become more prevalent in my mind. Forget being shot at over the green felt of a poker game because of a cheating scandal, that was too tame. Try being in a plane, spearing through clouds and turbulence and then getting struck by lightning, only to have parachuted out and grabbed the one harness that didn't click properly before flattening like a pancake as soon as I smacked into the ground (and then bounced).

That was more my mindfuck.

"Are you coming?"

Theo's question brought me back to sanity, and I clip-clipped over to him like a lame mare. Along with the hoodie, I should have definitely fished my sneakers out, but Lurch had them now.

Theo held out his hand, but I avoided it and climbed the stairs myself. The feel of his skin was better left in memories.

When I tottered on the second last step, I held my palm up to prevent Theo from assisting. I would do this, even if I acquired infected blisters along the way.

Upon entering the aircraft, I shouldn't have been blown away, but of course I was. How a metal tube could imitate a luxury hotel penthouse suite was beyond me, but this did. There was a lot of buttery toffee leather, thick beige carpeting, and some kind of bronze marbling along the side. Four seats of the same buttery color were directly in front, two facing each other on each side, with space to sandwich me in the middle of two people in each. Behind them were two long futons—or, in ritzy speak, *lounges*, that could fold down and convert into twin beds. Continuing the fancy language, a door to a lavatory was in the back in the same coppery marble as the interior framework.

"Take a seat wherever you like," Theo said, coming up behind me. The beginning whir of the engines vibrated beneath my feet.

Theo's Lurch entered after him and a flight attendant appeared from somewhere between me and the cockpit.

"Welcome aboard. My name is Andrea. Can I get you a drink?" she said. Her cheeks were luminous, her auburn hair even more so. The uniform she wore was tight-fighting, navy, and short, and the way her dewy lashes glossed over me and locked on Theo made me wonder if she was a conquest or if she had already yielded.

"Sure. Tonic, please, with lime," I said.

What did it matter, anyway? Theo's sex-life wasn't my concern. His brother, and making him pay for his sins, did.

I pretended like I wasn't serving myself a reminder and took a seat facing the cockpit. Theo sat directly in front of me, and zero surprise showed on my face.

"Are we expecting other guests?" I asked as Andrea busied herself in the galley at the back of the plane.

"Just us."

I inspected everywhere except Theo himself. "You must be back in your family's good graces, to be able to use this plane."

Theo shrugged. "The FBI aren't the only people Trace did a runner on."

This time, surprise couldn't be hidden. "Are you saying what I think you're saying?"

He raised his brows. "That depends. What do you think I'm saying?"

Goddamned poker players. "That Trace isn't talking to his own family. His father, specifically."

"Then you'd be right."

When Theo didn't offer anything further, I said, "Is that why you're doing this?"

"Doing what?"

"Look buddy, I'm here on this plane with you because you went out of your way to find me in order to tell me to go away. Except you secretly wanted me to come with you, since out there on the docks, you had your own plan despite me thinking I was in control. Now I'm here, and you know what I'm after." I was interrupted when Andrea bent between us and set down our drinks, but continued as soon as her airy perfume departed, "So, being obtuse may work with others, but not with me. Kai's no longer beside me, there's no further FBI or police involvement, so be straight and explain what your true motives are."

Whew. Through my pounding heart, I reached for my drink and took a long, fueling gulp. That was the longest I'd ever looked straight into his eyes and didn't flinch away from the hurt.

"That's only fair," he said, then bent forward. "But let me be clear. You're with me because you're a liability."

His words hit me. Though I didn't expect niceties from him, Theo's perception was still affecting.

"If you kept running games on your own, you were going to be killed. There was already talk in the wrong circles about taking care of a woman who was making too much money."

"And you had to assume that was me."

"There aren't many women who do what you do."

"So what? Because I'm good at poker, I have to die?"

"No." Theo tipped his bourbon to his lips. "But you have to admit you were losing your subtlety. Getting careless. And that's when they'd swoop in."

My cheeks went hot. "I take severe offense—"

"You offered your body in exchange for a bet."

Everything went quiet. "That was premeditated," I nearly whispered. "And under control."

"You don't think it was going too far?"

"Not that I have to explain it to you," I said through my teeth, "But Neri was heavily researched, all my actions carefully implemented and timed. He wasn't going to hurt me."

"But you were willing to do whatever it took."

I detected the undercurrent of meaning, and my lips parted. "Do you really think I was willing to have sex with him?"

In an instant, Theo went from staring at me to directing his attention out the window, I knew. *Oh my God.*

"You wanted to find my brother that badly," he said.

I caught the immediate defense before the sound left my throat. I could have stood over him, pointed my finger, and shouted, *how dare you judge me? You don't have the first sense of how I'm feeling or what it takes to be a solitary woman in this dangerous industry, or how many times I've been scared senseless. Nor do you even want to think on why my relations with Neri would bother your ego so damned much.* But, the part of me that wanted to harm him, to exploit his flaws and protect my weaknesses, won out. So instead, I countered with, "So what if I did?"

He lazily turned his attention back to me, whatever thoughts whirring in his mind drawing down the shutters in his expression. "And what is it they say about best laid plans?"

"Is this why you wanted me here? To criticize my strategies?"

"If you consider prostituting yourself to be a strategy."

There it was. That flare of jealousy—I hoped, dreamed, denied—was there, cracking through his concrete. The question was whether I was willing to exploit the flaw and spread it further.

"Well, it got your attention, meaning I'm as close as I've ever come, so I guess it worked."

"You were brash before. Now you've claimed idiocy."

I opened my mouth to snap at him, but the pilot had come out and was aiming for our seats. I clamped my mouth shut so hard it had sound, but I certainly didn't stop glaring at Theo, even while the pilot introduced himself as Steve and said that the skies to London looked good and we shouldn't be more than eight, eight and a half hours, tops.

"Don't pretend like you can get into my head the way you did before," I seethed as soon as Captain Steve left. "I've been more successful than you and Kai combined—I'm sorry, London?" My back went stiff. "Why are we going to London?"

Theo ignored all my statements, but he stayed steady on me. So much so that it was unsettling and alluring all at once. "Admit that you were looking for me," he said.

"No."

"Confess, Scarlet."

"I wanted nothing to do with you the instant you left."

"So you haven't thought of me? Wished for me?" His tone went low. Deep and velvety despite the plane gearing up and rolling across the tarmac, readying for takeoff.

"The only thing I've hoped for is your suffering."

I slammed back into my seat, using my arms as a barricade for my heart. His words couldn't wound me there. The meanings behind them wouldn't slip through. The *kiss* wouldn't be the dagger to wrench open my ribs.

"Then good for you. Part of your dreams came true."

My attention skittered to his scar, then just as quickly found somewhere else. "Don't make me feel sorry for you."

"*Pity* me?" For once, Theo sounded surprised. No, that wasn't the proper description. Deeply aggravated. Possessing enough ire to sound more emotional than in the entire few months I was with him before everything shattered.

His hand moved to his armrest, where he pressed a button. "Stop the plane."

"Wait—what?" I lifted off the back of my seat.

"You're getting off."

"I'm ... no, I'm not."

"You damned well are."

I frowned, then leaned over and pressed the same button. "Keep the plane going."

Unfortunately, I felt the thing slow down, to which Theo inclined his head and eyed me blandly. "They listen to me, not you."

"You'll have to forcibly remove me, then."

"Don't tempt me."

Half of my gusto disappeared. "I'm sorry. I didn't mean..." I gestured vaguely to his face. "It wasn't my intention."

"This was a mistake. You're better off with Kai."

"I haven't come this far, risked this much, to go backward." Against my better judgment, blunt curiosity crept in. "What happened?"

The directness fazed him. He blinked. "We're not here to share our traumas." Again, with the head-cock. "Or are we? Do you want to talk about things in our past? Your sister, perhaps?"

All organs, all bones making up my body, went rigid. "Don't you dare," I whispered. Wetness coated my bottom lashes, but I didn't so much as swipe the damp away. Further response would only prove he hit his mark. "Don't you *dare* mention her."

"Then I suppose we're in agreement," he said with all the inflection of a stone. His index finger compressed the button. "False alarm. Continue on."

Should I be feeling relief in this moment? Or was the offense of bringing up Cassie enough to make me depart this plane—this plan—on my own terms?

Theo answered my questions before I could. Not through more talk, since we were both done with that, but through unclipping his seatbelt, standing up, and moving away.

"I'll be in my family's quarters for the rest of the flight." He wasn't even directing his words at me. "Andrea will be able to meet any of your needs for the duration."

"Not yours?" I sneered, though even for me, it was a low, unnecessary blow that I instantly regretted.

Theo didn't bother with an answer. Instead, he said, "For the record, the reason we're going to London is because of the information you downloaded off Neri's phone. I knew Trace had spent time with him by speaking in the same circles you were, but that he'd since left the property. Neri was my dead-end on finding my brother. Until you surprised me by accessing data I didn't have." He bent down, close to my ear. "Over there, at the docks? I had nothing," he repeated. "It wasn't until you boarded this plane and Andrew accessed your bag that we had an additional clue. You fell for my bluff."

Cold air swept against the side of my face as he strode to the back, through the door I thought was the bathroom, but instead was a private suite for the Saxons, and disappeared behind the expensive wood.

"Fucker," I hissed. My shoulders pressed into the leather seat as the plane picked up speed and the engines grew in sound and power. The wheels lifted off the ground and sank into the plane with air and jet fuel replacing the need for rubber. We lifted off into the dark, cloudless sky. My windows went black as the cityscape shrunk in view and distance, and I played with the straw in my drink, allowing the circulating oxygen to dry anything wet on my face.

I didn't see him for the rest of the flight.

"MISS?"

I smacked at the fragrant, soft pressure on my shoulder.

"I'm sorry, Miss, but the plane has landed."

Turning in bed wasn't supposed to be this hard. It felt too upright, overly stiff, not at all like the regular hotel mattresses I'd been marshmallowed into—

"Miss!" *Thwack.*

"Ow—hey!" I blinked and swatted at air this time, as Andrea was smart enough to have backed off the instant my eyes opened.

Or ... so I thought. My hand had fisted, and I might have swung at her instead of slapped.

"Oh, God," I said, shifting straighter. "Did I hit you? I'm so sorry."

"It's fine," Andrea said, rubbing at her arm. "I'm glad you're awake."

"That's not ... I didn't..."

Too late. Andrea was already making her way to the galley at the back of the plane—*yes, a private plane, not in bed at a hotel, or in my apartment. Did I rent an apartment anymore?*—and I rubbed at my eyes, uncaring of whatever makeup I smeared across my cheeks.

Somehow, I'd fallen into a deep slumber. I remembered the wake time before, with Theo across from me, the scar bridging his nose whitening with anger, my cheeks boiling with heat-fueled rage. In essence, what was quickly becoming a typical Scarlet-Theo teté-a-teté.

I spun around in my seat. "Is Theo awake?"

Andrea paused in pouring a seltzer, hissing as it hit the ice. "I don't believe he slept."

She resumed pouring and clinking, steadfastly not looking in my direction, and it was all too tempting to read into her actions. Instead, I flipped back around and aimed my attention at a random magazine stacked beside me in the armrest. If I were flipping the pages a little too aggressively, well, no one knew that but me.

The crackling and bubbling came closer to my ears, and Andrea set the drink, with a lime curlicue on top, beside me. "There's a change of clothes for you on the lounge behind you."

"Oh?"

My wrinkled, navy blue formal gown must not be adequate dress anymore. The stitching was starting to rub under my arms, and I had to admit, it was *not* like sleeping in a nightgown. Especially upright.

"I have clothes in my bag...." I glanced around. "Wherever it is."

And frankly, where was Lurch, anyway? I hadn't seen him at all during the flight, which was probably a good thing, since he probably was the Andrew that stole my phone.

"These will be more adequate." While perfectly polite, Andrea's expression communicated the necessity of less dilly-dally and more gung-ho. "The pilot says it's about forty-five minutes until our descent."

I sipped the seltzer—wishing it were coffee, but I'd accidentally hit Andrea and probably didn't deserve the service—while padding over to the long, creme-swirl of a couch, where an unobtrusively folded stack of clothes was waiting. I didn't have to touch them to understand the complexity of the stitching and the utter softness of the fabric. When I pressed my fingers into the top piece, it crinkled musically with the tissue paper stuck between it. Unfolding the shirt, a waft of my usual perfume hit my nostrils, the tissue floating silently and fragrantly to the floor.

I checked the tag. It was an expensive silk blouse, European, and in exactly my size, lightly spritzed with my perfume.

How did Theo remember...?

Then I frowned. The better question would've been, *how did Theo* expect?

He had my presence on this plane so preplanned that these clothes had been ready for me the instant I touched down in Los Angeles. And oh, it *irked.*

Only one person had the capability of checkmating me, and damned if he would win the next round.

I unzipped out of my dress and slipped the blouse on. And *double-shit,* his taste was on point.

Sadly, I stripped it off and laid it with the dark, fashionably distressed and likely hip-hugging designer denim he'd also acquired.

My bag had been shoved between the seat and the couch on the other side, as I spotted the naturally-distressed strap hanging out. With a quick heave, I dragged it to the center aisle, unzipped it, and rifled through until I found what I needed.

Theo stepped out right when I was hopping one leg into my cut-off shorts.

"Ahem."

His throat-clearing gave me pause, but I recovered enough to stand and button my shorts. I looked over my shoulder and realized his gaze was still on my ass. He'd totally seen my hot-pink G-string.

At least, I thought with relief, *he didn't see my scar.*

My back had been to him, my cauterized wound well-hidden from view. No one except Kai had seen it, as I was incredibly protective. I didn't wear two-piece bathing suits anymore—not that I'd had much cause to be on a beach—nor did I need to cover it during sex, since I had none of it, not since Theo.

Which was better left unthought of.

"You're not wearing what I chose for you," he said.

"Nope." I bent down and hooked my shirt, a plain white tee, and pulled it over my black-lace scalloped bra. Then, I faced him.

He was dressed in low-slung jeans and an army-green V-neck tee. All designer, I was sure, hence the flawless pec-hugging and likely, butt-cupping, of the clothes.

"Why not?"

"Because I'm not part of your winnings," I said. "I'm here because I want to be, and I'll wear what I choose."

He shrugged. "Your decision."

After being caught under his too-long stare, I wanted to squirm. It was if he could x-ray right through my shirt and see all I was trying to hide—scars on the outside as well as the inside.

"Can I help you?" I said after a time.

He gestured with a glance over my shoulder. "You're blocking the aisle."

"Oh. Right."

God. I'd essentially become a black widow of poker these past two years but put me on a charter plane with the infamous Theo Saxon and I became an awkward pile of hormones who couldn't get out of her own way.

I shifted, and he passed, our arms barely grazing, but enough that the static charge flowed into my fingertips. I pretended it didn't happen and busied myself repacking my bag and tossing it onto an empty seat.

"Is there a bathroom I could use?" I asked.

Theo replied, without looking up from the newspaper he'd somehow acquired, "Through my quarters, toward the back."

I muttered under my breath but headed to where he directed. I supposed in addition to the kiss that didn't happen, last night's argument didn't happen, either. Theo was treating our interactions like a business meeting at a denim conference.

Once in the bathroom (surprisingly tiny for a private plane), I gave my face a good, cold scrub. I avoided looking too long in the mirror, knowing what I'd see. A tired, jaded, twenty-four-year-old. No need to reminisce.

I'd scouted my makeup bag and clunked it onto the marble countertop. The clicks and clacks as I sifted through were familiar and unconsciously comforting, like I was in my natural habitat, putting on makeup, like I always did at the start, or end, to the day—at the apartment with Verily, or at home with my parents, with Cassie coming up beside me, shouldering me out of the way so she could get in front of the mirror.

I allowed myself enough time to stare at my reflection, mouth *I love you* to my sister's living ghost, then moved on.

I quickly applied concealer, a little navy eyeliner, and some tinted gloss. My hair was a lost cause, as having it blown around by a helicopter's blades, tasting the salty air while on a yacht, and then playing poker on a dock didn't exactly create tamed tresses. I finger-combed it up into a messy bun and called it a job well done. There was a shower available, and, from peering around the glass partition, some excellent travel-sized Chanel bath products, but there was no time.

So I did what any person in my particular position would do. Swiped the bottles into my cosmetics bag and zipped it up tight.

When I came back to my seat, Theo was still there, ankle crossed over knee, sipping a coffee and flipping through the news.

"Anything interesting?" I asked once I took a seat across from him, still hoping for caffeine instead of diluted seltzer.

"You mean, is Trace on the front-page, the FBI having collared him after years on the run?" He flipped a page. "No."

"I see you have the funnies this morning." As Andrea passed by, I asked, "Could I also get a coffee? Cream and sugar?"

"Sorry," she said. "We're starting our descent. I have to sit down."

Figured. Theo probably could have asked for his drink now and Andrea would've bounced to give it to him. Unfortunately, I didn't have his sizable, perfect dick.

Stop thinking about sex with Theo.

Having him for real brought back the chemistry between us, the explosive sex and the orchestral orgasms. The fact that he could bring me to the brink with his teeth dragging across my breasts. An image of him on top of me, of me on top of him, my nipples tightening the instant his lips locked onto them, the idea of him kneeling in front of me, using his tongue on my—

"Are you a nervous flyer?"

I tore my attention from the window. Theo had been studying me, that half-lidded gaze of his noting every tic, every flush.

"Hmm? No." I wiggled a bit in my seat. No need to let him in on my desires. Not anymore. "Not exactly."

"It'll be dreary when we land," he said, his face remaining neutral. "You may want to put on the pants I got you."

"No." My mother's hissing warning resounded in my ears. "I mean, no, thank you."

"I appreciate the pleasantry," Theo said with a wry smile, and contrasted with his scar, it was the grin of Lucifer. "You'll regret it."

Regret what, I wondered? The taste of him on my lips, experienced a mere few hours ago? His hot breath on my neck as I rode him, which, if we spent any longer together, I'd want to do again, and again, heartbreak be damned?

"I'll add it to the list," I said. "What's next in your plan of plans, anyway? Are we showing up on Trace's doorstep?"

"Don't you wish."

"Can I have my phone back? Or can you at least tell me the information you found from Neri's?"

"Yes, and you'll find out soon enough."

Theo made no moves to get my phone.

The wheels touched down on the tarmac and the plane rocked side-to-side against the roaring wind. Once the engines slowed down, the pilot came over the speakers. "We've arrived at your destination Mr. Saxon, Miss Rhodes. Welcome to London, where the temperature is fifty-seven degrees with overcast skies with a sixty percent chance of precipitation over the next few hours."

"Is it not *June*?" I asked no one in particular. I glanced down at my exposed thighs, expecting them to preemptively be covered with goosebumps.

Theo shot out of his seat and tossed a canary yellow raincoat that fell across my legs. Stupidity wasn't in my vocabulary, so I accepted the jacket with a glower.

"Time to go," Theo said, tossing on his own leather coat over a hoodie. He flipped the hood up, half his face disappearing beneath the folds.

"Where?" I asked, shoving my arms through the raincoat.

"Haven't you figured it out, Scarlet?" He flashed me a wicked grin within his cover. "We're continuing our game."

Aren't we just, I mused, and swiped and swallowed the rest of his coffee before following him off the plane.

A BLACK CAR rumbled idly as we disembarked. I half expected a red carpet to be laid out to the vehicle, lest our shoes touch upon pauper's dirt.

"Is this the same private airport the Royals use?" I asked Theo's back as he loped in front of me.

"No," he said, without even a half-turn in my direction.

"Huh." I fixed my purse on my shoulder as I walked. "Guess the Saxon reach isn't as far as I thought."

I felt his eye-roll through his hood.

"No dinner with the Queen?" I asked, rounding the car to reach the passenger side. "I don't suppose it's proper monarch etiquette to host illegal poker games?"

"Do I have to listen to this the entire time we're here?"

"Give me my phone and I'll shut up."

Theo strode around the hood—or, now that we were in England, the *bonnet*—of the car until he was almost flush against my chest. I half choked on a surprised swallow, both at the sudden heat of him and the closeness of his mouth, about all I could see due do the clouds smoking up the grey skies.

"Can I at least meet one of the royal Corgis?" I asked.

There. Properly recovered.

Theo leaned against the closed door, his arm draping across the roof. His perfectly drawn lips parted. "Passenger side's that way."

I bit my slightly asymmetrical lower lip. Instead of giving him any satisfaction by stuttering or apologizing, I hiked the purse strap up my shoulder again and passed him to get to the other side, making sure at least my elbow brushed against his arm.

It was almost desperate, the way I wanted to prove our chemistry, even after all this time, even if only physical. Even if I knew it couldn't come to anything.

Aside from a light jostle, Theo didn't react and opened the driver's side door. By the time I reached the other end, he'd slid over and propped open my door, which I caught on the first swing.

"Ever the gentleman," I muttered.

Once I was in, he kicked up the engine. "I thought you didn't want any special treatment."

"I don't."

"Mm." He turned the car in a smooth arc and out of the private airport. At some point, our bags must have been put in the trunk—*boot*—but as usual, Lurch's maneuvers were a silent mystery. As far as I was concerned, I had my wallet and passport tucked into a small cross-body clutch that I would keep near at all times. No Lurch or Saxon would get their hands on it, just in case I was forced to escape and make a spontaneous quick exit.

I relaxed against the ebony leather, cool on the backs of my thighs and probably soon to be sticky. "Are you going to let me in on more of the plan here?"

"I already told you," Theo said as we drew up to a light in a small, two-way road. In fact, many of the roads here were smaller, all the cars whizzing by us more compact. Totally unlike the keg barrels of SUVs and six lane highways of the United States. "We're getting ready for another game."

I parsed through the hidden words in Theo's vocabulary, something I would need to brush up on now that we were back to exchanging dialogue. "Is Trace playing or running games around here?"

"Neither." Theo gunned it as soon as the light changed. My immediate reaction was to clutch what Cassie always called the *holy shit bar* located just above the window, but I resisted and clenched my hands on either side of the seat instead.

"Trace doesn't show his face in known game rooms anymore. He keeps his connections small, and then it's only when he has to. Like now, when he needs to make money somehow, and hires lackeys to do it for him."

The car veered as he passed a slower vehicle in front of us, Theo's speed never dipping during the lane change.

I unlocked my jaw to say, "Calling them lackeys is a disservice. I assume they're pros, able to get him the money he needs, plus a commission, in only a few games before moving on."

"You are entirely correct." Theo's lead foot continued, and to my dread, no other traffic—or lights—were ahead of us. He had free reign to speed.

God. My stomach heaved.

"He doesn't even stay in the same country for long before moving on," Theo continued. "He makes his plays quick, dirty and efficient."

"And what better way," I gritted out, "than to do so in Europe, when each country is a hop, skip, and lollipop away."

Theo tossed a quick glance my way, and if my eyes weren't glued straight ahead of us, I would've noted the flash of respect. "Your phone has told me, and history proves he won't be here for long—forty-eight hours tops—so we have to get moving, find his lackey, and follow the trail that hopefully leads to Trace."

"Would—" I had to stop to swallow the saliva quickly building up in my mouth. "Aren't we able to track him through bank statements or some sort of deposit? Something tells me his connections aren't only on foot."

Another glance to the left. "Are you all right?"

"Fine." I cleared my throat and commanded my spine to relax. "Are we in a rush?"

"Less than forty-eight hours to find at the very least, my brother's last footprints before he disappears again into thin air. I'd say we're in a hurry."

I couldn't handle it anymore. I closed my eyes. "What was on my phone?"

"A mistake. The Saxons are rare with them and for the most part, they're buried almost as soon as they happen, but not this time. Trace messaged Neri from a burner phone, a few hours before you landed on the *Hatari*, and Neri must have forgotten to delete it."

"How'd you know it was Trace? He wouldn't have used his signature in the text."

"The nickname Neri had for him," Theo said. "Nylon. Something Trace is ... known for ... in our inner circles, regarding the women he consorts with."

"I—" Dear Lord, Theo rammed the gas again, the trees and fields flashing by like a Wonderland nightmare as I fell down a deep, dark hole. "Can you slow down?"

"Why?"

The motor rose in sound, a beast purring out of slumber.

"Is it bothering you?" Theo asked.

The question wasn't out of concern. It was our usual spar, coupled with the unquenchable urge to win, even during a pointless episode such as this. And how could I be mad at it? It was exactly how I would've approached any weakness on his part.

"Not at all," I replied, but my voice vibrated right along with the engine.

"Good." Theo smiled through the windshield. "Because I'm only driving at half-speed."

The road gently curved, but as soon as we made the turn, there was nothing but straight, flat tar.

My heart plummeted at the exact moment the engine roared, the beast fully awake and flexing its muscles.

"Get ready, Miss Rhodes," Theo said, his arms relaxed, his fingers calmly curved on the wheel. "Maybe bite the seatbelt if you feel the urge to scream."

My shoulder blades smacked against the seat, my butt pressing into the leather exactly like it was on the plane, except we were on a road, with plenty of unknown obstacles, unlike in the air where the greatest risk was hitting a cloud.

"Theo, stop."

It was a whisper. He couldn't hear it over the car, the wind, his own cackle.

"Jesus, this is fucking freeing," he said, his lips wide. "Have you ever done donuts in a vehicle like this?"

Any other time, I would've been fascinated by the kid in him coming through, the wall he so carefully cemented together coming down brick by brick, all because of a fast car. Typical male bravado. I would've laughed. Shaken my head. Rolled my eyes.

I wasn't laughing.

"Stop. Please stop."

He flicked his focus up to the rearview mirror. "No one behind us, no one in front of us. I'm fucking doing it."

My knuckles were white. Nails cut into my palms and were slippery with blood. The backs of my thighs were sticky, but not for the initial reasons I thought. Fear equaled sweat. Hurt turned into blood.

I lifted off my seat as much as I could. "No—"

"Trace taught me this," Theo said through his teeth as he slammed the break, torqued the wheel, and put us into a spin.

"*Theo!*"

The sheer terror in my scream had him fumbling, slipping out of the carefully crafted spin, and we wobbled, jerked, the brakes squealing as he tried to regain control.

Cassie. Trees. Fear. Sweat. Blood.

"*My sister died from this!*"

The sounds the car gave off were shrill, worse than my screams, a thousand tons more powerful than my fear, and we skidded off the road and into the brush.

We came to a stop. Didn't hit anything. Theo turned the key and the only sound louder than my gasps was the cooling *tic-tic-tic* of the engine.

"Scarlet."

I kept staring ahead, eyes so wide and dry they hurt, but there was no care left, no idea that I'd survived. I was dead, like my sister. I was going to feel pain, like Cassie did. All I had to do was wait.

"*Scarlet.* Look at me. You're okay. Hey." Hands searched for mine. Theo swore when he noticed the blood, but he pulled them together, cupped them with his own. "You're all right. You're safe."

"N-no. Not safe. Not with you."

"Sweetheart, take a look at me. See my eyes. Come on. Turn. I'm not going to force you."

My neck felt stiff, like scrap from the car had lodged itself into my cervical spine. If I did as he asked, the bones would fracture. I'd be paralyzed. I'd die here in an English village that had no name because I didn't have the foresight to ask what the place where my life ended would be called.

"Nothing's going to hurt you. The car's off. No one's here but you and me."

Carefully, I moved so he was in my vision. It was painful to think that eyes so pure and blue could be owned by such a sinner.

"Good girl. Now breathe with me. Nice and slow." He pulled in a long breath and let it out, timing his to mine, and eventually, timing mine to his. "In ... out. There you go."

He squeezed my hands before raising one of his to cup my cheek. My spine bowed, relaxed.

"Nice and easy."

My lower lip trembled. "How could you?" I whispered. "How could you do that?"

Theo's lashes rose above the blue. "I'm sorry."

"How could you not *remember*?" My voice broke. His beautiful, marred face smeared under my tears. I pulled away from him.

He leaned back. "I remember."

"I'd told you everything." I wrapped my arms around my body. "Gave you all of me, including my most precious memories. And my worst nightmare. You used it against me."

"I remember," he repeated, harsher. "Your sister was in the passenger seat. Her boyfriend was driving. You were in the car with them."

My lips shook, and I pressed them tight.

"I wouldn't undermine you that way. It was only to scare you, to continue this stupid joust of ours where we keep wanting to one-up the other. I wasn't thinking. It was never, at any point, something so fucked up as to make you relive what happened to your twin."

I said nothing.

"Tell me you believe me," he said. His hand lifted like he was going to touch me again, but he dropped it back to his thighs.

I shook my head. "I knew the Sax from two years ago. I don't know you now. How you got that scar, none of it." I looked up. "For what it's worth, you haven't become a better man. You're worse."

The muscles in his jaw jutted out, and he looked outside, where long white-gold grass blew with the wind. The small amount of trees interspersed throughout followed suit.

"I can't counter that," he finally said.

I took in a hard inhale. "I don't expect you to. We're here for one reason. If this has taught me anything, it's to keep it that way. Don't duel with me." I paused. "Don't kiss me."

Theo turned on the engine. Surprisingly, it came alive without a sputter, despite the car leaving black skid-marks horizontally across the road. "My family wants to find him. Your FBI friend wants to cuff him. You must know, only one of us can win this war."

I fingered the necklace Kai gave me, underneath my shirt, remembering my promise. *Both brothers.* My obligation.

"You searched me out for a reason. I agreed to come along with you. We'll use each other for as long as we need," I continued. "No more."

While rocky, Theo got us back onto asphalt. He said, "And when one of us is done?"

I kept my attention forward, careful in my reply. "The other will be discarded."

THE CITY of London greeted Theo's and my awkward silence by screaming through it. Cars puttered past, honks ensued, music pulsed out of open windows and storefronts, and crowds of chattering people crossed intersections. The clog of pedestrians yelling at each other in a clipped English accent seemed to be the only difference between sounds of the UK and New York.

Well, that and the brief but polite *beep-beeps* rather than the prolonged leaning on car horns preferable to pissed-off New Yorkers.

Now wasn't the time to tell Theo that my bladder was also screaming, but I hoped we would reach our destination soon. My throat was parched, too. It was unfortunate that in my raiding of the private plane, I didn't think to swipe bottles of water, lime curls included.

We stopped at another light and I uncoiled my legs, wincing at the small space the car offered my bottom half.

"We're five minutes out," Theo said. They were the first words he'd uttered in over an hour. Granted, I hadn't provided any of my own, either.

I nodded and shifted again. "Good."

"Do you have to...?" Theo quickly took his eyes off the road to glance at my thighs.

"That obvious?" I asked.

"You've been twitching around like a toddler for the past fifteen minutes."

"Nice of you to notice." I gave him the side eye. "And offer to pull over somewhere."

"I told you, we're in a rush." He turned left. "Just past this block, and we're there."

I fisted my hand against my stomach, like that would stop the torrent of need coursing through my gut.

He found a spot on the side of the road, and his parallel park was seamless.

Why was it so sexy to see a guy one-hand a steering wheel while turning and looking out the back window of a car?

Did parallel parking *really* turn me on these days?

I winced. *Ouch.* my lady parts shouldn't be prodded more than necessary at this point.

Theo flicked off the engine. His movement, after being frozen in the driver's seat for the past hour, reactivated his scent, and his familiar smell, a smoky amber wood, drifted below my nostrils.

"Let's go." He shouldered open his door and I followed suit. Theo parked us in a small, cobblestone alleyway, where the sounds of Central London were present, but muffled. It was midday, thus the bustling lunch crowd we'd driven through minutes ago, but here in the shade of Victorian architecture and hand-placed stones beneath my sneakers, it was more like I was meeting for tea in the nineteenth century.

I'd never been to London before. It would have been wonderful to see Big Ben, or the Tower of London, or Westminster Abbey—all the touristy places that somehow, in London, seemed not so ad nauseam and more essential to one's education.

Did I want to see where King Henry VIII cut off his wives' heads? Abso-fucking-lutely.

But sadly, the Clyde to my Bonnie had other plans.

I trailed behind him, taking stock of everything in this alleyway, from the modern trash bins to the Gothic-era stone carvings framing doorways and window sills. The gray wasn't so gray here. It was entrenched, an essential color of history that fascinated and gave me pause. There was a light drizzle, but it didn't feel dreary. It fit perfectly within this scene of silent spirits and historical homes. How many footsteps preceded mine? Hundreds of years' worth of ghosts moved through this street, despite the modern bleats of traffic and calls and curses of pedestrians clad in the latest trends.

The pull in my gut wasn't so physical this time. It was a loss, being unable to explore the bones of this city.

A creak sounded, and I realized Theo had unlocked and opened a wooden door while I'd been standing on the sidewalk with my face tilted up underneath my raincoat.

"Coming?"

I scurried over as he swept a hand inside. A gentleman at last. I went in, wondering what the catch was in walking through first.

A light turned on behind me and the entrance sounded shut. Theo's close presence caused tangible pinpricks along the backs of my arms and shoulders, until he swept in front and gestured up the stairs. Then it was just his scent, tempting my nose and causing me to fall into step like a cartoon cat following the smell of cooking fish.

Another door greeted us on the second floor. We were in some sort of walk-up, with wallpapered blossoms on the walls and wainscoted stairway railings. Now that Theo's cologne had tempered, it was stale in here, airless and clogged. Without electric light, we would have been groping around in complete black.

Theo knocked with a loose fist, the other jammed in his coat pocket. Me, I hastily pulled the hood down and smoothed out my tossed salad hair, as if royalty would be greeting us and not a smarmy connection of the Saxons'.

A muffled "Yeah?" could be heard through the thick wood.

"It's me," Theo said.

A couple of metal clicks, and the door opened. A very tall, bald black man stepped into the light.

It took me a second, but—"Omigod, I remember you."

His opaque eyes slid in my direction and he looked me up and down in much the way he did when I'd made my first foray into the poker underground.

"You were the bouncer at Theo's games."

A brief nod, and right when I thought I'd thoroughly unimpressed him in the exact way I had when we'd initially met, he said, "Where'd your rainbow hair go?"

I was surprisingly flattered by his remembrance. "The way of my innocent youth."

Again, he nodded, but it was to Theo with a bemused expression. I was about to ponder why, until Theo gave him a hard nod and asked, "She inside?"

"Hasn't stepped outside since we got here," the bouncer responded.

He pushed the door wider, and Theo stepped in. Intrigued, I followed, feeling Bo's survey of me as I passed.

"Who are we meeting?" I asked Theo.

"The mistake."

I chewed on that, recalling Theo's explanation in the car—heard amidst sheer terror—and recalled him speaking of a mistake Trace had made.

The dim hallway had our forms taking shape only because of a single bulb above our heads. The wallpaper had gone from floral to a deep red and white damask pattern, the white curled and yellowed with age and cigarette smoke. The dark wooden floorboards creaked beneath our feet, evoking sympathy toward the downstairs neighbor, if the apartments below were occupied.

The feel of the place was slumlord, or at the very least, a squat house. If a rat scurried across my feet, I wouldn't have been surprised.

"Um."

Both of them paused in the hallway at my voice.

"Can I..." Good God, I didn't want to, but I had to.

"Bathroom," Theo surmised.

The bouncer said, "Go right when we go left."

I dipped my chin in thanks and separated from them when the bouncer directed. I turned the heavy brass knob, horrified that I'd be forced to use these facilities that could very well give me scabies—

The white was blinding. The porcelain sink even more so. Every part of this John had been cleaned so thoroughly my nose tickled at the smell of lemon and bleach still in the air.

Feeling much more relaxed, I went about my business, washed my hands, and exited, taking the first archway on the left, where Theo and his bouncer had gone.

Upon rounding the corner, a sofa chair came into view and the person in it. I gasped, then covered it up with a cough and a hand over my mouth. Theo cast a cutting look my way and I waved an apology, muttering, "If you would tell me about these things beforehand, maybe I'd be more prepared."

A skeletal girl—woman?—sat within the stained, pilled green fabric, an IV bag dripping to her right. Her brunette hair hung in lanky hunks, tangled with clotted blood, her spaghetti strap red dress that draped over her shoulders reminiscent of a clothes hanger, but none of that gave me pause.

It was her face, and the flesh that coated it. There was no pink flush, no Caucasian beige skin the way the rest of her indicated it should be. It was purple, mottled. My molars ached for her. One eye was swollen shut and her lower jaw hung as loose as her clothes. Her lips, which upon closer inspection, should have been plump and dewy with youth, were cracked and bleeding. One cheekbone was higher than the other, and a deep slash, stitched haphazardly, marred the velvet smoothness underneath. A bandage, already dirtied with rust-colored blood, covered her nose.

"What happened to you?" I whispered.

She looked up, her jade green eyes spearing into my core, and I realized I'd spoken louder than I intended.

"It's difficult for her to speak," Bo said as he stood behind the girl's chair. "So it's advised that any questions asked be essential." He said to Theo, "We should get her to a hospital soon."

"She hasn't been yet?"

Again, me with the trigger-happy mouth.

"We needed to talk to her first," Theo said for my benefit.

"But—"

"One of our doctors has seen her and okayed a few hours," Theo cut in.

"She needs a bath," I demanded. "Or if you would so deign, a wet sponge. Something to indicate that she's not a wounded animal here for your inspection."

Theo turned. "How many times do I have to convey to you that time is of the essence?"

"I understand that," I said patiently. "Yet you seem to forget that innocent people are often caught up and very nearly killed when they associate with your brother. And they deserve respect. Attention. Kindness."

His expression turned grim and I closed my mouth. I'd hit a mark, unintended but true. The girl before us had craved tenderness and been beaten. Left to fend for herself, but by God, she did. The kind of fight it took to get over that kind of threat was like an infection that infiltrated the blood, becoming an autoimmune response with no cure. I wasn't about to let Theo walk all over this woman.

"She'll receive it," he said quietly. "And while it doesn't look like it, Drea has been cared for. She is under watch, and a doctor associated with the Saxon name sees her three times a day. She needs a place to rest, yes, and a quiet room to recover—all of which she has. But for our visit, she's been moved—with her consent—to this chair for a short time. I am not the beast you make me out to be."

"And I'm not the innocent beauty you still think I am." I indicated the room around me. "Does she sleep in the bathtub? Because that's about the only thing that seems sterilized in this place."

"And also one of the only areas my brother won't think to look." Theo signaled to the bouncer. "Bo, get Drea some water, please. Now." He turned his attention back to me. "Can I get on with our mission, or do you have any other concerns you feel compelled to air out?"

I glared at him in answer. Damn it, I wanted some water, too.

"Good." Theo knelt in front of Drea. She stiffened at the proximity, and I had the urge to rush over, drape my arm across her trembling shoulders, and murmur reassurances. But, considering her reaction to a man two feet away from her, I didn't dare give her that kind of heart attack. I stood back, watching carefully and absently playing with my necklace.

Theo's shoulders sloped and a hand relaxed on his one bent knee. By some sort of witchcraft, that same flow of calm reached his features, every muscle softening into a standstill. The scar seemed to disappear. His eyes became kind.

That same stare regarded me in the car. After the fishtail, his face, those airbrushed lashes, the dark shadow of his stubble, the clear blue of his irises, were all I could see. Pleading that I focus. That I'd be okay, if only I breathed him in.

"Can you tell me?" he asked Drea, his voice remaining low, a soft-flowing river of words.

She responded to his voice the way a beaten horse would. Shying away, skittish, but ultimately, painfully, looking upon her captor since there was nowhere else to run.

Those cracked lips parted, a ribbon of black between the bruised red. "He ... hurt ... me."

"I know." Theo didn't touch her. His tone was his only tool of comfort. "That's why I'm here. To find him. Contain him, so he never has the opportunity to do anything like this again."

"There are ... more? People like me?" Her brows furrowed, the action causing her pain as she hitched a small gasp.

"Than you'll ever know," Theo said grimly. After a moment of quiet, he murmured, "I'm one of them."

Her attention flicked to his scar.

It was the most information I'd gleaned since running into him on the bottom floor of a yacht. *Trace did that to him.* And the when of it, the why, the *how*, would remain a mystery. Would he ever come out of the darkness? To this girl, to me? It was a harsh reminder that I didn't have a right to know anything about what he did. I never had that honor in the first place.

Especially after what I'd agreed to do to him when this was over.

Drea reached up, tentatively touching her fingers to the stitched-up gash on her cheek.

"Tell me what happened. If you're able," he said.

Her fingers trembled and she pulled them to her chest.

"If you can't, or don't want to, that's okay, too," Theo said. "I'm not here to force you to do anything." Somehow, he remained in a half-kneel, despite the fact that his muscles must have been protesting. "But you must know, you are the first person we've found, in a long time, who could provide us with something, anything, that we've been missing for years."

Drea hesitated, unable—or unwilling—to look away from Theo. I stepped forward. "Even what he was wearing."

Theo's rumble, low in his throat, was a warning, but as usual, unheeded. "Was he in a suit?" I tried further. "A t-shirt? What colors can you remember?"

Theo may not know where I was going with this, but when I was in the hospital and so many questions were bombarding me, spewing out of stern faces and blue uniforms, notepads pulled out, handheld radios spurting static, the beeps of machines and the intercoms, the patter of nurse's feet—it was all too much. Nothing could come to mind, not with the cacophony of concern spiraling out in silly-string tangles, filling my room.

Sometimes, the simplest question could jump-start the tiniest of details.

"Don't think of it as bad things you have to tell us," I said. "Even though, yes, it's terrible what happened to you. Think of it as things that will help us find the man who did this to you."

"P-police," she said.

"They've been searching for him for two years and haven't been able to discover where he is," Theo said. "The FBI, task forces, all of it was conducted to find him. And he was still able to find you."

Harsh, but true. I contributed to the silence.

"Suit," she eventually said.

"Okay. Good." I knelt beside Theo, using his shoulder as leverage. The old bullet wound gave off phantom cries, especially when I wanted to use my abs. Theo's glance was quick, but full of concern.

"Did he arrange a meeting with you?" I asked, redirecting his attention.

Drea shook her head. "I met him ... in a tavern. I'd gone in for a pint. It had been a long day at my desk and—"

Theo frowned. "You're not a working girl?"

Her brows jumped. "A prostitute? No. I'm not."

Theo held his palm up. "That's Trace's preference when he does things like ... this."

Trace lost his temper on a young professional? "How did you two meet?"

I said it like it was a blind date, or a meet-up after swiping right. It had the effect of casual conversation, prompting Drea to open up.

"I was ... just having a pint," she repeated. Then elaborated, "I probably appeared stressed, or down. I don't remember looking up a lot. Then someone came up beside me at the bar. Told me the weather looked stormy, then smiled." Drea said to me, "It was perfectly sunny out."

"He meant your mood," I said, letting her know I was following her train of thought. "It endeared you to him."

"Quite," Drea replied. Her shoulders settled against the chair. "And when I saw his eyes, well, they were exactly like yours," she said to Theo. "Bright, bright blue. And so nice." Her chin drooped. "I'm such an imbecile."

"To smile at a nice guy?" I said. "That's not dumb. It's what we all do."

"We started chatting, small talk, really." Drea shrugged, then winced. "He bought us another round, then offered to pay for shots. You Americans, you prefer your liquor hard."

I wanted to protest, then thought back to yesterday evening and the vodka I wanted to funnel just to get through the night. Couldn't argue.

"I became tipsy," she admitted. "Then *really* tipsy. The pub was closing, and he offered a top-up at his place. How could I say no? He was very kind, quite polite. And..." Her tongue darted out, in the space where it could, as she glanced at Theo.

"It's okay," I said.

"I've ... done this before. Gone home with men. A one-night stand sort of thing."

I nodded.

"That's what I thought this would be. We had the drink, whiskey I believe, and he started to get all handsy, and I allowed it because that is exactly why I was there, until ... his hold became hard. It was all in jest at first, or so I thought. Maybe he liked it slightly rough, and I was all right with that. I endured his smacks, until it stung, and when he b-broke skin, I—"

Drea sputtered, coughed, then began retching, seriously compromising the stitches in her wounds.

I guided her forward, my hand on her back, rubbing, but my message to Theo was urgent. "She needs a hospital. Now."

"One more question," Theo said when Drea's coughs subsided. "Did he say where he was coming from? What he'd been doing before he was at the pub?"

"P-possibly," Drea said, her inhales turning quick. "I can't— remember it all, due to it being a blur now, but ... he shouted, kept yelling. Accused me of forcing him to spend all his money in order to get into my..." Her mouth wrenched. "I won't say the word. It's foul."

She took some time to think, and hopefully relax, her lungs likely straining from the effort of providing both voice and oxygen to this small, battered body.

"A game of some sort," Drea said, coming up for air. "We bantered about winnings at the pub, which is how he was paying for our drinks. Stated how he was running low, but I was worth the additional risk."

"Okay." Theo looked to his shoulder and I jolted, my hand lifting off it in the same action. "Thank you."

He rose. I took his proffered hand before thinking. The dry warmth had me clutching firmer as I stood, my fingers disappearing in his steady grip.

At full height, I almost didn't want to let him go. But released his hand all the same.

Before I could remind Theo—"Bo, call the doctor," he said. "Make Drea comfortable immediately."

"'Course boss," Bo said, stepping forward. I'd forgotten he was in the room.

"Come," Theo said to me.

"I'm not your dog," I replied, but it was to his back. I said to Drea, "You did well."

"Did I?" she asked. "It doesn't seem so, the way your friend rushed out of here—*oh*."

Drea succumbed to more coughs.

"Sax is scampering away because you gave him something." I reassured with a quick hand-squeeze. "Believe me. I know."

"Good," she said, then, more fiercely, "*Good*."

"I'll tell you the instant we have him," I promised. And I meant it.

"Thank you ... wait."

I paused in the entryway.

"I ... I never got your name."

"Scarlet. But you"—I thought a moment, took a breath—"you can call me Letty."

"Letty," she repeated.

There was no time for second guessing. I smiled my good-bye, then hurried out of there.

"TRACE IS PLAYING CARDS," I said to Theo once I caught up to him outside.

"That he is." Theo opened the driver's side door and curved himself in, the motor emitting a throaty growl before I reached my side.

"There's gotta be a million poker rooms around here," I said as I clipped into my seatbelt.

I could admit, I was intrigued and looking forward to infiltrating England's version of the poker underground.

"There's only one person whose House would allow Trace in," Theo said. He took a corner, glanced at me, then let the wheel spin smoothly against his palms onto the straight roadway.

"You think Trace is playing these games *himself?*"

"I don't know." Theo tapped his index finger against the taut leather. "So much of that man alludes me, despite our blood ties."

"But that's about all you have," I said, and despite the urge to, I didn't take my eyes off his profile. "I remember, too."

The tapping stopped. "We were close once."

I faced the front window, but my thoughts remained with Theo. He was never one to offer up some history. Despite becoming so close to him and tracing the mold of his body—the line of his shoulders, the veins in his arms, his very sinew and licking my tongue across the border of muscle on his stomach, shivering each time I was able to touch his skin. His physical essence was forever imprinted into the rest of my life. But mentally, he was a deliberate ingenue. Hearing a word regarding his Before was a treasure. This tiny moment was no different.

I still wanted to know him.

"When you were kids?" I asked.

His brows came down as he thought. "I'm not even sure we could ever call ourselves children."

The Saxon brothers' father was known for brutality outside his family, earning his title from intimidation, cheating, and death. Trace was close to becoming the next Gordon Saxon. Vicious, prideful, uncaring of infamy and ideally craving it. His overt exertions made that clear, the one child to lay claim to the Saxon throne with the drive to maintain it just how it is.

Sometimes, I wondered if Theo worried he had the same temptations inside him.

Trace, Theo, and Ward, Gordon Saxon's three sons, are like a sliding scale in aggressiveness, Trace being the worst. If they were treated the same growing up, how could Theo possibly come out clean?

"What happened back then?" I dared to ask.

His throat bobbed.

The feel of his fingers, his calloused skin *whisking* against the small blonde hairs on my thighs, had my hand slamming on top of his to stop the shivers.

He still drove as if he were ferrying Miss Daisy over the London Bridge. Eyes straight ahead, one hand relaxed on the wheel.

"I know what you're doing," I said, but inwardly cursed at how unsteady I sounded. "Stop trying to distract me."

His palm pressed harder into my skin, the pads of his fingers dancing their way up. "Tell me to stop, and I will."

My front teeth dug into the soft flesh of my lips as I curved them in to stop the groan threatening to unleash. He traced, so lightly, my inner thigh.

"Answer the question," I said.

"Answer mine."

"You didn't ask me anything."

"Do I have to?"

He braked at a light, using the physics of the stop to come closer to the denim cutoff of my shorts. He played with the threads.

"You promised," I whispered.

"You're right, I did." But he didn't stop dancing. The flash of blue in my periphery told me what he was looking at. The strip of white that followed had me anticipating his next words. "No kissing. I'm not kissing you, am I?"

God—"No," I breathed out.

"Undo your top button."

His fingers came closer to the seams.

"I..." Chin tilting up, I stared through the skylight into clear azure, exactly like Theo's eyes.

"Slide your zipper down."

"But..."

His warm palm slid against my underwear, the lace but a textured prelude to the performance laying underneath.

"You drive me insane," he said, looking straight ahead. "Make me crazy. I lose my focus when I'm around you, because all I want to do is make you crazy right back. Take my frustrations out on your through pure, pleasure-ridden torture. Am I torturing you enough, I wonder?"

Without any warning, my subconscious had me unzipping my shorts before the light turned green.

At Theo's acceleration, his fingers hit home.

"*Oh.*"

I moaned, my hand finding his wrist, gripping it, bringing him deeper. I lifted off the seat, staring sky-high, groaning his name and trembling against his mercy.

You can't fall for it, Letty. You can't be beholden to him again. Don't. DON'T.

Shut. Up.

It felt too good to listen, and since it was my subconscious that got me into this predicament in the first place, I labeled it confused and would rather give into ecstasy than logic. It had been so long, since Theo's fingers had last laid their claim hundreds of nights ago.

"Don't stop," I said, panting.

A purr sounded to my right, and at first I believed it to be the car, its multiple engines or horsepower or whatever the fuck was vibrating the bottoms of my legs, causing increasing sensations, coupling with Theo's intricate weaves and heaving me off the edge of a cliff I hadn't seen in *years*—

"Scarlet, you're making this impossible."

The purrs, the rumbles—they weren't from the car. They were from Theo.

I reached over with my other hand, spreading my fingers across the hardness of him through his jeans.

"Fuck—" He rocked against me, and with a sharp jerk of the wheels, brought us to a stop at the side of the road.

I said with a smile, despite my heated breaths, "Now you know how it feels."

In a smooth swipe, Theo had me unbelted. "Take your shorts off."

"N—" The denial almost left my lips, until he took his hand away and left me aching, empty, *wanting*.

I pulled my shorts and underwear off without utterance.

With a surprising amount of strength, he hooked me around the waist and arced me on top of him, bringing his seat down in the same manner.

Sex did that to a man.

There wasn't even a tangle of my legs. No awkward moment with the gearshift. This man was as flawless in action as I remembered him to be.

And now we were face-to-face.

"I'm following your rules," he said, grinding against my core. I mewled, the effort at containing myself causing our noses to touch. "I think it's time you follow mine."

He reached down, and I braced myself on either side of his seat. His dick released and I didn't have to look down to remember the gorgeousness, how the size fit me perfectly and filled every empty corner I possessed.

"Yes," I said into his ear. "*Yes.*"

In one heave, he was in, my cry of finally being complete again filling the car's interior. I pushed onto his shoulders, becoming the driver this time, and rocked, rolled, swayed, until he hit every part that sang with pleasure.

Eyes up, then closed, I gave myself to this man. His hands centered on my hips, relinquishing control. Our breaths went in sync with our movements, my chin lowering, lips brushing against his temple, his cheek.

This is wrong. So very hurtful. But God, I want it. I can't stop.

I moaned, our pace quickening, the slide of him, in and out, pounding, thickening, pumping, until sweat turned to dew on my arms and his became a sheen across his cheekbones, his mouth delectable, made for me to bite down on.

I couldn't.

I cried out once more, this one drawn out and timbering into a whisper as I sagged against him, my face burying into the cologne on his neck.

"Scarlet…"

He rubbed my back, his caress gentle. Kind.

Dangerous.

I reared up. "Fuck."

His hands immediately left, the warmth of him trickling away as I lifted and slammed back into my seat.

I felt around the floor until I found my shorts and shimmied into my underwear while he buttoned up his pants, but his face was unreadable.

"That was a mistake," I said.

"Admit we both needed it," he said, then turned on the engine. He moved into traffic as if we'd just made a minor pit stop for snacks. No hitch in his breath, no heaving of his chest, a complete absence of trembling in his fingers.

That was all coming from me.

"The amount of tension between us, it needed to be fixed in order to keep what's important at the forefront," he said.

"We've just complicated everything," I said, close to tears, but I swallowed them back.

"You and I haven't seen each other for years, and when we left each other, it wasn't because of lack of sexual attraction."

"You left," I corrected. "*You.*"

"I've wanted you this entire time," he admitted.

"And what? You think you left me aching, vulnerable, ready to ride you the instant I saw you?"

He flicked his attention over to me, then back to the road. "No, the instant you saw me, you slapped me in the face."

I barked out my frustration, my shoulder blades burying into the buttery leather of the seat.

"Don't punish yourself so much," he said softly. "And give yourself more credit. I didn't take you right now because I knew I could. I did it because the instant you walked within my horizon again, all of me responded. I couldn't stand being so close to you and not knowing you again. Not touching you."

Me, too.

I refused to answer. The rest of the drive, I said nothing, and Theo, never one to ignore hints, didn't prod me into conversation. We'd done it. Both of us. And hell if I didn't want to do it again. Inexplicably, I felt swollen heat between my legs as soon as he spoke, the caramel of his words melting against my body, priming me for more.

"That's it," I said as we rolled to a stop in front of a very expensive townhouse.

Theo didn't comment at the sudden use of my vocal cords. "Trace isn't in there, no. But the person who runs the underground house is."

I shook my head. "Not what I meant. Us. We're not doing that again. That was the only time."

His eyes contained feral sparkle in the fading light. "Whatever you wish. You're in control."

"I may need to be more specific in the rules, I agree."

Theo hadn't argued, yet I still felt the need to put him in his place. "No kissing will now become no *skin-on-skin contact*."

"Understood," he said, then pulled himself out of the vehicle.

"Where are we?" I asked after exiting.

The double doors above the stone staircase opened, their beveled glass revealing a curvaceous shadow.

"I think you'll remember her when you see her," Theo said.

She stepped onto the terrace, her hands on her hips, the rest of her voluptuous in a black, silky thin fabric.

I took a step back, my butt hitting the car. Instantly, the alarm began shrieking. I shot forward, tap-dancing my apology.

Theo clicked a button on his keys, bringing silence to the night once again.

It seemed no matter where I was, what country I happened to stumble in or what year it was, this woman would always be better, more charming, more calmly seductive, than I would ever be capable of.

"Rada Khalaji," I said.

"DON'T YOU HATE HER?" I asked Theo through the side of my mouth as we took the staircase, where Rada awaited.

"The transaction you're remembering from two years go, Rada and I have long since come to a truce," Theo said in answer.

"I'm sorry I'm not up to date on the Saxon profit-and-loss sheet, but maybe you could give me a little more than that before we hit the last step."

It was exhausting, entering into situations I wasn't prepared for. Granted, I failed to utilize our car ride to elicit more information like I should've and instead jumped on top of Theo like a spider monkey, but I was determined to change. In the end, I had to remember one crucial detail: Betrayal.

Once I turned he and his brother in, Theo was never going to forgive me. To add sex to that, to mix his feelings, if any remained, with mine, would be such a brutal, irreparable mistake. Which I'd already made.

I tripped over a step and Theo steadied me. I'd gripped his helping hand too hard and let go as soon as I had balance.

"Are you all right?" he asked. Rada was now a few feet away.

"Yeah, fine. Might've just ... pulled a muscle."

It was clear, by the tightening of his face, what I'd caused him to reflect on. What we'd done in the car, me writhing on top of him, our mouths so close we could taste each other's orgasms. His expression went hard with dark promise.

My pulse ricocheted in more directions than one, as my words had the dual effect of putting me in the same flashback, but I schooled my expression into dark threat.

"Don't even think about it," I said to him.

"About what?" Rada interjected, her accent light, unplaceable. She'd lived in so many countries, I surmised, and originally from Pakistan, that it was hard to root her anywhere based on her vocabulary alone.

The years between us hadn't aged her in the slightest. Her black hair remained flat and shiny as a placid river, flowing down her back when she moved. Her wide, brown doe-eyes, while showcasing innocence, disguised the calculated reflection going on underneath. She was a head taller than me without heels, a gorgeous tower with them on.

"Sax here wants to prevent me from joining in on a game," I said to Rada. Then added, "How nice to see you again."

Theo proved his displeasure by gripping my elbow. Not so tight as to leave bruises but included enough of a squeeze to let me know that I was approaching restricted airspace by daring to speak first.

I turned to him briefly, my smile saying, *If you don't include me in your plans, I'll just do the talking myself,* and left it at that.

Rada did a double-take, her gaze turning sharp. "My goodness. I never thought I'd see you again."

She looked to Theo, curious for clarification. Was I still Theo's girlfriend, she might be wondering. What other possible reason would there be for me to be accompanying him again?

I also wondered if Theo kept in contact with Rada, took protection from her and entered this house, maybe even her arms. He knew where she lived without searching for her address or picking up his phone. They greeted each other like they'd only seen each other last week and *that* had been much too long.

Rada lingered when she kissed both his cheeks hello, her eyes steady on mine.

I hoped she could smell me on him.

"Come in," she said, sweeping her arm out.

I could tell by her careful blankness, for the life of her she couldn't remember what the hell my name was.

"Take a right into the drawing room," she said behind me.

Theo, wearing chivalry like he would a top-hat that he could take on and off, stepped aside so I could enter first, then Rada.

I followed her directions and turned left into a minimalistic environment in various shades of gray, with thick-cushioned suede couches and tufted upholstered leather ottomans framing a gray, wood-bordered glass coffee table. Heavy smoke-colored drapes framed the three floor-to-ceiling windows facing the front, and the most ornate piece was a fireplace, the mantle seemingly beveled straight from the wall. The only hint of color was a close-up painting of ocean waves above one of the couches. The whole space exuded the word CALM.

This was probably where she took prospective clients and various henchmen before she threatened them with imminent death on behalf of her father.

The property was, at least in my value, worth $25 million. I'd played in enough places like this to catalogue them.

A subtle peek on my part showed that her biceps were still as cleanly-lined under her brown skin as they'd been before. She put my once-a-month spin classes to shame.

"Can I offer either of you a drink?"

Theo nodded, and I followed suit, carefully picking my way over the duvet-like carpeting to a couch.

Rada stopped in front of a sterling-framed glass bar cart, the ice clinking as she set them into crystal highball glasses, then poured golden-brown liquid.

She was clad in an all-white wrap jumpsuit, and with her back to us, showcased her perfect, peach-shaped rump. I subtly cast over to Theo to see where his attention might be, but he was busy frowning at his phone.

Speaking of which—

Rada silently made her way over the carpeting with a sterling tray and gracefully set it on the coffee table between us. Theo set down his phone by his thigh and reached for a glass, crossing his leg at the ankle when he settled back.

Rada took a seat across from us, artfully crossing her legs. "So, what can I do for you?"

"I'm sure you've deduced that by now," he said after a careful sip.

"Still searching for your brother, I see."

"I've tracked him here, and since you come to my city often claiming you own this town, now is the time for you to prove it."

One expertly plucked eyebrow. That was the extent of Rada's tell. "Are you still smarting over our negotiations years ago?"

"Tell me where Trace is, Rada." Theo bent forward.

Instead of being intimidated by Theo's scarred face in full afternoon light, she relaxed against the pillows and tipped the glass to her bright red lips, maintaining eye contact the entire way.

"I admit, I could be of assistance," she said.

"What's the price?"

"Are you not enjoying your drink?"

I startled out of my repose, accepting that Rada was acknowledging me the way she would an invisible dust mite in her sheets. "Uh, yes. I'm fine."

She angled her head. "Perhaps you'd enjoy coffee instead?"

I suddenly became aware of the purplish bruises under my

eyes, the state of my hair. "Sure. That would be..." Theo didn't seem to mind the interruption, going back to his phone. "That'd be great. Thank you."

Rada arced into a stand. "I'll let the kitchen know. One moment."

Theo looked up from his phone. "Can you provide one of your butlers while you sort out the coffee?"

"It'll cost you," she tossed over her shoulder.

"I'm aware."

A middle-aged man appeared in the entryway, hands politely folded behind his back and thin-rimmed glasses perched on a small, pug-ish nose. He was belly first, his white button-down straining against the material, but his legs were surprisingly thin.

"Can I be of assistance, sir?"

"Yes." Theo set his drink down and gestured for the butler to approach. He murmured something in the man's ear.

The butler, ever used to strange requests from his employer and her friends alike, cast a strange glance my way before recovering and nodding to Theo. This man was a pro, his half-second stare at me not something any layman would notice. But I was on the type of alert I used at the poker table.

"Right away, sir."

I watched him exit, then turned to Theo. "What was that?"

"I'll explain later."

"No, you won't. Tell me now."

He sighed. "In a minute, Scarlet."

"You'd better," I warned, noting Rada's approach. "I didn't come across the ocean just to be your lap dog." I paused. "Or sex doll."

He shot me a look. "You'll get to flex your muscles soon. That I can promise."

Sated for the moment, I sat back.

Rada returned, a petite woman trailing behind her with an

artfully-designed silver tray containing a single-serve French press and a gorgeous little teacup with light pink floral print along the rim. It was completely at odds with the gray, but so cute I instantly wanted to lift it with my pinky finger sticking out.

And the instant the waft of coffee beans hit my nostrils, my brain *zinged* with incoming stimulation.

"Here you are, darling," Rada said as she resumed her position.

The—maid?—went about pouring, but I stopped her with a hand out and a smile. "It's okay. I got it."

The maid nodded politely and departed.

"Tell me about the games in this town," Theo said to Rada.

"Looking to pass the time while you're here?" she asked. She put her index finger to her lips. "I can think of a few things we can do."

"Enough."

I paused with the coffee halfway to my mouth. Theo's bark was often worse than his bite, but that didn't mean it had no teeth.

Rada did nothing but cross the other leg.

"You'll get what you want," Theo said in a softer tone. "But in turn, I need to get what I want. And that's the top games here in London. Where are they, who runs them, and how many times have you seen Trace?"

"There are a few well-known houses around here," Rada admitted.

"I want your favorite."

Rada made a sound with her tongue. "There's one I can think of, tonight. It's a large one, though—I doubt your brother would dare."

"How big?"

"A room full of security cameras big." Rada leaned over to lift up her drink. "The most categorically recorded clandestine game in the neighborhood."

"What's the buy-in?"

Both seemed surprised to hear from me. Funny, considering out of the three of us, I was the most active player.

Rada deigned to regard me. "Twenty-thousand."

The Scarlet of yore would've been stunned and dropped her nice teacup on the expensive carpeting. I merely quirked my lips.

"Doable," I said to Theo. "If you can stake me."

Theo opened his mouth, probably to argue and say there was no way he was putting me in a room full of dangerous Englishmen—

"I'd be happy to," Rada said.

I jolted. Rada's eyes, so stark against the brown of her skin, the rimmed eyeliner, the white of her outfit. They possessed the depth of a goblin shark.

"Good," I said, at the same time Theo proclaimed, "Absolutely not—"

"You, like your brother, are hard to welcome at games right now," Rada interjected. "She, on the other hand..."

At least I'd graduated to a "she."

"I can do it," I said to Theo. "If you think this house can find your brother, or he'd show up, I can be there. I can be your eyes."

"It's a terrible idea," Theo said.

"*She* said it herself," I said, including Rada in my periphery, "There are a ton of cameras. If you want to continue to be incognito, it's not a good idea for you to go in."

Theo rubbed the spot between his brows, right where his scar crossed onto his nose. To give him time to think would be gifting him the moments he needed to figure out a credible excuse. And we were on borrowed time. I had no idea how long Kai could keep the police at bay. And I needed time.

"It's settled," I said to Theo, hopefully in the vein of, *don't argue with me.* "If you don't mind," I said to Rada, "I would love to use your facilities. It's been a..."—I avoided Theo's study—"busy day."

"I can do even better, darling. If you're going to the estate of a duke," Rada pressed a napkin to both corners of her mouth before making sure to include me, all of me, in her perceptive study, "You're going to need a better outfit."

RADA LED me up an ornate staircase to the second floor. Theo stood at the base, watching us ascend. I glanced back once—only once—and kept my pace with Rada. It was strange, the sudden *yank* I felt in my chest, like I'd been tied to Theo but was now thinning out the string.

This would be the first time in twenty-four hours I wasn't in the same room as him.

"Here we are." Rada pushed open the double doors to what must have been her master bedroom. It, like the gray room below, exuded a soothing sanctuary, with that effortless flair I wished with all my being I had. If there was a time I'd ever own my own property, it would be designed exactly like this.

Creams, silky whites, pale blues. The king-sized bed wouldn't dare house any springs and would be the pricey, squishy foam that fitted to one's body like a lover. The pillows were long rectangles, temporary cuddle-buddies for those nights when the lover wasn't available, all ensconced within a billowing, silky canopy.

My eyelids went heavy at the sight. All I had to do was merely rock forward and I'd land face-first in the divine comfort.

"In here," Rada said.

She'd disappeared through an ornately carved wall, potentially the entrance to a walk-in closet. If I didn't trail behind her closely, I'd lose her in this maze of a house.

"I've found the perfect dress for you."

I followed her voice, discovered the line in the wall, and pushed it open. Rada stood among soft chiffon, intricate lace, designer cutouts and red soles on shoes.

Now, I'd have to add all items of her closet to my property list.

"I think we're the same size," Rada said. She held out a red floor-length dress with a deep V at the cleavage. It would fit me like an hourglass.

I approached, running the material between my finger and thumb.

"Beautiful, isn't it?"

"Yes," I breathed. The real thing didn't come close to my rentals, or the few dresses of my own I'd acquired and left folded in Verily's closet. I turned in a slow circle, eyeing every piece of silk, sequin, and crystal in the custom-designed closet. The smallest drawers caught my eye, four nestled one on top of the other underneath shelves for handbags that cost more than a year of Verily's rent. As I gently tugged on one, I half-knew what would greet me but was still bowled over by the sheer sparkle.

Diamonds, pearls, emeralds, other jewels I was unfamiliar with, and ... what was that? I peered closer. On instinct, I picked it up, inspecting it, then shoved it under my shirt as insurance for later.

"Try it on," she said when I turned back around. "I'll be waiting in the bedroom."

It wasn't until I raised my head and realized Rada had walked out and shut me in her closet, that I got a clue. Rada was being much, much too nice. The dress dropped with a clatter.

That bastard. Theo locked me in here so I wouldn't accompany him to this duke's estate and play him under the table.

"Hey!" I yelled.

Theo was going to leave me in his house until he deemed it necessary to let me out. Damn if I'd let him, damn, damn, *damn* him—I'd show him what it meant to take me out of my country and into someone else's only to have me safely stored away in designer clothing like a rich, trophy wife—I'd friggin' bare my teeth at the asshole and bite whatever exposed skin—

"Trouble with anything?"

The closet door opened without a struggle. Rada lay supine on her bed, sipping champagne that she had brought up when I wasn't looking. There were two glasses.

"Um," I said. "No."

"You don't like the dress?"

"Actually—" I was halfway to turning back into the closet but changed my mind. "I do have a question."

She waited.

"Why are you being so nice to me? Right now, I mean." I gestured to the bedroom door. "Downstairs, it was like I didn't exist, and now..."

Rada tutted. "Darling, after all this time, you must understand the play by now."

I crossed my arms, then re-crossed. "I..."

My radar couldn't be *this* off. Even in the presence of a woman whose sense of the people around her rivaled mine, it wouldn't neutralize my powers. Yet, Rada remained a mystery. One to watch.

"It's Sax, isn't it," I said to her.

"You must admit, there's something about him that is utterly feral." She savored the last word. "And fascinating. I want that man, have wanted him for a long time."

"And you consider me competition?"

She chuckled, a low, feminine sound, that had I been a man, I would have drifted forward. "Darling, no. We're both aware that Sax chooses his women, whether or not he has one currently."

Um, no. I didn't know that. But my expression remained passive.

"In the end, I'm a supporter of women, especially those in this realm. We're rare dolls, as players. The kind that not a lot of men can find easily on the market. I dare say," she said while leaning to the side and topping off a second glass of champagne, "Sax might have a type. He always enjoyed the rare jewels."

I wondered if Rada knew of Theo's high school girlfriend, the one his father tortured in front of him until Theo agreed to do his bidding. The one he watched be mutilated, forever scarred, because of a father's deeds he inherited as his own.

"As such, I feel it is my duty to say, be careful. You might not understand as much as you think," she said.

"Is it all right if I take a shower first?" I asked, with as much composure as I could. The red dress still lay in a discarded pool on the floor of the closet, growing deeper creases the longer it lingered. Rada maintained the power, but I could control time, and the faster I was primped, the more I could allocate to Rada and understanding the duke, the members, the cameras.

As for bedding Theo ... well, I wished Rada the best of luck with that.

"You may use the guest quarters down the hall, in the secondary wing to the house." Rada set the champagne bottle down with an audible *clink*.

Something I said—or didn't say—rattled her. Pissed her off. Perhaps it was in my facial tics, the utter disgust I had, but whatever the reason, I was not to be allowed to use her en suite bathroom.

"Sure. Thanks," I said, then sprinted out of there.

As I rounded a corner, Theo was in the hallway, commiserating with the butler he'd had run an errand a little while ago. The instant the butler saw me, he said some last words to Theo, then disappeared around the bend.

Something seemed off—in the slant of Theo's shoulders, the drooping of his eyes, how he shifted his weight.

"What's up?" I asked.

Theo turned to face me, and I noticed a white pharmacy bag in his hand.

"Did you need ibuprofen?" I asked.

"No."

Fine. Wasn't my business. "I need to take a shower, so I"—*we were back in the car, me riding him, his breath hot on my neck, his dick hard inside me*—"um, I'd like to freshen up, so if you could please move aside..."

"It's for you." Theo lifted the bag he held with two fingers.

"Me? Why..."

With his free hand, Theo pulled out his phone. A few taps later, he turned the screen toward me. "You've made the news."

THE LACKLUSTER COLOR of my driver's license photo stared back at me.

Even though it was taken four years ago, my eyes looked older, strained and dulled, the flecks of blue blurred and pale, the watery circles drying up in the years after.

Time should have smoothed over the edges in my smile, the curves of fatigue. In a way, it did. Cards assisted in burying the grief, the dirt that covered it fertilized by illegal addiction. Adrenaline helping it grow.

"Scroll down," Theo said.

I took the phone from him, first going above my picture and reading the headline:

INNOCENT GUNSHOT SURVIVOR FROM WILLIAMSBURG DRUG BUST NOW GUILTY FUGITIVE

24-year-old Scarlet Rhodes from Croton Harmon, Westchester, narrowly escaped death-defying odds when she was at the receiving end of a bullet shot from the gun of one of Manhattan's most notorious crime lords and currently one of New York City's Most Wanted, Tracey Saxon.

Rumors spread that Miss Rhodes was the girlfriend of Tracey's younger brother, Theodore "Sax" Saxon, also a fugitive from the law, and in doing so, found herself amidst an underground world heretofore unknown to the former honor roll student at Croton-Harmon High. A high school dropout who lost her twin sister, Cassandra Rhodes, almost ten years ago in a horrific car accident, Scarlet has since acquired a taste for the bad boys. A little over two years after barely surviving the well-documented Saxon fury dominating these streets, Scarlet has once again teamed up with this familial crime syndicate and can now add "criminal" to her non-exhaustive list of ways to rebel against her parents, and I daresay, living out a Bonnie and Clyde fantasy—

"What kind of rag mag is this?" I asked Theo.

"A blog," he said. "Read by hundreds of thousands a day."

"Explains why it's so unnecessarily wordy," I muttered.

"This isn't a joke. The FBI knows you're with me now. It's only a matter of time before the major news outlets catch on and people start to recognize you."

"Even on London's streets?"

"I repeat," he said, "Over a hundred thousand hits a day."

"We knew this was going to happen eventually." My heartbeat drummed, but my hand was steady when I passed the phone back to Theo.

"You're blond in the picture."

"I—what?"

"The photo they've uploaded. You're blond."

"And?" I asked carefully. My attention slid to the pharmacy bag he held. "Is that ... oh God, what color did Rada's butler choose for me?"

"You have to do this," he said. Theo's tone had me focusing back on his face.

"I mean, fine. I have no problems changing my hair."

"Good." His relief was palpable.

"Did you actually believe I'd fight you on this?"

"You fight me on everything."

I fake-scoffed. "Not for something involving me being caught and arrested in a foreign country."

"Are you still sure you want to do this?" he asked, searching.

I didn't hesitate. "Of course."

"I don't mean the at-home salon treatment, Scarlet. If you leave now, we can come up with something completely unrelated to my family as to why you're here. They wouldn't be able to prove otherwise. Unless—"

"Kai wouldn't dole me out," I cut in.

"Okay."

"Do I have to worry about Rada?" I lifted my chin in the direction of her bedroom.

"No. Do you want out of this?"

I shook my head and made for the bag, but he jerked it out of reach. "Answer me honestly."

I hope I exuded calm when I said, "Why go to all this trouble then, Sax? Finding me on a yacht, playing pretend-poker with me in the docks, plonking me on a private plane, taking me to the UK. It's clear you need me for something. Maybe it's about time you tell me why."

After an exhale, Theo let me take the shopping bag. "I need you to play."

My fingers grazed his as I hooked the plastic handles, the tension between us amplifying from a *zing* to a *bang*.

"That, I can do."

We'd moved closer somehow, this bag of hair dye bringing our lips within inches. He smelled of scotch, a sharp, nutty scent mixing with his woodsy cologne. Theo was the essence of an evening hike up a tree-lined cliff. Fresh air and smoke. Fire and stone.

God, I had to touch him.

"Scarlet," he warned.

Each shade of pigment in his irises was visible, the dark blue of an ocean bottom, the bright of the sky, the navy of the horizon. A mosaic of blue beauty. His favorite color, and mine.

I'd moved so my lower lip grazed his. My lids were half-mast, my hand reaching up then sliding down the suit-sleeve of his arm.

Cold hit much too soon.

Theo had stepped away. "We don't have a lot of time." He gestured to the bag. "Do you need Rada's help with that or…?"

I cleared my throat, then had to do it twice, since my heart had nestled in my windpipe. "I can do it." Trying for a joke, I added, "Do you have any idea what it takes to maintain this unnatural blond shade?"

Theo didn't smile.

I stepped around him. "I've been directed to a certain bathroom. I'll be in there if you need me for anything else."

"I don't."

My back stiffened, and I skipped a step, but kept walking.

"Neither do I," I said, but it was too quiet for him to hear.

I threw the plastic bag in the cream-marbled sink, gold flowing through the expensive stone like small rivers. This wasn't an estate that would install shower curtains, so I bent around the glass partition and twisted the monogrammed tap to HOT.

In a single strip, I was naked and ready for a few moments of gloriousness. I readied to get this gloppy hair dye business over with, because every cell in my five-foot-seven frame was looking forward to that spray. I'd shave my legs while waiting for the color to set—I didn't care, as long as I could get that rain shower system battering my shoulders like a little marching ant army.

The steam added a light dew to the bathroom, coating first my mouth, then my lungs, with delicious moisture. I rifled through the plastic that was quickly becoming damp and sticky and pulled out the box.

When the model's face flashed up at me, she fell to the ground.

"No," I said, then it became a whisper, "*no, no, no.*"

I retreated, the backs of my legs hitting the toilet and I tumbled, grappled for the marbled walls but found no resistance and smacked to the floor.

"*No*," I sobbed, pulling my knees close.

The memory hit anyway.

Brunette hair tangles in the wind, strands spat out with laughter because she can't keep her mouth closed, can't stop talking, about the school's new running back while sitting on the high school's lawn, her sundress hiked up enough to tan her legs and kicking out at my shins when I throw pieces of my sandwich at her.

At first, I didn't feel the waft of cool air against my shins. I'd burrowed into my legs, the barrier offering meager protection to the battering, endless remembrance.

She'd only been alive for seventeen years, and yet Cassie would stay with me forever.

Light footsteps sounded, but I didn't look up, barely cared, how Rada or any of her staff would see me. Too immersed in self-pity, grief, fear, it was a state that didn't—couldn't—happen often anymore, but when it did, it hit like a bear. Limbs quaked, sounds escaped, but if they were from me, I couldn't tell.

Weight fell across my shoulders and pulled me against fabric. Large hands spread out on my bare back and stoked.

I lifted my forehead from my knees, squinting through the steam. A black lapel brushed against my nose, and as I looked up, the mist parted and cleared against the sheer concern on Theo's face.

"It's okay," Theo said, still stroking. He studied every aspect of me that he could, grazing for wounds, blood, anything to indicate why I was curled up on the floor in a cloud of fog.

He'd unbuttoned his shirt, the collar flayed open to expose his clavicle, beating rapidly as it assisted pumping to his brain, his heart, his very lifeblood pulsing in the center of my vision.

Why I fixated on this was unknown, but I lifted two fingers anyway and pressed down on his neck.

"Scarlet, what's going on? I can't help you if I don't know."

The beats hit my fingers, his adrenaline making it harder, faster. *Alive.*

"Sweetheart, you're crying."

His thumb scraped across my cheekbone, and he spoke. "What's happening here?"

My hand found his wrist, squeezed. "I don't ... I can't."

"Can't what?"

I swallowed. "The..."

He followed my gaze, his hand never leaving my face, cupping my cheek, stroking my jaw. "The hair dye?"

"It's brown," I said, as if that contained all the answers he needed.

He settled back into his crouch. I still gripped his wrist. He said, with the way of trying to understand where a baby's pain is coming from, "You don't like the color?"

Against every internal warning, my eyes welled. "I haven't been brunette since..."

Realization dawned. "Ah, shit."

Theo's curse was like an ice cube being thrown at my nose. I shook him off, let him go. "It's—stupid, I know. I can do it. I'm being a child."

"No, you're not."

Theo's cadence, the pureness of its meaning, made me want to bawl in his arms. But, crying didn't make it better. Wouldn't bring Cassie back.

"I had a moment. I'm sorry—"

"Don't apologize."

"Sometimes it hits me out of nowhere," I said over his words. "Stopping at an intersection, waiting for a light to change. My head hitting the pillow at night. Raking through clothes racks. Staring out a goddamned window." Theo's thumb was stroking at the crook of my arm, but I barely noticed, shame replacing sorrow. "Looking at a box of fucking hair dye."

"It's not the hair dye."

I bit down on the inside of my cheek.

"You don't want to look like her."

"I don't want to *see* her. Not like this. Now that I've turned into everything she hated, I..."

"Come here."

He pulled me to him, but I said, "No. I'm fine—"

"You're not."

Theo was strong, and if I actually resisted, he'd let go, back off, stand in stone and allow me the time to get myself together. But...

Oh, but...

I didn't want to.

I fell into him, his blazer cloaking over me, my nakedness so exposed yet protected. I sighed into his neck, allowing the tears to come.

Theo rocked us on the ground, easy, massaging the tightness, combing back my hair, kissing the top of my head, and while the steam escaped, the heat didn't.

My grip turned into a clutch on his arms, and I burrowed deeper, uncaring if I ugly cried. In a sudden, brutal *yank,* I missed my sister desperately. Needed, wanted her here, or where we would've been, back in Westchester or in Manhattan, college roomies, sibling rivals, loving friends. She'd work in theater, would've gotten a job manning backstage at a Broadway musical, readying for the chance at her big break. I'd be enrolled in engineering, or biochemistry, destined for a science background, the way I was able to move numbers and probabilities around in my head by the age of seven. She'd be here, *I'd* be there for her, the way I'd never been when she was alive. Too into my books, studying, ostracized from making any friends and dismissing my sister's friendship.

I failed. Had the chance at a full life with her and I blew it.

The stubble of Theo's cheek scraped against my temple. If I could evaporate into his scent, I would. I could become the air, forget…

You're going to fail him, too. Betray him.

"I can do it," I said.

"What?" Theo tipped me back to hear better.

"The … I can change my hair color to brunette."

"We can get you a different color. Black maybe. Hell, pink, if it would stop making you feel so limp in my arms. I won't do this to you, Scarlet."

"There's no time." I forced my voice to be stronger. "We've already … how long have I been in here?"

Theo hesitated. "Something close to forty-five minutes."

"Jesus. We really have no time. Okay." I inhaled and loosened from his hold, though I wished I could stay. "Just give me, like, twenty minutes. Or thirty." I calculated the time to use the hair dryer. "Forty. An hour."

"You think I'm leaving you?" Theo uncoiled from his crouch. If comforting me on the ground brought him any stiffness, he didn't reveal the pain.

"You want to stay?" I asked. "While I...?"

He picked up the box. "I want to help."

Theo set the box on the counter and pulled out a plush stool that had been hidden under the vanity. He then reached around me, his mouth dangerously close again, and pulled a towel off the rack.

Gently, he wrapped it across my torso, stroking under my chin for a moment, our eyes locking, before he broke the contact and led me to the stool.

"Sit."

I sank, reuniting our gazes in the mirror. Theo lifted the hair off my shoulders, smoothing it back. Tingles hit my collarbone as his fingers played their notes. My spine felt him next, his touch grazing across my skin, before he leaned over and became nothing but scrutiny as he read the directions.

"First time coloring a lady's hair?" I tried to joke.

His focus didn't stray. "I need to wear gloves? Chemicals that can burn through skin? What the fuck are people putting into their hair?"

Laughter danced in my ears, my own, unexpected and genuine. I helped by opening the box and pulling out latex-free clear gloves. I put them on his hands, and dubiously, he took out the rest of the bottles and went about shaking and mixing. Theo didn't fumble, make faces, or comment on the smell. As he treated all tasks, he took this one seriously, and it was with true somberness that he applied thick brown paint over my sunny blond locks.

The silence was killing me. "Have you always preferred blondes?" I asked him.

He glanced at me in the mirror, then went back to spreading the dye. "I prefer the rainbow."

I said with a wry smile, "That hasn't been my color of choice for a long while."

Unwillingly, I went back to my reflection, watching my hair turn darker, the brown setting off the blue in my eyes, the natural rouge of my cheeks that wouldn't go away no matter how little sleep I allowed myself. His dark-haired Scottish princesses, my dad had always called us.

All I had to do was smile, see a flicker of dimple on my left cheek, and I'd be Cassie.

Theo lifted a panel of hair, his gloved hands crinkling gently in my ear. "Tell me how you learned poker so quickly. How you became so good at it during my time away."

"As if you didn't know," I said, adjusting the towel around myself. "The House always knows."

"Maybe you were a distraction," he said. "And I wasn't as keen as I usually claim to be."

"I was always good at numbers," I admitted. "By eight, my favorite subject was math. I never thought to apply it to card games, though—"

A chunk of my hair landed against my neck and shoulder with a wet *thwack*. "Poker is not simply a *card game*."

"Which I quickly realized as soon as I started serving your patrons in lingerie," I said. "And watched. Learned. When I met your resident dealer—"

"Fucking Kai. That narc."

"Can I finish answering your original question?"

Theo went back to painting. "Yes. Fine. Go."

"Kai's tutorials, coupled with the patterns I was noticing on the felt, brought out a hidden talent. But you know all that." I shook my head, then remembered Theo was still tugging on the strands. "Sorry. So, when you left ... I don't know, keeping up with the game, helped."

"With what?"

I met his eyes again. "Don't make me explain that part, Sax."

The idea of detailing my heartache to the very man who broke it was something I never envisioned I'd do. But it was the explanation of working for the FBI I was eager to gloss over and pretend wasn't real. Theo didn't know the deal I made, even though he knew about Kai. Which come to think of it...

"Did you think I betrayed you? By continuing to hang out with Kai?" I asked.

Theo thought about this. "Kai and I had a close relationship, FBI or not. As evidenced by my contacting him to contain your ass when it was becoming clear you were throwing yourself into situations where you weren't thinking first."

"I was *fine*."

"No. You weren't. Aren't."

"Which means you still care about me," I deflected. "What made you come back, Sax? That night in the hospital ... I never thought I'd see you again."

It was as if the atoms in the air hardened, or sucked up all the oxygen, or simply popped into vivid, thick existence.

"I said I'd protect you," Theo said, in the darkest tone I'd heard him speak. "I don't break my promises. You're done."

"Huh?" Dread collected like tiny, metal magnets in my gut.

Theo settled his hands on my shoulders. "I'm finished."

"I see." I breathed in fresh, lightened air. "As evidenced by you staining my skin."

Abruptly, he lifted off. "Oh. Sorry," he said, and peeled off the gloves.

"It's fine." I stood. "It'll wash off. How long did it say I had to wait?"

"You don't have to. You've surpassed the time suggested."

"I have?"

Theo shrugged, offhand, but I detected the strategy behind his expression.

"I've been done putting this glop on your hair for a while," he said.

"You wanted to keep me talking." I said, softer, "Keep me distracted."

Again, a one-shouldered shrug. "I sort of just ... pulled. On your hair. Pretending application."

"Thank you."

He looked me dead in the eye. "You're welcome."

"So I'll head in then." I indicated behind him, where he was blocking the entrance to the shower. At some point, he'd turned it off, maybe as soon as he came in and saw my crumpled form. I'd only just noticed it, which gave me pause. Normally I was much more observant.

"Let me come in with you," he said.

I faltered, my hand pausing in midair.

"I'll help you wash it off."

"That's not necessary." I stepped forward, but his touch stopped me from moving farther.

"No," he allowed, "it's crucial."

Now would've been a good time to gulp. But I wasn't a fan of facial tells, audible or visual. "I thought I told you in the car that it wasn't going to happen again."

"I want you naked."

Crap. I didn't contain the catch in my throat. Theo used the moment of weakness to hook my towel and peel it off, his fingers trailing across the exposed skin of my chest slowly, delicately.

So enthralled with the moment, my body priming for him—

nipples hardening, blood rushing, clitoris dancing, that my brain stayed five seconds behind. Turned out, those seconds would become crucial, because in peeling off the towel, all steam dissipated, bathroom lights bright, he could see everything.

All of me.

"Christ," he whispered, and there, right then, is where my brain caught up.

He delicately brushed against my scar.

"Oh, I—no." I bent down to retrieve the towel, fumbled in wrapping it back around.

"I knew it would be bad," he muttered, still focused on the spot even though thick cotton now covered it.

"It's not, really." As usual, I tried to brush it off. The recovery, the phantom pains, the random tightness from skin so stretched thin it would forever be a dark reddish mar against my pale beige coloring. "As you can see, I'm fine—"

"Don't."

I faltered at the look on his face, my fingers still clutching the towel as some sort of protective barrier.

"Don't play it off, pretend like it's all right. I did that to you." He pointed at my torso. "Right there. That's me."

"It's not," I said quietly. "It was your brother, not you."

"And I'm about to ask you to walk right back in on him." He spun, his fingers clumping into his hair. "What the fuck is wrong with me."

"Absolutely nothing," I said, sharper now. "You seem to keep forgetting, I'm not your little puppy. I'm doing all this because I *want* to."

Theo rounded on me. "How could you want something like that? Or choose to return to a situation where your attempted killer is known to hang out?"

"You mean, what the fuck is wrong with *me*?" I stepped so close, my toes hit the tips of his shoes. "Why don't you just ask what you wanna ask, Sax. Like, how am I so screwed up that I'm right back in the situation that nearly killed me? Or, why is it I'm so mental that you were forced to reveal yourself at the sake of getting arrested? Of contacting an FBI agent in order to trap me? Of doing all the things that expose you, because your ex-girl-friend can't seem to get her act together—"

"Those are your issues, not mine," he snarled. "I'm only here to get my brother back to my father, as requested."

I reeled, anger popping like a soap bubble. I was nothing but a task at hand. I needed to remember that. "How can you be so...?"

"Cruel? Because telling me you got that bullet wound will-ingly is like me saying I got *this*"—he indicated the scar on his face—"because I volunteered for it."

"How did you get it?"

Theo balked, as if he were readying for my retort but received honest concern instead. I was surprised at myself, since I'd much rather spar with an opponent than try to understand them. But this was Theo. *My* former Theo. And he was hurt, when I wasn't there and stopped looking for him, when I'd given up. Somehow, that added a layer of guilt to my anger, in the way that during these years, I assumed I was the only one who suffered, and how utterly wrong that was.

You still love him because he's broken.

Brows pulled in, I dismissed the thought.

"I..." His lips pressed together, jaw hard.

"Was it Trace? Did he do that to you?"

Theo remained silent, but I caught the almost imperceptible movement of his chin to the side.

"It was your father," I said.

"It's nothing for you to be concerned over," he said, and it shouldn't have, but the dismissal hurt.

"Why? What happened?"

"I told you. Don't worry about it."

"Talk to me, Sax."

"Scarlet," he warned.

"Do you think I'd consider you weak if you told me?"

Theo had been staring at something behind me, refusing any sort of contact. But, the instant I asked the question, his eyes *clinked* against mine.

I should have heeded his warning.

He strode forward and tangled his fingers with mine, still gripping the towel.

"My scar is apparent every time you look at me," he said. "Yours isn't. You can't know what that's like."

Unblinking, I pushed his hands away. And dropped the towel.

He hissed in a breath.

"I changed my mind," I said, watching how he roamed, a panther stalking its territory. "Stare all you want."

"This is how I want you," he said, though it was gravelly. Not his natural voice at all. "Naked and standing."

Somehow, I felt strengthened, despite being in my birthday suit while he was fully clothed. Standing straighter, my quickened breaths heaving my breasts, I was empowered in front of him. Not on the floor, not folded up into a protective ball. Standing, as me. A natural brunette.

A scarred woman.

"Take my clothes off," he said.

I grasped his suit jacket and pulled it down, locking his biceps in place. Then I unbuttoned his shirt as he heaved out his breaths, chin down, mouth parted, those crystalized blue eyes watching my every move. Gripping the sides, I peeled his shirt open, untucking the flaps and exposing the deep V of his pelvic muscles.

The belt was next. I unbuckled it within the electrified

silence and pulled it loose in a smooth arc. Button, zipper, *peel*. I shoved his pants down and he stepped out, and after I released his arms from the lock of the blazer, he assisted with the rest. But it was smooth, unhurried, and had me pausing. I expected Theo to *take* me, to throw me against the bathroom tiles or prop me against the sink and thrust. My body ached for it.

Instead, he offered his hand and guided me into the glass-walled shower.

He twisted the faucet. Almost like a waltz, he had us change positions, my back to the spray. Ever so gently, he tipped my chin up, then combed his fingers into my hair, stroking, coaxing the color to leave in dark rivulets down my body and pool at my feet before disappearing down the drain.

Theo's massage had me closing my eyes, giving in to his tender touch. When I reopened, droplets had collected in his eyelashes and put a shine to his lips. In the lackluster lighting, his scar seemed to disappear, just like mine had, as he continued to comb and stroke. Still, he made no moves to press me to him, to feel his erection, to do anything other than simply be sweet.

I lifted to my toes, nuzzling against the stubble on his jawline, closing my eyes again as he finished washing out my hair.

A man like this wasn't supposed to know how to be kind.

These moments were too tender. These seconds too special. They would turn into the kind of memories that had the power to ruin *everything*.

I landed on the soles of my feet.

Grasping his chin, hard, I threw him off-balance enough to step closer. Yet, I stopped the propulsion mere millimeters from my lips.

"Control, Theo," I murmured. "Do you have it?"

He allowed enough time for one quick breath. "Fuck, no."

Theo's mouth slammed against mine.

Theo's body was a water slick against my fingers, but I hopped on the slide, gliding down the ridges of muscle, the hard lines of him satin beneath my touch. The spray of the shower washed over our faces, pooled against our lips, but my tongue was only wet from him. He tilted me to the side, kissing me with tongue.

My arms wound their way around his neck while his traveled down my torso, met my hips, and lifted my thigh, balancing it between the glass partition and his body.

I felt him between my legs, the stiffness of his against mine, but he didn't demand access and instead drew out the tease.

"*Please...*" I breathed.

"Tell me you want it."

I told myself to exhale through the swell, the ache of having him near, but not near enough. "I..."

"Admit you want me."

"I've..."

He lingered near my opening, the tip of him stroking, tempting, a temperance of demand where, if he didn't make a move already, I was going to take his dick and ride him on my own terms.

"Stop fucking around, Sax." I sounded out of breath, though I hadn't even exerted the effort of lifting my own leg.

"That's exactly what I aim to do, but you need to ask for it."

"You know I want this."

"You want me inside you."

"Yes, Sax."

"Say it. Say my name."

"*Sax!*"

"Wrong one." Theo pulled back, the shower's tears trickling down his nose, bringing his hair flat against his forehead until he flicked it back. His stubble glittered, his lips so dewy I wanted to suck on them like my favorite cherry lollipop.

"Goddamn you," I said. "Theo. I want you, *Theo*. I've always wanted you. I haven't had anyone since you."

That admittance, though completely unplanned, had his pupils flaring, his growl of dominance echoing within the shower walls. His irises had gone dark, the grey-blue of an incoming coastal storm.

"Don't you dare stop now," I breathed out.

We're making a mistake.

I staunched the conscious thought, giving into my subconscious need instead. For him. For Theo, the man who'd left a second hole in my heart and made no promises to fill it up again. And I showed it by gripping his neck and pulling him back.

Theo released his hold—so briefly I barely felt when he used two fingers to part me—but *God*, I felt it when he plunged.

The wall tiles were ice against my back at the slam, the hot and cold of the mixing temperatures culminating into my voice-filled gasp drenching the air between us.

He lifted my hips, positioning so he could have the deepest access, and I torqued my head back, drowning from the pleasure of having him fill me. The shortness of breath I felt could have been from the water cascading over my mouth until his lips covered mine. Theo's fingers tangled at the back of my neck, the white noise of the shower doing little to disguise his moans and my cries.

"Theo, I'm going to..."

Theo brought his mouth near my ear, his head dipping with passion and landing near my collarbone. "Not until I want you to."

He pulled back, emptying the space between us, and before I could voice my disapproval, he spun us on the wet stone floor, throwing me off enough so that my hands slammed against the shower wall, and entered me from behind.

"Oh ... yes," I said when he hit my G-spot, my palms skidding across the tiles. "Don't stop. *Don't stop.*"

His smacks became pounds, and he palmed my ass, squeezed, before yelling out and thrusting as deep as he'd ever gone.

Both of us, in tandem, yelled out our orgasms, muscles in my thighs twanging and releasing, a flow of pleasure I hadn't felt in years, since *him*, replenishing my bloodstream, awakening the woman lying dormant inside, her sexual prowess released with a wave of true, ultimate pleasure.

Theo's hands cupped my waist, the water doing nothing to prevent the bruising that would surely show the imprints of his fingers. Theo's marks of passion on me, indicating the ecstasy both of us received, was not something I remembered missing until the instant his grip released.

In pure cliché, my legs turned to jello without his steadying hands. I straightened, but shoulder-bumped into the wall, breathing heavy, lids so low Theo's movements were mere flickering shadows in my vision.

He rubbed a hand across his jaw. "That was..."

Amazing.

But I said nothing, catching my breath and my balance in the moments it was taking him to come back to reality.

His chest rose and fell, Theo's body receiving all of the spray, a sparkling dew outlining every border and crevice on his delicious form. "Do you need time to finish getting ready?" he asked through his hard exhales.

I couldn't help but crack a smile. Movies never panned to this part, where literally, right after the sexual crescendo, people had to finish making plans while naked and recovering in a place that didn't contain a bed.

He remained exposed to me, and I to him.

"Yeah," I said, pushing off the tile. "Sure."

Theo nodded, scratched at his jaw again, and stepped out, giving me a perfect view of his taut, round melon of an ass, golden just like the rest of him.

Orgasm abated, I re-entered the spray, tilting my face up and letting the hot water coat my breasts, run down my stomach, collect near my thighs.

It wasn't nearly as hot as Theo.

Sighing, I turned off the stream. When I exited, I was one towel down and Theo was nowhere in the vast expanse of this bathroom. Probably for the best.

I toweled off and helped myself to the various lotions and potions on the vanity. Once thoroughly scented and moisturized, I turned on the hair dryer, allowing the dry heat to evaporate any remaining water from my hair as well as my eyes.

I did it all without looking in the mirror.

God, I was afraid.

Cassie hadn't been in my life for almost a decade—that newt-finger of a blogger had been correct in his article—yet, it would always feel like I'd lost her this morning.

Time was meant to be the ultimate Band-Aid, a healer of all woes, the giver of strength. But it seemed to have skipped me, because thousands of days later, my heart couldn't stand to be a twinless twin.

Save for surgical modification, I'd done everything possible to stop looking like her, and I'd managed it for a record eight years. Hell, I'd become a different person on the inside *and* out, Cassie properly buried both in a cemetery and at the bottom of my soul.

Now, for reasons unknown, she was asking to reappear, and I wasn't sure I could handle it.

After blow-drying for twenty minutes, my hair was so dry as to resemble burned tumbleweed, and I couldn't find any more excuses.

"You've become a strong-ass bitch in the poker underworld," I reassured myself. "You can handle a little self-reflection time."

Okay. One, two...

Closing my eyes, hands to my stomach, I turned to the mirror, and ever the strategist, even to myself, I opened my eyes before three.

"*Cassie*," I wrenched out. Hands bracing the countertop, I leaned forward, her smoke-filled blue eyes stared back, her straight, Roman nose, the high cheekbones, the slightly-pointed chin.

The dimple, although it didn't appear in her smile this time. It showed with a trembling frown.

"I can't do this," I said to her, legs beginning to shake. "I can't—"

You can.

"No," I whispered.

Look under your right eye. See? No freckle.

I gulped but strayed to where the dot should be.

And your chin. Where's the scar after flying over the front handles of your bike and landing jaw-first on summer-baked asphalt?

Not there, because that was the day I'd had a stomach bug and Cassie was forced to bike to swim class on her own.

Your freckle, Scarlet Rhodes's beauty mark, is under your right brow, low enough that the corner of your lashes touch it when your eyes are open.

I touched the spot, my lashes flickering against my finger.

And your stripes are on your hips, the lightest white stretch marks, from losing weight so rapidly then gaining a bit of it back after my death. Whereas mine are right on top of my ass.

That was right. Cassie often bemoaned her randomly acquired stretch marks when we were changing in the locker rooms or in our bedroom swapping clothes, whereas I had none. Not at that time, when she was alive, complaining, and being the most annoying person on the planet to share a room with.

And your scar. It's on your ribcage. See? A bullet wound I never received, because I'm not you.

"I'm not you," I said, grazing over the wound.

You're not me.

"You're dead."

I waited for a response, but the voice, whatever or whoever it was, said nothing. It was gone.

With its absence came a steadying of my trembles, a rhythm to my breathing. I was the sole resident in this bathroom, had always been. It was only me, contributing to the silence.

A knock came at the door as I was smoothing down my newly glossed strands.

"Scarlet?" It was Rada's voice. "Are you ready for the dress?"

"Yes—" I scrambled around the floor for my underwear. Out of the corner of my eye, pastel blue caught my attention. Upon further inspection, it turned out to be a neatly folded (and perfume scented) bustier and lace thong. "Just a second!"

When did Theo do that? Did he reopen the door as I was drying off and quietly sling an arm around the frame, dropping off the expensive, fragrant package? Or did he do it when he originally came into the bathroom, before seeing me curled into a ball on the floor? Did *Rada* drop this off during Theo's and my water-soaked sex?

"Jesus, this place," I muttered. But shook out the bustier anyway and clipped it on.

Expectedly, it was gorgeous and hugged my curves in all the right ways. Theo flung himself into my vision, his gaze raking up and down, drinking in every lace detail before moving to reveal the skin underneath. I told his image to fuck off.

The shower scene would be the last *last* time, damn it.

I opened the door to Rada, who held the red vision on a hanger, her other arm crooked at the mid-length so it barely touched the floor.

"This should fit you seamlessly," she said. Her expression showed no indication she knew what Theo and I had been up to, but I'd be a fool to take Rada at face value. I was dealing with people who'd mastered the art of poker long before I entered into their town. Rada earned her crown years before me. Possibly at birth when she was born to a crime lord.

"Thank you," I said, taking the dress carefully. "I truly mean it."

Rada's attention lowered, then stopped at my collarbone. "Don't take that necklace off. It will go lovely with the dress."

I unconsciously fingered Kai's gold chain but dropped my hand as soon as I became aware.

"I ... uh, I'll be out soon." I started to shut the door, but she gently palmed it to remain open.

"Sax and I will be waiting for you in the drawing room. We have a few things to discuss before you go."

"Of course."

She nodded, and clicked the door shut.

I slipped into the dress, finding it slightly difficult to zip up on my own, but I wasn't about to call Rada or Theo back in for help. There weren't any shoes provided, and I realized, with a deep, despairing sigh, I'd have to wear my bear traps again. After folding up my old clothes and hanging my damp towel, I made my way back downstairs in bare feet, idly wondering why, in a mansion with so many rooms, we were returning to the drawing room. I would've been keen to see the rest of this place, but perhaps Rada had her own secrets to keep.

The room was directly to the left of the staircase, so I had no trouble re-finding it. Theo was already there, in his surprisingly unrumpled suit, his short brown hair still damp from the—*our*—shower together. He was turned away, his profile a lemon-soaked outline from the setting sun out of the tall windows.

At the sound of my approach, he faced me, and his carefully constructed mask of indifference slipped. In that remarkable way he could, he took in every part of me, so much so that even my pores were exposed to his scrutiny, before he landed on my hair.

"You look beautiful," he said.

Theo never met Cassie, but I felt as if he were staring like there were two of me, one beside the other, and it was with rare endearment that his lips lifted as his brows came down. My hand unclenched, as if I could hold Cassie's through the air.

I opened my mouth to say thank you, to hopefully extend this unique, stupefying moment that was between Theo, me and Cassie, but it was broken.

"Are you hungry?"

Rada appeared on my left, and at her suggestion, my stomach rumbled my answer.

"Good," she said. "I'm having a few small things made, so we can pick while we talk."

I suppressed a sigh. Playing often caused a lot of hor d'euvres to be passed under my nose, as it was easier to eat small bites in order to play big games, but I sorely missed big steak dinners and the buttery mound of mashed potatoes that usually went beside it.

"Shall we lay out the ground rules?" Rada asked, perching on the same sofa-chair she'd chosen previously. It was the perfect position to take in the entire room, and everybody in it. A hidden throne. It resembled every other gray decoration, but so thoughtfully placed that one wouldn't miss a thing—from the archway into the foyer to the hidden door carved out of the wainscoted wall leading to what I supposed was a hallway to the kitchen. Rada's staff came and went only through that entrance.

On cue, a staff member unobtrusively pushed through the door carrying a tray of finger sandwiches.

My stomach frowned.

Theo thanked the woman as she set down the tray in the middle of us but seemed to sense my disappointment because he cut a warning my way before reaching for cucumber-stuffed bread that was maybe a third of the size of his palm print.

"I've spoken to my source," Rada said, with no acknowledgement of her staffer between us. "And he's confirmed Trace's presence, of a sort, at the game tonight."

"Any chance you want to name that source?" Theo asked.

"Of course not," Rada said.

"Then how can we know he's credible?"

"If you consider me to be trustworthy, or," she allowed, "trustworthy *enough*, then you may also consider him to be so."

Theo tensed, but I cut in. "This is what we have, Sax. We might as well go with it."

"Considering Trace isn't even keeping his own family in the loop, I would say you should," Rada added. "Why is he keeping away, anyway? I thought he and your father were close."

"They are," Theo said. "But my father tends to ... punish. After the bust involving Scarlet, Trace didn't want to return. I assume he wanted to make an independent name for himself, make our father proud."

"Yes, and how's that going?" Rada asked.

"He's making money," was all Theo said.

"And piling up bodies, from what I hear." She slid a glance over at me. "Female ones."

"Trace is out of control, which is why my father wants him back."

"Assuming you can catch him," Rada said. "Do you really think you're the only one who's looking for this man? The eldest Saxon brother is making enemies as much as he's collecting bodies. The FBI has him on their Most Wanted list, don't they? Which makes me wonder..." Rada leaned forward as I stiffened, "what price is all this to you, Sax? What terrible situation have you gotten yourself into? And bringing her in, no less."

To give myself something to do other than slap the sneer off Rada's carefully lipsticked face, I reached for a stupid mini-sandwich.

"Enough family history. Give us what we need, Rada," Theo said.

"*Oh*, I do so love it when you say my name," she purred.

This time, I stiffened for all too different reasons.

"Explain the room."

Theo's tone left little room for argument, and while it was clear Rada still wanted to play, she relented and sat back. "It's at the Duke of Buchanan's house."

"Do I have to..." I scratched at my left arm, wishing I had a drink to hide any nervous movements. "I dunno, approach him in a certain way when I'm there? Curtsy?"

"Not at all." Rada waved me off. "Many families have royal titles, cousins of cousins of in-laws of heirs, though they're more decorative monikers these days. I wouldn't pay much attention to it. In any case, this particular House is run by his son, Henry Wittacker. Young, often stupid, but knows how to run games."

"Security?" Theo asked.

"Plenty." Rada paused to sip her wine. "He has a room

devoted to it, monitors displaying cameras located all throughout the playroom. Two men manning it, usually. One is a retired detective, the other is a former MMA fighter."

I raised my brows. "That's some polarity."

"To add further color, the fighter is named Edgar and the detective, Steve."

"Huh."

"Why would Trace go to a game so heavily taped?"

Rada raised a brow. "What makes you think he's going there personally?"

Theo shook his head, thinking. "That's not like him. To do work he can easily assign."

"He's desperate," I said, and they both glanced at me like I'd magically *poofed* myself into existence. "Trace needs a big play. So far, he's been collecting in side games, not making too much, or too little. Drawing the least attention possible. You agree with that, right?" I asked Theo, and he nodded.

"Now, well, it's been two years," I continued. And thought of myself. "He's tired. Not as careful. Essentially, ready to come home but afraid to, and so he's taking it out on random victims he's coming across. Scraping as much money together as he can. And becoming paranoid. Trace is losing his touch, which is not only bringing us closer to him, but—"

I cut myself off. I'd become so absorbed, thinking so hard of Trace and his motivations, I'd almost brought the FBI into the conversation, and the least I could do to talk about them, the better. Theo was watching, and I'd be a fool to assume I was so talented I could continue flying under his radar.

Not if I couldn't *shut up* about the police.

"We need to catch him before they do," Theo surmised, and while he was calm, I worked overtime to remain the same. "How do you assume all this?"

"Drea. Her bruises." *The look on her face.* "That's not the sign of a man in control."

"You're right," Theo said. He put down the sandwich he hadn't bothered to eat. "This may be our last chance. You were able to find him," Theo said to Rada.

"There's nothing to stop the cops from doing the same kind of research," Rada said. "Our families have deep, loyal ties. Just as if you would call me for help, I'd assist, and just as you'd ask me to keep a secret, I would. Trace used a connection, and if the police get close to me, I'll swear up and down I haven't seen him and don't know anything about where he could be."

"*Have* you seen him?" I asked, and Rada startled. Yet, there was something in her tone...

"Of course not," she said. "Any man smart enough would know to play under pseudonyms. His happens to be a form of communication we use when we're down on our luck."

"I'm sorry, we?"

Why did I continue to feel like I'd just walked in on an intimate conversation between Theo and Rada?

"Yes," Rada said.

Neither decided to fill me in. Perhaps they were waiting for me to answer my own question, and given enough time, I did. *We.* The mafia.

It was easy to forget what kind of chain Theo was a part of, titanium and strong. Unbreakable. It was an underworld family containing so many links, far-reaching, worldwide. Always there when you needed them, as well as when you didn't. The Theo I remembered wanted to break away from such strangulation. Yet, here he was, working for his father again in bringing his psychotic brother back into the family.

I went to his scar. *What did Gordon Saxon do to you to bring you back into his clutches?* I wanted to ask him. It had to be something so sinister, so nightmarishly cruel, that Theo couldn't refuse.

I thought of Chenko, and the promise he made me swear to.

Theo had made sure he had nothing left of value to give. Nothing except ... himself, in favor of others.

But who?

Theo's younger brother. Theo loved Ward, that I knew. Their father now resorted to threats against his youngest and last son.

Disgust curdled on the back of my tongue. Of course Gordon would. And of course Theo would do anything protect him. Including submitting to permanent mutilation on his angelic face.

Gordon W. Saxon. Oh, how I hated that man.

"You've played there before?" Theo asked Rada. I jarred back to the present.

"Many times," she said.

"All right. Tell us the layout."

Rada outlined her mental blueprint of the poker room, and while her staff drifted in and out, refilling our waters and her wine, I paid particular attention to her description of the players. Eight took to the table, including the duke's son. Investors mainly, venture capitalists, a couple of others with royal monikers, including a knighted Sir Kingston. It was rare to have a female player at the felt, but foreigners often came and went, so having an American at the table wouldn't be uncharacteristic.

Trace himself wouldn't be there, due to the notoriety of his face. That was a relief—Trace would recognize me on sight, even with new chocolate locks.

"How do you know he's Trace's horse?" Theo bent forward, resting his elbows on his thighs.

"Trace has chosen a great player, but Mel is a talker," she said, then smiled. "And I love to be spoken to."

"Is he Trace's only horse?"

"He's the only one I know." Rada gave a dainty shrug. "But if he were smart, he'd have many horses playing at many tables."

"I don't get it," I spoke up. "Why would this Mel agree to Trace as his backer? Does he not watch the news? Trace has got a reward on his head, both by his family and the FBI. Why isn't he giving Trace up?"

"Because the split is eighty-twenty," Rada answered.

I fell back against the chair. "Wow. Shit."

"Then Trace has to have more than one horse," Theo said. "We're lucky we found one."

"We have to assume Mel's a liability," I said to Theo. "He's already spoken to Rada. Who knows who else he's bragged to."

"Yeah. Trace is going to put an end to it soon," Theo said.

"Or end Mel," I added.

"He wouldn't—can't," Rada said. "Mel's too well known."

I snorted. "That won't stop him."

"Your job tonight is to watch Mel's plays," Theo said to me. "Knowing my brother's desperation, Mel will be playing to win as much as he can, but not so steep that it'd be out of character for him."

"And I need to do what I can to encourage a high pot, and allow Mel to win," I said.

"Yes." Lifting, Theo splayed his hands on his thighs. "Then we can follow him once the game has ended, see if he leads us to my brother. Are we set?"

"Yeah," I said. "I'm confident."

"Wonderful." Rada snapped her fingers, and the butler appeared with a wad of cash. She then handed it to me. "Welcome to my stable, little princess."

I gifted her with my most special smile. "Is my cut also eighty percent?"

She laughed. I took that as a no.

One of these days, I thought as I stood, *I'm going to play for me only. And keep all the damn money.*

Theo cupped my elbow and I used his assistance to slip on my heels.

We said our good-byes to Rada, and while I knew we were committing to a deal with a snake, at least I knew the type of venom this one carried. All Rada wanted in this instance was money, and I would give it to her.

Many thought poker was a gamble, based purely on luck. It was nothing like that. Probabilities, statistics, knowing how to keep the pot low when you had a precarious hand or the subtleties of tricking your opponents to bet high required both a skill for mathematics and people. It was a type of tai chi that if done right, one could make it a lucrative career.

"The plan is as follows," Theo said as we exited Rada's mansion and went down the steps. I made sure he couldn't see my eye-roll at his *as follows* part. "Draw no attention to yourself. Bet well, play better, but don't astound anyone. Can I count on you to do that?"

"Of course."

"I mean it, Scarlet."

"I'm not an idiot. I'm aware how important this night is, and no greed of mine is going to ruin it."

"Or ego."

"Yes, because that's something you're unfamiliar with."

"Scarlet," he warned.

"All *right*. No, my ego will not become a part of this night at all. Not one iota."

"You're over-selling it."

"The way this conversation is going, if I didn't know any better, I'd say we didn't just have shower sex."

Theo skipped a step.

I smiled and walked ahead.

Point, Scarlet.

When we reached the car, Theo said behind me, "I'm only trying to keep you safe."

"I know," I said to him, but it was with unintended sadness.

"If all goes well, tonight will be it. You do this, then we're done."

I nodded. Went back to playing with my necklace, my stomach whirling with washing machine precision.

"I get it," I said, but added a smile to my flat tone. "It's just sex."

"You think I'm not putting your interests first?" he asked, pulling open the passenger-side car door. My gut was shot by that annoying trigger called *hope*. Theo stitched over the ache by adding, "I'm getting you some hamburgers first."

THE WAXY BURGER paper crunched beneath my grip and my fingers now smelled like cheese, but my stomach had formed into a full, meaty smile.

I reached into the cupholder between Theo and me, nabbing some fries.

"You were hungry," Theo said, staring out into the road.

"Famished. What I'm wondering," I said once I swallowed, "is how you've managed to subsist on half a slice of cucumber. You haven't eaten anything."

"I'll have time once you're inside."

I paused in licking salt off my fingers. "Oh?"

"I'm not going anywhere," he said, the left turn signal clicking in the resulting silence.

"But ... it could take hours."

"I'm aware."

"And you're just going to stay in this car?"

"There's nowhere else I'd rather be."

The car coasted to a stop on the side of the road, a golden wash covering the hill in front of me, a curved horizon to my right. The glow of the duke's house created its own sunlight during what should be moonlight.

Theo turned so he faced me, dead on. "I want you to feel like when you're in there, you're covered. That no matter what happens, I'll be here in case anything goes wrong."

The interior was so dark as to be black, but Theo's eyes glinted through like chipped, broken glass.

"I'm pretty good at having my own back," I said, but it wasn't with my normal gusto. Any time Theo caught me in his sights, my resolve unraveled. Not so much as to become loose strands pooled at my feet, but enough to think I needed him.

"I have no doubt about that," he said, and what was left unsaid was, *I forced you to be that way when I left you.* "But I'm here now, so keep your phone on."

"I get my phone back?" I dropped the napkin I'd been using to clean up, but then thought, "They'll search me. There's no way MMA Edgar and Detective Steve won't notice my phone lighting up."

"Your phone can be traced by the FBI. So this is a burner. And Rada made a call. You're being treated as a VIP so you'll avoid the search."

"Oh, yeah? What have you guys made me to avoid something like that? A sheik's son's fiancée?"

Theo said nothing.

"You've *seriously* made me the heiress to a sheik dynasty?"

"Named Vivienne Mathis. Rada also has a special relationship with Henry Whittacker."

"Meaning she's slept with him," I said.

"Just keep your phone on," Theo repeated. "I'll hear what I need."

"All right," I sighed.

Theo started the car and drove slowly around the bend of the hill and up a long, curved driveway. "I'll drop you off, then stay close by. The code word for if you need me immediately can be..."

"Cassie," I blurted. He glanced over, and I nodded my affirmation. "I can bring the name up in conversation easily enough, but it's not something I'd be forced to say unless it was deliberate. It's perfect."

"Yes. It is."

"Cassie for the win, then," I said as we reached the entrance to another, more acre-driven mansion. "Okay. This is it."

"I'm not going to wish you good luck."

"Don't need you to." On impulse, I leaned in to kiss the rasp of his cheek. "That's enough."

I'd been studying him closely. It was why I noticed the subtle softening of his features, a crack in his shell before he paved over the vulnerability.

"Don't screw up," he said.

I didn't answer, and instead swept out of the car, the red gown whisking at my ankles and adding a decadence that was lacking at the heart of me.

I fished in my small clutch for a mint, popped it in, then stepped toward the doors.

"Name?" asked the man at the doors, clad in a black-piece suit.

He was the only one out here, save for the purr of Theo's engine as he drove back off into the night. The neighborhood was expansive with land but light on houses. It was a borough on the outskirts of London, probably something ending in "-shire" or "-heath." An exclusive, protected suburb in which London's elite traveled into the figurative underworld to meet their Hades. In this case, the devil was in the cards.

"Vivienne," I said to the figure. He glanced at his tablet. "Mathis."

"I see you. Go on in. A man named Edgar will assist you. He'll be waiting beside the metal detectors."

Edgar? Interesting. I assumed he'd be in the camera room

only, but it seemed these men played multiple roles. In tables like these, run by families with reputations, these circles were kept small and trusted. Henry Wittacker didn't simply invite anyone, which was probably why it hadn't been difficult for Rada to find Trace through Mel. Trace likely was forced to use his last name in obtaining a seat at this lucrative table. He needed money to get out of the UK, fast, and short of robbing a bank, poker was a way of making quick cash. Underground, even more so.

It occurred to me that Rada had put her reputation on the line for Theo. Members of the poker elite didn't rat on each other. Politicians, restauranteurs, celebrities, Russians, the mafia, the code of this brotherhood was simple: Keep your mouth shut.

In fact, it wouldn't surprise me if this man were Steve.

"Thank you, sir."

I picked up my skirt and stepped through the double-arched doors the man swept open for me. If the outside of the house was basked in a golden wash of sunlight, the interior was even shinier, the unobtrusive light fixtures glinting off brass accents—or likely gold, and vintage at that. The small table under the diamond shaped mirror with delicate gold legs could have been gifted by the royal family, as well as the Renaissance paintings guiding my way to the left, where two largely obtrusive metal detectors waited, right before marbled stairs with gold railings descended to the bottom floor.

Hades indeed.

"Miss Mathis?" a very tall man asked, also in an all-black, three-piece suit. My head maybe reached his shoulders. He appeared lean in his outfit, but I was confident his arms and thighs were roped in muscle, a man adept at combining martial arts and wrestling, bare-chested, with no protective armor against his opponent. A visual representation of poker, if you will.

"I'm Edgar. Follow me."

We strode around the metal detectors and the two people

manning it, and I clip-clopped down the staircase, my fingers running across the cold golden railing, one step behind Edgar. A one-second check in my handbag to make sure my phone was on, and—

"I hafta be honest, it's not often we have a lady in the house," Edgar said.

I refocused. "Yes. I get that a lot."

"You must be good, to come here."

"I'm all right," I said as we reached the landing.

Edgar was fishing, but that was okay. I was well-used to men attempting to "know" me, or in their version, have presumed aspects of my personality that no matter how I answered, would remain prominent until I drained the pot. The potential for Edgar being no different was high, but I played along anyway, though not too hard. I was to be above-average, but not amazing.

"It's interesting, you know, how you landed on the VIP list mere hours ago."

Hmm. Edgar was also observant.

"It was a last-minute detour into the UK. My fiancé, well, he has his quirks. One being diverting our"—my mind raced to recall the charter plane Theo had flown us in on—"Bombardier en route to Persia because he just *had* to have the world's most expensive burger. Have you heard of it? Involving gold and lobster? Regardless," I waved a hand at him like I pictured a sheik's princess would do, "If I smell like a cheeseburger, that would be why. He's now asleep at our suite, and I'm bored and waiting for him to wake up so I can reboard my plane."

Yeesh. I hope I sounded fancy enough. That, right there, was *so much* pulled out of my ass in record time.

Meanwhile, Edgar probably had a delicate internal monologue beginning with, *rich people. They don't pay me enough for this shit.*

Couldn't agree more, buddy.

"Interesting story," Edgar said, then stuffed his hand in his pants' pocket and pulled out a brass key. "Just so you know, I'll be watching you carefully."

MMA Edgar. Also smart.

Lucky for me, nothing untoward was planned at this game, other than monitoring another lap dog. My job was simple. Sit down, play decent hands, wait for Mel to finish up, then call it and leave. So easy peasy that it was obvious why Theo allowed it to happen. This was the safest thing I'd been up to since the routine of getting up and making it to my morning high school classes every day.

"This key allows you to re-access this room," Edgar said. "Show it to security upstairs whenever you have to exit to have a smoke, or other ... ladylike things."

Ah, men. Always assuming women will constantly need the bathroom.

"Thank you," I said, palming the key and dropping it in my purse. It was small entertainment to think the *clank* of it against the phone could've hurt Theo's ears.

"Good luck."

Edgar trotted up the stairs, and I waited to see which direction he turned when he reached the top. Right, which meant that was where the security monitors lay.

I pushed the door open and wandered into an environment that had become my home.

There was no focal point in this room. No shiny fixtures, carved Renaissance-style wood, diamond chandeliers, nothing. I was in a secret add-on, a room unknown to any guests passing through the main entranceway and onto marble tiles rippling with precious stone. The duke's son—Henry—had a man-cave that, with any other guy living with his parents, would have contained video game consoles and special gaming chairs, computers and a flatscreen as the centerscape. Here, there was thin carpeting as to mute distracting footsteps, a single medium-sized flatscreen showing a recording of the French Open, and one circular table, stapled over with the most expensive purple felt money could buy.

Wasn't purple the color of the Royals? Ballsy.

As the men quieted their conversation and chips stopped *clicking* against each other, I murmured to the man seated just at the door with an open lockbox, trading cash for chips. He ran the cash through an electronic money-counter. Its *whirrrrr* echoed through the silence, but at its end, he nodded with satisfaction and passed over a plastic tray containing four rows of chips in green, blue, purple, and red respectively.

Five people were seated at the round table. I took the second-to-last available chair on the right, sitting down with a vague smile. A few flickers of interest, but otherwise, the men stayed with their chips. Henry sat across from me and lifted his fingers in hello, an acknowledgment of my presence. The others were in form-fitting designer suits, tailored with Englishman's precision. All blazers fit them perfectly—a sign of true wealth.

And as usual, all men.

My clutch lay unobtrusively on my lap, the clasp open, and I hoped Theo could hear. I pictured him in his car, sheltered by the night, the only light coming from the reflective screen of his phone as he listened carefully, earbuds in, and tapped his index finger anxiously against the case. It was one of his very minor tells —just a few taps before he caught himself and schooled both his body and his mind. I wanted to be beside him, palming his cheek and smoothing out the lines.

"We're all here," Henry said. He'd unbuttoned his collar, and if he had a tie, it was discarded. In his House, I supposed he could dress however he wanted.

"Nope, we're missing one," a man seated two from my left responded.

A quick scan of faces, and I noted Mel had not yet arrived. Was he going to come at all? Our planning assumed he'd be here, that Trace was eager for more cash so he could leave this country and his crime behind.

"If he ain't coming, we ain't waiting," Henry said. "I'm ready to play."

"As am I," I said.

The players jolted at my voice, sounding so light but playing so hard on the vowels the way their accents didn't. It was crucial to speak up, both so Theo could locate my voice and to utilize my best weapon. I chose icy-cool, unperturbed, graceful, and sweet-toned. It was enough to get even the savviest players to look up at the sultriness, glance over, and study—if only for a second. It was in that single second of appreciating the sexiness of a woman that they gave up their tells.

"Who are you, again?" asked the first man who'd spoken. He remained crisp in his navy suit, mid-fifties, with more salt than pepper hair. His eyes were keen.

"I apologize for not introducing myself. I'm Vivienne. A pleasure."

"Mm."

"A sheik's princess, is that right?" Henry added. "You have a spare yacht you can loan us?" He laughed at his own joke.

"I believe my prince has three." I smiled.

"What's he doing allowing you out, looking so beautiful without him?"

This came from the man on my right. I thought of Theo. "He knows that if he doesn't loosen the leash a little, I'll bite him."

The man guffawed, then patted my arm in a fatherly way. "I like 'er. Let's play."

"Is Melrose coming?" Another man asked, this one in a midnight blue and black two-piece suit. These tailorings would truly send Kai into an orgasm. It almost made me do the same—

picturing Theo in these pieces, striding into the room, commanding attention with the fit of the lapels over his chest, the cup of fabric over his ass—good *Lord*, he would put these skinny, pot-bellied men to shame.

Henry's half-hearted head shake snapped me to attention. "Nuh. He asked a friend to take his place."

"A lot of 'friends' taking position at this table, Henry." It was the first man who spoke, the one with the keen eyes.

Henry shrugged. "They come from vetted sources, no need to get your knickers in a twist, Sal. I've been in charge of these games how long? And nothing's 'appened."

"Yeah," he said, and I got the impression he *hated* that a kid was in charge of the best game in town.

"Right, then when's *he* coming? This friend? My wife has me going to a charity gala in a few hours. I'd love to get some more plays in," another man said.

"Any second now," Henry said. "Let's keep going. He can join the next flop. Xavier?"

Henry looked to the man who had a white chip with DEALER in front of him. Since this was a small game with no casino elements, each of us would take a turn as the dealer.

A cocktail waitress appeared from a hidden door, tray in hand. As she placed the other player's drinks to the right of their elbow, she looked to me. She appeared to be exactly my age when I started this career, her fine brown hair pulled high and tight in a pony-tail, all the better for men to tug at when they thought they were being cutesy and attempting to get her attention. Her bodice was red and tight, the lace garters under her leather mini-skirt even more so.

It was not an outfit she would have chosen. It would be all Henry's work.

"Gin and tonic," I said. When she passed by, I put a green chip on her tray as tip.

"Much obliged," she said quietly, and disappeared back through the secret portal. Not without a few appreciative studies in her wake.

We played. With each hand, I grew increasingly nervous, waiting for Mel to come through those doors so I could begin the task of becoming a mentalist.

Five hands later, the door stayed shut. In my distraction, I lost more money than I intended, which had me thinking *fuck it*, and refocusing on the game. I couldn't let these players completely dismiss the sheik's mysterious princess.

"Sir."

With the stealth of an alley cat, Edgar had walked in and was leaning into Henry's ear. Henry nodded at whatever Edgar said. "Let him in."

"Are you ... sure?"

The hesitancy in Edgar's voice heightened my attention.

"I'm sure. He owes me."

"Princess Leia? You're up."

Keen-Eyes wasn't so keen on me. A brief study of my two cards gave me the answer before I went back to Edgar and Henry's conversation. "Check."

If, when Edgar went to open up the room, it was Theo on the other side, I wouldn't be surprised. This plan of ours would be crap if Mel never showed, and it had been two hours without his presence. I was playing with Rada's money, which, if I lost any more, would cost both Theo and I in ways I'd yet to measure. And to lose tonight would mean Trace was back in the wind. At each point in our trifecta, fire lay.

Why then, would Theo risk going on camera? I glanced up at the black lens in the corner right as the tiny green light flicked off. A subtle glance to my right, and another camera's light went black.

"Mel's friend's here," Henry said for our benefit.

My hand was slack against my face-down cards, every joint of mine carefully schooled so no outward emotion would show.

Edgar pushed down on the door's lever and the ornate wood opened. In its place stood a man with sinful blue eyes, arms with the power to lift me and shoulders to withstand my weight. Narrow hips sheathed in a suit expertly crafted to display the Adonis underneath. A wave of hair, burnished and silky, that when during sex, would fall against his brow.

Everything about this man was so familiar that if I wasn't careful, I'd mistake it for love.

But it wasn't Theo.

MY OLD WOUND THROBBED. I tasted real fear, acrid and rancid, at the back of my throat.

Trace.

He was here, and in two seconds his scan of the room would land on me.

My elbow scattered chips to the floor and had the man next to me swearing like I'd just spilled his drink. I hunched under the table to collect them, mentally going over various plans on getting the hell out of here without being noticed.

I didn't have many to go on.

The cocktail waitress bent down at my feet to assist. I grabbed her wrist to keep her there, and well versed in antics of her rich clientele, she covered her squeak of surprise nicely. Her wide brown eyes landed on mine.

"I need you to help me out of here," I whispered. I hoped, with my earnestness, I instilled in her the sheer urgency of the situation.

"I don't understand," she replied, and I covered a curse.

"That man that just walked in? He's my ex. An abusive one. He can't see me. He *can't.*"

The pain of Trace's bullet throbbed at my ribcage, a silent

alarm my body crafted as a reminder of the pain he could inflict. The death he almost accomplished.

The gorgeous suit he wore most definitely housed a handgun. There were no illusions that once he noticed me, sifted through his memories and saw through my brown hair, that he would shoot me on sight. Nobody here owed me anything, much less protection.

The waitress hesitated.

"Are you all right down there?" the fatherly man asked.

"Oh, yes," I said, making my voice higher than normal. "Just cleaning up my mess. I'm so clumsy. Um..." I looked to the waitress, and, well-versed in the subtleties of this room, she understood my silent question and answered, "Rebecca."

"Rebecca is helping me count my chips. Ensuring I didn't lose any under your shoes," I finished.

Another pair of shoes took up position across from us. Trace was sitting down at the table. If I popped up, I was done for.

"Rebecca, *please.*"

She blinked a few times as she thought. "Yes, okay." She hooked my waist and we both lifted off the floor.

"Oh, dear," she said to the men. I remained at her elbow, facing away from the table. "It seems we have an issue."

Playing along, I tottered against her, and she balanced us into a wobbling stand.

"She been drinking before coming here?" someone asked behind me, and I heard the scoff.

"Nice *friends*, Henry."

"If you don't take the game seriously, sweetheart, we don't want you here."

"Jesus H. Christ. Take better stock of your players, Henry."

A shadow covered us, and I coughed through the *yip* of terror that wanted to come through instead, but it was Henry. "Get her out of here," he said to Rebecca, then looked upon me with disdain. "Permanently."

I mouthed a pitiful *I'm sorry*, then pretended to retch.

"Good Lord." He jumped back. "Your fiancé will hear about this. And you're not getting your buy-in back."

"I—I—" another well-timed retch and Rebecca and I were practically pushed through the hidden door.

My clutch was making an indent on my belly, the clasp automatically shut as soon as I grappled it against my stomach and scuttled out of there. As I straightened, I clicked it open and yell-whispered, "*Cassie*. Cassie, Cassie, Cassie!"

"What?"

"Nothing," I said to Rebecca. "Thank you. For helping me out of there."

"Of course. That man..." Her eyes slid to the side and down. "He's not very nice."

"You know him? The one who just walked in?"

"Yes," was all she would say. "He's one of Drea's regulars, but she quit abruptly and now I'm pulling shifts every night."

I raked down her body, as if I could x-ray through her clothes and detect any bruises. Something chewed on my brain. I asked, almost off the cuff, "You know someone named Drea?"

Her gaze *pinged* onto mine. "I thought you were saying the name Cassie."

"Yes, but now I'm thinking of Drea. You know her."

"I—no. I do not."

She turned, and I clasped her elbow. "Rebecca, you don't have to be afraid of me."

"I'm not," she said, avoiding my eyes again. "I'm afraid of *him*."

"Did Drea work here? Was this a side job of hers?"

"I can't be gone for too long. They'll notice." She started to walk away.

"I used to be one of you. The exact same. A cocktail waitress at these underground houses," I blurted to her back.

She stilled.

"I know what it's like," I continued. "I was even stupid enough to fall in love with one of them. Is that what Drea did? Did she fall in love with Trace?"

"I've told you—I don't know who that is."

"You *do,* Rebecca. I can spot a tell a mile away. And you know how I learned it? By being a server to these men who think that a hot chick in a sexy costume just for them is too stupid to notice how poker is played. Or who's behind the cards."

Her shoulders slumped. She spun on her heel to face me. "She wasn't here very long."

"But Drea worked here." My mind flicked through memories as I attempted to find the right one. "Was there ever a man here named Mel, or Melrose, who played as a horse for someone else?"

Rebecca's brows furrowed. "I really can't stay here and discuss this with you. I'm the only one on the floor—"

"Tell me one more thing. Please." As soon as I saw the hesitation in the flicker of her lashes, I barreled on, "Was Drea hooking up with Trace?"

She sighed, licked her lips, then said, "Yes."

Trace was a regular here.

This was a trap.

"Now please, I have to leave," she said, and this time, when she trotted away, I was too frozen to stop her.

Drea was a liar. Those bruises—her cuts and swells, the tremble of her lip—were all real. Trace did beat her, but was it with her permission? Did she love him so hard and fast she was willing to be crushed near-to-death in order to please him? No. I couldn't envision any woman who would submit to that. She loved him, yes, but his cruelty wouldn't have come through while she was falling. It was only when he heard his brother was looking for him that he'd switch to that beast inside him, both crafting a plan and submitting to his yearnings at the same time. Drea was a pawn—she had to be. There was no way that girl looked me in the eye, her cheekbones cracked, her brain barely back to its regular size, and deliberately led us here as lambs.

Theo.

I snapped out of it, fumbling for my phone. When I found it, I pressed it to my ear. There was no connection. Theo would have hung up as soon as I yelled out the danger-word. I tried to unlock it with my fingerprint, but either I was too sweaty or trembly or all of the above, because it wasn't working.

"*Shit*," I squeaked, then tore down the hallway, envisioning where the best undisclosed entry would be.

Theo was on his way, and he was going to walk into a slaughter.

Still attempting to unlock my phone, I made the command, "Call *Sax*." When my phone brightened, and an icon popped up stating "*the definition of "saxophone" is...*" I nearly flung it into the wall.

"Call *Theo*," I said with as much pronunciation as I possessed.

The speaker replied, "calling Theo," and I exhaled with so much relief, my back bowed forward.

I pictured Trace, grinning at the stupidity of my farce, when all the while he knew who it was trying to get away, despite my new brunette sheen. Drea would have told him Theo had someone with him, a female. Theo wasn't known to bring his consorts round-trip. If Trace were also keeping an eye on my activities, much like his younger brother had these past years, then he would have noted my absence and put two and two together. He must also have known that as soon as I stumbled out of the playing room, I'd try to reach Theo.

Trace would have planned for it.

God *dammit*, how do you stay one step ahead of a cheetah?

"By picking up the fucking phone, that's how!" I yelled at my cell once Theo's voicemail clicked through. With one hand bunched in my skirt and the other holding a useless device, I stampeded up the stairs, around the corner, and through the kitchen. Two surprised chefs looked up at my flurry, but I was through the service entry and outside before either of them could say much.

I flew onto the terrace, peering through shadows since those were the only pockets Theo would stray. I couldn't spot the shape of him, the slope of his shoulders or his broad back, nor his scar, a crack of white against the black. He wasn't coming through the landscaped trees or the privacy fence, there was no sound of foot-steps up the small staircase leading to a perfectly tended vegetable garden. Theo wasn't here, not where we agreed upon. He wasn't meeting me at our designated meet-up point, our escape plan scratched.

I spun, glancing up at windows, grazing over clouds, thinking maybe I'd gotten it wrong. This wasn't where we agreed.

"Think, Scarlet, *think*."

Tilting back to the door, I thought maybe there was a side entrance I got mixed up, or another service entrance I'd missed.

Then I heard the gunshot.

WHEN A CERTAIN CRACK of sound hits the air, the noise too quick to be a car backfiring, cutting off too fast and hard to be considered a firework, the *pop* so viscerally recognizable, so spine-chillingly accurate, an ancestral instinct deep inside of us immediately recognizes it as danger cutting through the air, target unknown.

Human nature is to run away from it.

I sprinted toward it.

Taking the same route I used to escape this house, I tore through the hallway and burst through the door leading into the poker room, and what greeted me was *not* what I exited mere minutes ago.

Men were toppled over on chairs, one spread eagled across the felt table. The fatherly one, the only kind man in here, remained prostrate in his seat, but was rubbing his forehead. There was no blood on any of them that I could detect. No bullet wounds. My own throbbed.

Quickly, I tallied the men, one key player missing.

Two, actually, my gut reminded.

Rebecca, the cocktail waitress, cowered in a corner, not quite standing, but not quite sitting, either. I ran over to her.

"What happened?"

"I..." she looked at me like I was shining a light into her eyes, and she flinched. "It was so fast."

"What did Trace do? Rebecca, look at me. Please. Take a breath and tell me what happened. There's not much time."

She swallowed, and I took that moment of her hesitation to reach behind me and grab someone's drink on the table that somehow remained unspilled. "Here. Gulp deep."

She accepted the glass and drained the golden liquid.

"Someone was arguing outside the doors," she began. I nodded my encouragement, outwardly calm. My heart drummed in my throat.

"It was a man, and he was angry. He and Edgar got into it. I..." She paused, thought. "Edgar didn't win."

Theo, I thought.

"So the man busted through the doors, and he asked"—She met my eyes quizzically— "He wanted to know where 'Scarlet' was."

Yes, definitely Theo.

"He was so demanding. Frightening, just like ... he looked exactly like Trace."

"I know," I said quietly.

"They saw each other," she said, louder now. "They saw each other, and Trace grinned like—like something *evil*, and next thing I know, his lookalike was on top of him. Literally. They fought, the other players tried to intervene, but then Trace pulled out a gun and shot at the ceiling..."

Ah. The one area I hadn't scanned. I followed her gaze and noted the small black hole in the molded fleur de lis pattern above.

"Everyone froze," Rebecca continued. "Trace said he had Scarlet, that if this man wanted to see her again, he had to go with Trace. He did."

"Did what? He went with Trace?"

"Yes. I told you it happened fast."

I rescanned the room while I straightened, the men mumbling to themselves or smoothing out their shirts. Only a rivalry of the Saxon brotherhood would cause such a brief, potent scuffle, so much so that I doubted these men knew what to do with themselves during the aftermath.

"You all have to leave."

Henry regained authority and stood from his curled up position under the table. "I'll call the police if you don't. This night is finished."

Everyone here knew Henry wouldn't call the cops if Trace were holding a knife to his throat and threatening to take all the cash. To involve the police would mean shutting down the lucrative House income he gained through these clandestine games.

I indiscriminately slipped through the hidden door, but not before digging my hands in the toppled-over lockbox on the floor and stuffing the bills in my cleavage. You never know when you need extra cash, and I'd have to pay Rada back somehow.

Plodding my way a third time through the servant's quarters, I ended up in the backyard. At this point, I should have thought of something. A bell inside my brain should've rang, informing me exactly where Trace had taken Theo and why Trace used me as bait to lead Theo elsewhere.

Instead, my mind was unusually, traitorously silent.

I thought of going back to Rada's, but that held too much risk. Trace was aware of Theo's and my plans, that we were together, and our intentions of ambushing Trace. It was up to Theo how to stuff Trace in a plane and to their father. My job was to be the lure, and after that, after getting the two of them in the same room, I was to...

The FBI.

Now was the time to press the necklace. My deal had not

only come into fruition but graduated to necessary. Theo's life was at stake. I had to find them. Now.

Theo.

My breaths hitched, though I wasn't running. The mere thought of what Trace could be doing to Theo—what had already been done, Theo's *face*—tore into my mind with such warp speed that there was no room for anything else. But there had to be. I *had* to get it together enough to stop standing in a stranger's garden panicking and instead figure out where—

My brain clicked back into action.

Drea. *She* was the reason everything had gone to shit, which meant Trace knew where Drea was. And now that he had Theo, Trace had one more person to collect.

"You bastard," I spat out, and kicked off my heels. I ran through the lawn, out of the property and over the hill, my old scar screaming at the sudden impact and skin-stretching I was usually so careful to control. "You're not going to take Theo out of my life a second time."

Theo's car was idling, spare keys magnetized to the inside of the front bumper. I reached over the wheel, found the keys, got in, and whipped the car into gear.

It had been a while since I'd driven, but if Theo and I ever had a second chance, it was up to this stick shift to get me to where I needed to be.

Before we'd never have another moment together again.

By the time I figured out the navigation on my phone, gotten used to driving on the other side of the road, and re-mastered the stick-shift from my days of sharing an olive green Camry with my sister in Westchester, I knew it was too late.

I screamed at the wheel, my eyes threatening to spill salt-water all over my cheeks, and my face burned with the effort of containing the storm of emotion boiling its lava through my vocal cords.

I'd made it to where Drea was being treated, the place where Theo and I had taken steps a lifetime ago, in an old part of London, the stone moldings and uneven cobblestones made more Gothic and surreal in nightscape. The street was deserted, and though I knew the place where Drea was staying would be, too, I had to keep retracing steps. If I didn't, it meant I'd failed, and I couldn't accept that Theo had been so completely and success-fully ripped away from me. Again.

Somehow, escaping the FBI's radar and his family's clutches seemed a possibility. That of all the fairytales, Theo and I deserved a happily ever after.

I'd been so immersed in losing Theo all those years ago, so determined to forget him and what we were, that I missed the very real advantage that at least he was alive. Out there, somewhere.

Now? He could already be dead.

That realization wrenched me out of the car and had me stumbling to the peeling, wooden door with a tiny rectangle of a window that Theo had knocked on yesterday.

This was the only option left. My palms landed on the wood, again and again, the slams communicating into the once-silent night that this was all I had. After this house, there was nothing to go on, nobody to go *to*, except to the very people who wanted Theo as badly as I did. And they wouldn't want to save him, like me. They'd want him boxed in, handcuffed. Held captive.

To which did Theo deserve to go to? The devil's dungeon to claim his soul, or the people's jail cell to repent with his life?

I palmed my necklace, neck bowed, and turned, my back

smacking against the door that remained still, locked and impenetrable. No footsteps sounded on the other end. I slid down, allowing the tears to fall, too.

"What have I done?" I whispered into the street. "Who have I become?"

A couture gown that wasn't mine encased my body. I was in a foreign country, unfamiliar with both the accents and the land. My stellar poker ability was moot. Everything I'd worked for, the life I'd crafted after last seeing Theo, had been reduced to null. Losing my sister was a tattoo on my soul, the needle shearing through delicate skin, becoming a permanent mark on what once was flawless, but I'd reduced her life to nothing, because my survival didn't matter.

I didn't matter.

Trace couldn't be stopped. Theo couldn't be saved. Kai wouldn't be redeemed. In five simple moments, life was overturned.

But that was how it worked, wasn't it? One moment, and your sister's dead. Two moments, and the man you love has walked out for good. Three, and you lose your best friend. Four, and the FBI comes in, barrels raised, but there's nothing to shoot, because the deal you made no longer counts. There's no Trace, and there certainly isn't Theo. Five, and you're in jail.

My head hit air, then smacked onto sudden ground.

It was so quick I didn't have time to voice pain upon impact but raised my hands in an effort to find delayed balance.

"What the—"

"Bo?" I asked the upside-down face. "You're here?" Hope spiked like a lightning bolt. "You're *here!* Someone's here!"

"Lady, you need to find another stoop to sleep this off."

I scrambled to a sit, then tottered to a stand. "I thought this place was cleaned out. That there'd be no one left."

"Just me. Oh, it's you. What's with the new hair?"

"Where's Drea? Have you seen Theo? Trace—"

"Whoa. Slow down."

"I can't. This is an emergency. Theo could be hurt, or worse, and I don't know where to start. Except for coming here. I thought you'd know where they took Drea, or if Trace found her and took her somewhere with Theo. If he's holding them both hostage…" I trailed off, frustrated my thought process wasn't working properly. "What could Trace need from Theo to convince their father he shouldn't come home?"

"Huh?"

"Trace took Theo. Why?"

Bo took his time asking his next question. "Do you need to come in?"

"Yes." I nearly knocked his shoulder off when I barreled forward.

I tracked the hallway, then the bathroom, then the main room before coming to a stop in the middle of the creaky wooden floors. Bo acted as spectator for the entire process, his back resting against the main wall, arms folded.

"Satisfied?" he asked when it was clear I was done mentally ransacking the place.

"Where is he?"

"I don't know. And I mean it," he said when I opened my mouth to argue. "Drea left here on her own. Voluntarily. She finished her tea, went to bed, and when I woke up, her room was empty."

"She was gone as of this morning?"

"Yep."

I shook my head, attempting to make sense of the revelation. "But she was so injured when we saw her … God, was it yesterday? How could she have…" My brows smoothed out the longer I studied Bo's face. "She was faking it."

"Not all of it." Bo shrugged. "Her bruises and cuts were obvious. But as for anything on the inside…"

"But how did she manage to convince so many people? A *doctor*? If all she had was superficial cuts and bruises … Sax said he was getting updates from a doctor. A trusted family one who they used when in this country. Shit." Another realization-bomb hit me between the eyes. "The doctor could have been on Trace's payroll. Not Sax's."

"Don't look at me. I just work here."

"And you reported Drea missing to Theo when … this morning?"

At last, there was hesitation in Bo's features. I stepped forward. "Bo, what aren't you telling me? Need I remind you that Sax, your *boss*, could be somewhere under duress, and when he gets out, he'll be mighty pissed. At you. Especially if you're in any way responsible for his temporary incapacitation."

"Look, I don't get involved in their family business."

"I'm not asking you to. I only want the facts of exactly what happened today and your role in it."

Bo uncrossed his arms. "I'm not sure if I should get *you* involved in their family business, either."

"You don't think I can handle it?"

"I know what happened to you. A few years ago, when you got between the brothers back *then*. What'd you think will go on this time?"

"Yeah? Then you saw how I was. Naive, lost, grieving. Drawn to a world where sinners were favored over saints. I didn't consider myself a saint then, and I don't today, but I can assure you, my demons are smarter now." My voice broke. "Thinking of Theo with Trace, knowing he's only there because Trace used me as bait—again—I can't just leave it at that. I need to get him out of there."

Bo made a gargling sound in the back of his throat sounding suspiciously like scorn. "With what army?"

Oh, if only you knew. "The Saxons appreciate subtlety. So I'm doing this the best I can before involving anyone else."

"I don't believe you."

"You don't have to. Where are they, Bo?"

He shook his head, his eyes taking on a careful gleam. "You're too late, anyway."

"Too late for what?"

"They're long gone, honey. Probably in the air by now, flying back to New York City."

I lifted my chin and said quietly. "So you're on Trace's payroll, too."

"For a gifted poker player, you sure took a lot of events these past few days at face value."

Because you were distracted, Letty. Your feelings for Theo overrode anything else. Even your own safety.

"You know, everyone fears Trace the most," I said. "He's so overtly vicious, very direct with his threats. And usually comes through on any intended mutilation." I lifted my shoulders and spread my arms in a *what can ya do?* action. My heartbeat played on my eardrums like a one-man rock show. "But in focusing on Trace, you miss the quiet deception of Sax. He's as brutal, if not more, because he treats his intended victims with slow-acting revenge. They suffer for a long time. Remain alive with torture. These brothers, they're from the same family stock." I cocked my head. "What makes you think Sax would kill you any less brutally than Trace?"

At last, a flicker of uncertainty crossed Bo's face. "I'm not afraid of you, little girl."

"You don't have to be."

Then came a sneer. "You're so fucking rude. I despise cocky chicks. Especially when they know shit-all, like you right now.

You can't even *begin* to understand Gordo Saxon's intentions when asking Sax to track down Trace. Nor can you figure out why Sax approached you in the first place. Sure, you're a good player, but did he *really* need you to find his brother, who, as you said, likes to leave bloody footprints all over the place? Practically put a beacon on himself on where he was? Think about it, little girl, why are you here, all on your lonesome, with your lover boy once again sacrificing himself for you?"

My heels hit the floor as I backed up, his words like a scattering of glass shards raining down on my head.

"That's right, *Scarlet*. You're basically like that book—a big, fat red letter that Sax was better off avoiding."

"Wow, look at you, you can read."

His upper lip curled, strings of saliva spreading than detaching as he bubbled with rage. "Their father put a fucking *hit* on you, you dumb bitch. That's why Sax had to find you, *that's* why he kept you close, and *that's* fucking why he followed Trace like a rescue pup when Trace said he had you."

My lungs shifted, like my ribcage had become too tight and they were expanding for air. I parted my lips to say *what?* but my brain was working to fast, sifting too quickly, that my question was already made irrelevant.

Theo approached me on the yacht of an arm's dealer, waiting in a quiet room for my arrival. I never thought too hard on his explanation as to why he came out of hiding and found me again. The idea that he wanted to contain his brother was enough of an excuse. Given Theo's history with Trace, it was entirely viable that Theo would do anything to find Trace and prevent him from hurting anyone else. Look how he was with Drea, so tender and concerned. His roughened exterior immediately calming to a terrified girl who'd experienced the fists of his brother.

And that was where I'd failed. I'd forgotten to remember *why* Theo approached wounded females with such guided gentleness.

How could I be so stupid? Theo's history was laid out for me years ago, in glaring detail, yet it never occurred to me when he was kneeling in front of Drea that he remembered his high school girlfriend. That every time a woman was hurt at his family's hands, he thought of her, and her continued torture.

Theo's determination to protect was a well-known weakness exploited by his family, until he stopped loving. When he realized he couldn't have anything of his own and made it so he never would again. Then, their manipulation stopped.

Until me.

Two years ago, I'd walked into his poker room, and he'd looked upon me with such instilled pain that I'd caught my breath just noticing it. We couldn't have stopped our love if we'd tried. Not even a bullet could change it.

Fast-forward to the game with Neri and...

Neri showed deep interest in me during each hand, not to mention, Neri's careful handling of getting me alone in the middle of an ocean. In my mind's eye, I saw his neutral expression in a whole new light, especially when he said I wasn't to be auctioned, nor was he going to use the one night he won for his own pleasure.

I was there to be killed.

Except, Theo was there—intervened?—and convinced Neri he didn't need to go through with the hit, because Theo had money. He must have paid Neri more than the value of the price on my head to keep me alive.

Neri was going to have me killed, at the behest of Gordon Saxon. *That* was his intention from the very beginning, well before I set foot in a hotel ballroom.

Oh my God.

Neri and his bodyguard passing out from my drugs turned out to be crucial happenstance. No wonder Theo was so bowled over by it, and Kai even more so.

Kai? Did he know? Was that why he'd participated in Theo's plans to shepherd me out of the United States?

"How…" My throat crunched against the words, but attempted bravado was my only available weapon. "How much am I worth?"

"You're not the end game," Bo said, laughing. "But you're definitely at the end of the line."

I became aware of my slip of a dress, my bare feet, my tousled, useless long hair. Bo was leaning forward like he was about to pounce.

Bo ran his tongue across his top teeth. "And guess what? I want that money."

He leaped.

I was quick. And much lighter than his heavy, muscle-laden frame. I dodged his grab, sprinting to the far corner, bouncing against the wall, then tearing down the hallway. He caught me by the end of my skirt. My chin cracked against the floor and I rolled over, arms up in defense. Bo crawled on top of me, his meaty hands climbing over my thighs, latching onto my breasts, then heading to my neck.

Screaming, I clawed at the skin on his forearms and kicked at his weight, but any footprints I left on him were pain-free, because he kept coming, his fingers reaching until they landed around my throat and squeezed.

Stars came immediately. My vision wavered, my tongue bulged, and my face felt like it was about to crack into a thousand pieces that would never fit together the same way again.

Fumbling, desperate for time, my dress was hiked past my thighs, naked legs exposed. My fingers hit cool metal and slipped, then grappled for it again. I pulled it out of my garter—my other hand still digging into his wrist, arm, fingers, peeling back his nail beds, begging for life—I flipped the safety, pointed at his temple, and pulled the trigger.

His lids peeled back from his eyeballs, a garish picture forever imprinted on my mind, before the image exploded with blood.

Bo flopped on top of me, the full weight of him a crushing reminder that what was once a lively individual hellbent to kill me was now a dead person. I suddenly wanted him off me—off, *off*—the sounds echoing throughout the hallway sounding inhuman, animalistic, and containing the most basic language of survival. Eventually, I discovered those sounds were my own.

Trembling, I pushed out from under, his body making a flopping sound reserved only for the lifeless before rigor mortis set in. My shoulders were wet with warm, thick, syrupy blood, my feet slipping on the same, but I managed a stand, then a topple into the wall, before sliding into the bathroom and turning on the shower. I peeled out of the gown, my cheeks suspiciously dry throughout the process of washing somebody else's blood off my limbs. When I clambered out, soaking wet, I traveled from the bathroom to what was Drea's temporary quarters on the other side of the apartment. Bo didn't move as I stumbled by, and was in the exact same, face-down position I'd left him in.

I searched through drawers, finding a basic sweatshirt and leggings, and slipped them on. There were also a pair of worn-white sneakers that were a half-size too big, but I put them on, too. Still, no tears. But I dropped the clothing a few times due to my jerkier-than-normal movements, the trembles in my fingers that were refusing to ebb. Forget tying the laces.

Bo's body remained immobile when I went back to retrieve the small, pearl-handled gun I'd filched from Rada's closet and stuffed into my waistband. Despite my body's seizures, I remembered to turn the safety back on before doing so.

My gown, I shoved into a plastic bag. A jug of bleach was discovered under the kitchen sink, and I dumped it down the shower's drain. I wiped down anything I touched. Then, I exited the apartment.

Forty-five minutes.

That was how long it took to clean the parts of me that I could and remove any incriminating evidence from the crime scene.

I hadn't said a word.

Twenty Hours Later

Kai met me at the gate.

I deplaned from the public aircraft, having been curled up in a middle seat in economy class for the better part of seven and a half hours. My joints were stiff, my scar tissue even more so, and I winced at every step forward. I still wore the sweats I stole while Bo was lying dead on the hallway floor. The thought of him prone, the all-black of his outfit hiding the blood that had to be seeping underneath his body...

I swallowed.

"Hey," Kai said. He lifted my duffel from my shoulder and threw it on his, put his arm around my shoulders, and kissed my temple as we walked. "You look like shit."

"I feel..."

"I know, honey." He pulled me tighter into his side. "Once we get in the car, tell me everything."

"Is Chenko...?"

"No," he said. Too abruptly.

"Does he know I'm back?"

"Not yet."

"I couldn't press the button on the necklace."

"I know."

"I had both brothers, and I couldn't do it."

"Don't fret about that right now. Be glad the new ID worked, got you back here."

"Thank you." A lot of breath encased my words, but it was billowed with relief. I wasn't sure if I'd make it out of London, if as soon as I flashed my passport, Chenko's agents would be waiting, shiny metal handcuffs dangling.

When I called Kai, it was with nervous desperation. There wasn't much I could say over the pay phone without further incriminating myself, other than, "I need your help to get out of here. I'm in big trouble."

Any other time, I would have been over the moon to step into a traditional English phone booth, bright red and quaint as hell. If Verily would have been with me, we would've taken selfies in front of it, laughing as we tripped over each other's feet in order to both get in the shot. At least—the Scarlet in my memories was like that.

Kai used his connections, built through his time as an undercover agent for the Saxon mafia, to have a fake passport made. He directed me to a storefront advertising delicious Indian food, and when I gave my name with a voice seeming more autotuned than real, I was led to the back, behind the kitchen, where a nondescript tripod and an elderly lady with long, almost knee-length grey hair and a bright orange kurti took my picture.

Ten hours later, the passport was ready. I'd fallen asleep in the corner, adrenaline crashing like a kitten who'd gluttoned on too much milk, and was shaken awake by the same young man who'd met me at the host's table however many hours previously. He had a dish of succulent foot in his hand, tipping his head in the direction of the old woman as explanation.

After I finished eating and promptly paid from my pilfer of Henry the Duke's son's lockbox, the passport was shoved in my hands and I was ushered out the back door. When the blustery outdoor weather hit the bags under my eyes, I was reminded to check the booklet. The small square of my face looked back at me, and a few slow blinks later, I categorized it as me and not a war-torn, pale version of Cassie, brown hair askew, lower lip drooping in a tired, traumatized way. *Samantha Davis*, likely one of the most American names I'd ever seen.

I curled the booklet against my stomach and hailed the next taxi that crossed my path.

What could Theo be doing during the hours of my wait to get out of the UK, the time I spent in the air, the minutes I now spent with Kai? Almost a day separated us now, the last I saw of him in the interior of his car, the dark tint of him blinding in my memory.

Would he get another scar as punishment? How much mutilation could one son endure?

I'll find you, I thought. *I have to. You won't suffer alone.*

Kai fished into his pocket then sent out a *beep-beep* as he pressed the keyless fob to his car in the covered parking lot adjacent to the arrivals section of JFK. Somehow, we'd made it outside and across an airport road without me cataloguing it.

"In you go," he said, opening the passenger door. I slipped in without a peep, my exposed legs suddenly cold. I wished Kai had a blanket in here. I hoped I wasn't getting sick.

He got in on the other side and started the engine.

"Okay," he said once he backed out. "You're safe. Now talk."

I did. I told him everything. Out of everyone left in my life, Kai was the best trusted, the most understanding, the one who could help me figure out what to do to get Theo back.

"Are you fucking out of your goddamned moronic stupid mind?" Kai yelled once I was finished.

"Not the reception I was hoping for," I mumbled.

My voice sounded dry. I fumbled around for a bottle of

water, which I knew Kai often had on hand due to his many stakeouts—some mandatory, most being annoying—and found an unopened bottle that had rolled under my seat.

"What were you expecting? A high-five? You left a *dead body* in a mafia safe house."

"Which they'll assume was a mafia hit. I cleaned up, don't worry."

Kai dared an exasperated glance up at the car's roof. "He's American, Scar. This is going to come back—"

"To the Saxons. It's their problem, now. Add it to their list of transgressions."

"This is bad. Like, really. We have to loop Chenko in and I'm not sure if you can get out of this without charges..."

"He tried to kill me, Kai."

"I know. Jesus Christ, I know." He squeezed the wheel, so hard I saw the bones of his knuckles. "When you boarded that plane with Sax, we had a clear plan in mind. Get the two of them in the same room together. Press the necklace's button. Send in the troops. That was it."

"We left out an important problem," I said.

"Yeah?" he responded, somewhat angrily. "And what's that?"

"Humanity."

Tendons in Kai's cheek stood out.

"What went on in London ... it was unpredictable. We didn't consider *other people*. Rada, Drea, this duke's son, Bo ... Trace. I kept in front of it as much as I could, but their actions preceded mine. I'm convinced Trace knew, the entire time, where Theo and I were. And he had the plan to get his brother all along."

"But why?"

"That's where I hit a roadblock. I don't know. And considering there's a hit on me, why didn't Trace take it? He had all the chance in the world to take me out, and instead, he played cat-and-mouse with us. It's almost like their father had one agreement with Theo, and another with Trace. Like Gordon Saxon was playing them against each other for pure entertainment in order to see who would end up on top."

"Wouldn't surprise me."

"Not to mention, why did the king Saxon put a price on my head? What was I doing that angered him so much he wanted me dead?"

"Uh, let's see. You broke a major drug trafficking scheme spearheaded by his favorite son, Trace Saxon."

"That was a couple of years ago. He's holding that much of a grudge?"

"And instead of dying *then* like you should have—in his mind —you went on to become a major player in underground poker."

"Never in his houses. I made sure of that."

"Fine. Next transgression—you scattered both his sons to the wind. Heirs he'd been grooming since they had diapers strapped over their dicks. When grown, both were damaged by his unfatherly ways, yet carefully honed into taking over an illegal empire. And when you made them fugitives, all Papa Saxon was left with was ... who? The youngest brother? What's his name? I'm always forgetting."

"Ward. Are you saying he's blaming me for the break-up of his heirs? He's the asshole pitting them against each other!"

"You think he sees it that way?"

"How's my death going to benefit him? I'm a little piece of nothing, swimming around in his ocean like an ... empty plastic bottle."

"That will never disintegrate."

"God." I covered my face with my hands. "You'd think I'd've learned to stay away from the Saxons by now."

"I dunno. You talk about assassins coming after you like it's a day at a beach when the sun's too hot."

"I have to," I said, looking out my window. "If I allow it to compute, I'm a goner. All I wanted to do was find something I was good at, and that turned out to be poker. And in finding the game, I found Theo. I can't escape him." I paused.

"Are we talking about the Sax of two years ago, or now?" Kai asked as he made a right turn.

"I..."

"Fuck."

I glanced at him. "What?"

"Well," he said on a sigh, "You're talking about humanity putting a wrench in our plans, but I don't think you've considered your own."

"What are you talking about?"

"You're back in love with Sax, Scarlet." Kai braked at a stoplight and turned to me with the flattest expression I'd ever seen on his usually vivacious face. "If you ever fell out of it. And you've just made this a hell of a lot more complicated."

KAI TOOK me back to his place.

For a man who had taken a sick day to aid and abet a fugitive, he was doing rather well, but I guessed being an undercover agent for the purposes of a highly dangerous mafia sting would do that to a guy.

I also understood that my time as a free woman was severely limited. Kai had kept Chenko and his agents at bay for as long as he could, but now that I was back in the US (and with no Theo or Trace to show for it), if Chenko got wind of my presence, there would be no questions asked. I'd be immediately taken into an interrogation room, squeezed for information, booked, then put in a holding cell.

And I would be no good to Theo in jail.

We took the stairs to Kai's second-floor walkup, the thin, stained maroon carpeting doing nothing to buffer the creak of the wood as we ascended.

"Is Marcus here?" I asked.

My love for Kai's boyfriend spoke volumes. I was often the third wheel during their dinner dates, yet Kai's Trinidadian soul mate never once made me feel unwanted. He was funny, upbeat, sweet to Kai during rough days and stern during days of rest.

Always wanting to travel, explore, catch elevators to secret floors in the city known only to those that were "in." They met through a dating app, yet to see them together, you would have thought they were childhood sweethearts. But, the thought of seeing Marcus right now, of putting on a face, had me dreaming of going back to Kai's car and sleeping the rest of my dire situation off in his backseat.

Avoidance was my instinct, I'd come to learn. But having consequences smacked into my face, that was my fate.

"He's not," Kai said. He plodded up the stairs in front, my duffel so light it bounced against his hip.

I zeroed in on his lower back with suspicion. "Why did you say that in such a clipped tone?"

"No reason."

"Why aren't you talking to me directly?"

"Because we're climbing stairs."

"But your neck is so stiff, your footsteps really abrupt..." It clicked. "Kai, *who* do you have in your apartment?"

Kai sprinted the last two steps like they were taped with the finishing ribbon of a marathon, careening around the corner and flinging open his apartment door before I had my hand off the railing.

"She's here!" Kai yelled to someone inside. "Talk some sense into the woman."

Kai couldn't have called Chenko already, could he? Frozen, I clung to the railing, sensing its ability to assist me in increasing my velocity when I pushed off and back down the stairs. In fact, that was a good idea. There were only so many cat lives left. If I were detained now—

"Scar?"

A soft outline of hair appeared in the doorway, flashing copper-red from the sunlit windows behind her. Kai chose his apartments based on natural light. He boasted it was because he was a millennial increasingly concerned with environmental conservation, including energy, but we all knew it was so he could save on his electric bills. To which he replied, *two birds, one stone, Scar. Quit mouthing off.*

A lean body with toned legs in coral shorts and a plain white tee came next. The exposed skin was slightly freckled, pale to the eye and warm to the touch, nails painted in chipped pink because she couldn't kick her nervous habit of picking her cuticles. The long neck was bordered by a clavicle I was always jealous of, because it made strapless dresses look stunning on her.

She carried one difference, though, an addition I hadn't been witness to, since I'd been in the underground so long. A sparkle of white on her ring finger.

"Verily," I whispered. Inexplicably, my vision went wet.

"Oh my God, Scarlet."

Footsteps sounded, heavy and rushed, and before I drew breath she had her arms around me, squeezing, my neck dampening with her tears.

"You're okay," she said, her breath hot on my skin. "You made it back."

"I..." I lifted my hands, placed them lightly on her back. Over her shoulder, I tried to find Kai. He wasn't anywhere I could see.

Delicately, I pushed back from Verily. "It's not safe for you to be here. I can't believe Kai called you."

It was only a second, but I caught the burn of hurt in her eyes. "What isn't safe for me is also dangerous for you."

"You don't understand. The Saxons have—"

"God, you with the Saxons. The Saxons with you. It doesn't stop, does it? Will it ever? No. Scarlet." She caught my arm as I tried to pass her. "I'm here because I love you. I worry about you. You didn't hear Kai on the other end of the phone, how he sounded. He was terrified for you. And when *Kai* starts to worry, what do you think that does to me? To your family?"

I shook her off, avoiding her eye. "Kai's playing a dirty game."

"Why do I have to keep reminding you of how much we love you?" Verily's voice broke. "And why won't you come back to us?"

I paused, turned. "Your ring," I said, my voice thick. "It's beautiful. You and Noah deserve a beautiful life. I mean it. But I'm not meant for that."

"Oh, Scar. You break my heart."

I looked to the ceiling where a single spotlight flickered, laughing dully. "It took me a while to realize it, I admit, and I was really good at burying any reminders, but Theo walked back into my life Ver, and I ... I..."

"Sax. Fucking Theo Saxon." Verily rubbed at her lips while she said it, distorting the sound and somehow making it angrier.

"Yes. He's back. And fighting for his life, because I was too dumb to figure out that he'd returned to protect me."

"From what?"

"His father."

Verily slumped, her hip bumping into the railing. "You have to get away from them, Scar. All of them."

"It's too late."

"Never. Come with me right now, and I'll drive you to your parents. You can stay there, recover—"

"*No*, Verily." And I meant it viscerally. "Kai made a mistake asking you to come here."

Verily stepped up to me, her eyes searching. I let her, my lips frozen into thin lines. "Since when have you become so mean?" she asked softly. "Your parents are desperate to see you. *Noah* would love to see you, especially before we get married."

"It can't happen."

Through the silence, Verily's thoughts must have been ticking. Mine were on lockdown, because any weakness, any hesitation, and I'd be in Verily's arms asking her how she still loved me.

She broke the quiet by saying, "You know, in another life, in a better one, you would have been my maid of honor."

I tossed back, "And in that perfect life, he'd be marrying Cassie, not you."

Her gasp singed every space inside me, sucking up the air, hollow black smoking in its wake. Her mouth tremulous, Verily couldn't think of how to respond. *You bitch* wasn't in her vocabulary. Neither was *go to hell* or *fuck you* even though I wished she would fling that kind of hurt at me.

"Go, Verily. You don't belong here."

In my head, the tone was a croak, a barely detectable sound above baritone. But she understood. My best friend let it sink in, filling the vulnerable softness of her expression with stone, and cemented my words with a burning, unforgivable stare.

"Each time I see you, you get worse," she said. She paused at the top of the stairs. "Pretty soon, there will be nothing left of you. And before you tell me how little you believe in yourself, how you've decided to put no value on your life, think of it another way. Pretty soon, there will be no one left who cares."

Her footfalls sounded, laden with the burden of having me back in her life, only to watch me leave again. I clenched my hands, as my fingers trembled and stilled my tremulous lower lip. I blinked back the tears threatening to fall, but there was nothing I could do about the heat in my cheeks, the hot flush of emotion clogging my throat and making it difficult to breathe.

More footfalls came, these ones different, tentative and hesitant.

"She left?" Kai dared to ask, and that was all it took.

"*How could you?*" I shouted. His reaction was to throw up his hands and startle like a mouse caught with cheese.

"Shh! Easy, Scarlet, the neighbors are already pissed at Marcus's and my—"

"How dare you bring Verily here, to me," I hissed, but allowed him to usher me into his apartment and shut the door.

"Think of it as the equivalent to splashing cold water on your face," Kai hissed back. "It was either your bestie or Chenko waiting in my apartment. I figured you'd appreciate the former."

"No, I wouldn't." Without anything to pummel, I deferred to an open-palm smack on Kai's maroon stucco walls. They were thin, so the sound was somewhat satisfying. But not enough. Never enough. "If you want to put this to rest so badly, arrest me. Stick me in a room with Chenko. Do *not* bring Verily near me ever again."

"You talk like she has leprosy." Kai was genuinely shocked. "How could you not want her around, after all this time? I thought you missed her. I thought seeing the normalcy that used to be your day-to-day life would help."

It was easy, probably expected, to throw another punch at the wall, this time closed-fisted. Anger, blame, and screaming all served to prove the point that Kai screwed up. But it was oh, so tiring. And I was spent. Dangerously close to giving up. I said, with brine-coated rocks on my tongue, "It only serves to remind me how much danger I've put them in. Her. Noah. My parents. Gordon Saxon wants me dead, Kai."

At last, Kai was made speechless.

"How could you think I'd want Verily near me?" I gestured behind him. "Someone Gordon hired could've been in your apartment, or the one next door because he killed your neighbors for a stakeout spot, waiting for me, and instead getting Verily as a bonus. She was alone here, Kai. She was *by herself* when we both knew there are people out there wanting to kill me, and if that fails, hurting me where it would gut me the most." I said her name like an elastic snapping in two. "Verily."

"Jesus. Scarlet, I'm sorry. I didn't ... when you called me to come home, the first thing I thought of was to surround you with family. And when you told me about the Saxon hit in the car, I'd completely forgotten ... no, that's not an excuse. I'm supposed to be better at this. Sharper. It was a big fuck-up, and I'm lucky Verily wasn't hurt. I'm sorry, Scarlet. Truly sorry."

Kai's repentance was like a cloud, bloated with acid rain, landing on my shoulders. I felt the weight like it was something I personally gained, but not what I wanted. It was so easy to shrink my world into a pinhole, where only Theo and I existed and our actions solely affected one another. In that shoebox there was no Saxon family, no Kai, no Verily, no parents, and most importantly, no guilt. Zero fear. Since the only person I had to look out for was myself, it was a simple task to barrel forward. I wanted blinders like those poor horses in Central Park, where my periphery was completely black, and I wouldn't be spooked by crowds of pedestrians, the sudden acceleration and braking of cars, the screech of buses.

Tunnel vision. That was what I wished for.

Then I wouldn't see my parents on the sidelines, Mom's eyelashes thick and clumped with tears, Dad's frown lines deepened first by the loss of Cassie, then by watching the slow decay of his remaining daughter.

"No," I said. "I'm the one who's sorry. I should have figured out another way to get back here, without involving you or anyone else I care about." After a sigh, I realized, "I should've just called Chenko."

"Now, that's just stupid."

"At this point? Not too much sounds smart."

"If you'd brought the task force in, and I mean true, patriotic FBI agents with no attachment to you whatsoever, not even sexually, you'd be in custody and have no way—let me reiterate, *zero chance*, of figuring out where Theo is and getting to him first.

"Not to mention," he continued, finger raised over any counterarguments, "the shit-river I've had to cross in order to get us here in the first place. You go down, you take me with you, and hell if I'm going to let that happen. I'll go down harder. I had Theo in a room—nay, a *boat*—and I didn't inform my superiors. I knew where you were the entire time you've been listed as a fugitive. I'm aware of Theo's brand spanking new identifiable scar on his face, a fun fact that I am positive my boss would be over-the-moon to know about."

Kai grabbed my shoulders, and repeated, nose-to-nose, "I. Am. Fucked. If you go to the FBI now, you might as well have done it well before betting your body to fucking Neri. Because you'll be making everything we've done up until this point a piece of utterly pointless crap. You might as well shit on me."

"All right, I get it." I held up my hand, pushing his face away from mine. "I'd never betray you."

"Same goes, pretty. Now." Kai leveled his shoulders. "Let me get my gun."

"We can't go anywhere, even with weaponry."

"Why not?"

"Because I don't know where Trace could've taken Theo. Not to mention the price on my head."

"Then I'll trade in my pistol for my thinking cap. Come on." He gestured further into his apartment, seeming how we were both still standing in his small entryway. "Sit your butt on the couch, I'll brew us some tea, and we can conference."

I had one foot forward before my body froze. Stiffness traveled from my toes, rippling up toward my neck, but that was where it stopped. My face, it was left to crumble.

"Scar. Oh my—okay, come here. Come here."

Kai's arms came around. He was never a light hugger—the kind who tolerated reaching out merely to appear normal. Kai was all in, his bones pressing through his muscles in order to maintain a firm, steady, anchor.

"There's been so much delay already," I said into the fabric of his shoulder. He smelled of beach and ocean, musky with a touch of salt. "And I keep thinking back to why he came back in the first place, why he risked contacting you and seeing me again. It was to try and save my life. And I repaid by—"

"You didn't know."

"But I should have. Theo wouldn't just appear out of nowhere to say hi. There's always something going on under his skin. He was the best cold reader in poker—I should've remembered. He knew people's moves before they did."

"Exactly right. Which is why you couldn't have predicted what was going on in his head. Or tried."

"He's hurt, Kai. I know he is. He wouldn't have left without fighting..."

Kai released his grip, rubbing the sides of my arms instead. "You're close. Remember that much. You've made it back to New York, with my assistance, of course, but you're walking the same soil he is. We'll find him. I have extensive notes on the Saxons, as you well know. Trace's habits are like my own at this point, and I will go through them with a fine-tooth comb, with you by my side, and we'll figure out where Trace would have him."

"I was going to betray him." I swiped a hand across my eyes, dissolving the mist, but it didn't do anything to quell the ache, deep under my ribs. "Theo was trying to save me and I was willing to hand him over to the FBI."

"You need to remember." Kai kept his tone low, steady. "He's not a good guy. Sax has done a lot of bad things. It's not like you were sending an innocent lamb to slaughter. More like a wolf."

I looked at Kai then.

Kai's phone buzzed. It was loud enough that I heard the vibration through his pants. He pulled it out while apologizing, muttering that it was probably Marcus and if he didn't text something back within ten minutes, Marcus would likely call an ambulance.

That was pretty much the M.O. to anyone hanging out with me these days. Leaving worry in my wake. I wondered if Marcus even liked me anymore.

"Oh, Jesus."

"What?" I asked automatically, trying to read the look of surprise on Kai's face. "What is it?"

"Well..." Kai swallowed. Actually, he gulped. "I don't believe our research will do any good anymore."

"Did the cops find Theo?" I almost whispered it. I was so terrified it was true.

"Uh. No."

"Did Theo just *text* you?" That would have been the ultimate, wonderful dream come true.

"Not that, either."

"Fucking tell me." My voice had risen to a crescendo—no hesitation allowed. Spit, however, was absolutely welcome when aiming to scream my point in panic mode.

"It's ... it's..."

"Goddammit, Kai." I swiped the phone from him, read the text myself.

Literally felt the blood leaving my cheeks. Pooling at my collarbone.

"Oh, Jesus," I echoed.

Glad you made it back safe and sound, Scarlet.

If you're able, please come to my home at 8pm this evening.

I promise, no assassins.

Just my sons.

- G.S.

"HE MUST HAVE A MAN OUTSIDE. Even though we disguised you as best we could, Gordon Saxon figured out you were back." Kai paced the apartment, the wide-paneled wood floors unable to buffer the scrapes of his heels. "Where did we go wrong? No one is involved in this—literally no one. And I didn't fucking leak anything."

I shook my head, Kai's phone hanging loosely in my hand. "We were idiots to think otherwise. This man has more power than the FBI. More men than the ... the president. It was a matter of time."

"He's not going to get you." Kai dug his fingers into his hair, a motion that *banged* a vision of Theo into my mind doing the exact same thing.

Theo...

The answer was obvious. "I have to go."

"No. *Nope.* You were right before. We need to loop in Chenko."

"It's too late."

"They can go in your place. I'm sure we could get a warrant, harboring two fugitives. Yeah ... yes, we can do this. That text!" Kai pointed to his phone at my thigh. "Gordon admitted to having his sons, two of the Most Wanted. It's enough for any judge."

Again, I shook my head. "He'd kill them first before ever handing them over to the police."

Kai paused mid-reach for his cell. "You can't be serious. He wouldn't kill his sons rather than..."

"He'd still have one left. Ward. That's all he needs to run an empire."

I handed over the phone. Kai said, "Jeez. That's cold."

"I've never had any deep conversations with the Saxon brothers' sire, but I doubt that description even comes close to what he actually is."

"Either way, you're not going. This has gone too far. This man has put a fucking *hit* on you for falling in love with Sax. You cannot dip a pinky toe near his moat. Understand?"

"I'm going to grab a shower."

"There've been points in the past where you—wait, what?"

"You heard me." I peeled off my shirt on the way to the exposed industrial shower in the far-right corner, separated by the rest of the apartment with a single fogged-over glass panel.

"You're ignoring what I'm saying. That never bodes well. For either of us," Kai said.

"Your thinking cap is to carve paths in your floorboards. Mine is to take a hot shower and go over my options."

I didn't have to look back to know Kai crossed his arms before saying, "You've already made your decision, haven't you?"

My only answer was the creak of the pipes as I turned on the water.

"I'll call Chenko the instant you put your head under that spray," he warned.

"No you won't." I stepped out of my shorts, then underwear, and got in the shower, massaging my neck as the stream melted against my face.

"Yes, I—oh, come *on*, Scar."

Eyes closed, I smiled.

"Since when did you become a fucking pick-pocket?"

I spun so the water cascaded down the back of my head. "You learn a lot in the underground."

"Where is it? Where's my phone, you asshole?"

Kai came around the glass panel, hands on his hips, while I squirted shampoo into my palm.

"Where did you—oh, *come* on, Scar."

He spotted his phone in the toilet.

"This is my last chance," I told him. "It's a bitch move to destroy your phone, I know, and I promise I'll get you a new one. But if I don't find out what Gordon wants with me, if I don't get to see Theo ever again..."

"Do *not* Romeo and Juliet my ass while you're naked."

I stepped forward just enough for the spray to hit my lower back, keeping my expression free and clear. "My world stopped spinning when my sister died. It restarted again when I found Theo. Then ran into another wall when he left. My life's trajectory has been fucked up ever since I was seventeen years old, and for once, a clear path has been laid out in front of me. I need to get him out, Kai."

"Even at the expense of your friends? Verily? Your family?"

"If I don't do this," I said, tipping up to wash the suds out of my hair. "There will be nothing left of me to give."

Kai grew serious. "You've sold so much of your soul to the Saxon dynasty already, Scarlet."

"Yeah?" I turned the tap off, wrung out my hair. "Then what's a few threads more?"

It was with great reluctance that Kai said good-bye to me at his door. I wasn't escaping entirely, as Kai made me agree to wear his necklace as he monitored me on his computer, ready to call in the cavalry at my barest touch.

He was a true friend. While Kai didn't agree with my actions, he also knew that I'd jump through the fire escape if I had to, and it was with the path of least resistance in mind that he shook on a plan.

It was inescapable destiny. Once I had eyes on both Trace and Theo, I was to press the necklace and bring the FBI in. It was the only way Kai would let me go without following, as well as the only reason why Chenko wasn't standing in the doorway blocking my way out.

I wasn't going in alone. Technically. I had the necklace, an item that wouldn't be confiscated by Gordon Saxon's security team due to its innocuous appearance. I didn't take Kai's gun, as I barely knew how to shoot, and my confrontation with Bo remained on traumatic repeat in my mind.

You killed someone.

There wasn't time to dwell. I rubbed at my eyes, essentially pressing the memory out of existence until it would pop up again, likely at night, during the moments between awake and rest, those crucial seconds where all regrets changed to vivid flashbacks that wouldn't recede, no matter how many sheep were counted.

Well, I wasn't going to sleep, anyway.

This time, there was no formal gown adorning my body, no diamonds, or pearls. It was simply my denim shorts, which I washed in Kai's sink then blew dry with a hair dryer, and one of Kai's obscure rock band t-shirts. My hair was tied back and I wore minimal make-up.

As I took one last look in the entryway mirror, I thought this was a person I hadn't seen in a very long time. The maintenance, primping, and couture I'd become accustomed to were long discarded, and I was back to myself, a girl from upstate who moved to the city with little to no dreams, but nowhere else to go. I'd been lucky to find Verily, and through her a waitress job which ultimately led to an uncanny talent of playing with cards. Everything I'd been through culminated to this point.

There was nothing left to lose. I'd been labeled a fugitive, or at the very least a person of interest, in the United States, along with Theo. I was too pragmatic to believe we'd be sipping Mai Tais in a country without extradition, living out our lives under different names, never to be seen again by the Saxon family or the FBI. In order to get us out, I had to bring the FBI in. Complicated, fool-headed, but true.

"You'll be careful," Kai said as I entered the floor's hallway. It wasn't a question.

"Always."

To his credit, Kai didn't roll his eyes. "I won't take my attention off my computer screen. Not for a minute."

"I know."

"I love you, Scar."

At the emotion in his voice, I went into his arms and said close to his ear, "I love you, too."

"I'll see you again." There wasn't as much inflection in his words this time.

"Of course."

Without looking back, I descended the stairs.

It wasn't necessary to reply to Gordon Saxon's text asking for an address. His townhouse was well-known and ultimately impenetrable by any one layman. One had to receive an invitation in order to pass through the iron gate, and that included police, dirty and clean alike. No one crossed into Saxon territory without extreme vetting and specific intentions. It was a feat similar to an FBI agent's wet dream to see the interior of the home, never mind Papa Saxon himself. He kept himself carefully apart from any crimes, questionable deliveries and inflated payrolls. In the words of Chenko himself, Gordon Saxon was a slippery son-of-a-bitch who the government had spent a decade trying to collar.

As I walked toward the subway, conscious of any eyes on me, I hoped I'd have the chance to talk to Theo before I pressed the necklace's button and fucked him over a second time. Wouldn't that be wonderful. I could look Theo in the eye and say, *thanks for risking everything in an attempt to save my life, but I'm having you arrested. Enjoy your foreseeable future behind bars. Oh, by the way, I'm still in love with you.*

The mere thought of it had me missing a few steps. If I could get a chance to explain before the walls come crashing down, if he'd be able to look at me...

The only way. It's the only way, Letty.

And maybe it was. I traversed the lingering crowds poking around Chinatown, the cacophony of voices and cars rising into a cloud of white noise. Once I reached the subway entrance, I descended into the ultimate underground.

When a rat scuttled across the platform and down onto the tracks, it was too close an analogy to my journey to Gordon Saxon and I focused on the incoming lights of the subway train instead.

THE SAXONS' main townhouse was located in Williamsburg, an area one wouldn't think a crime lord would move into, but with the growing gentrification and the draw of trendy storefronts, it wasn't too much of a stretch to think Gordon Saxon and his fourth wife converted a piano factory into a brick-lined, industrial-styled, four-story mansion.

I stood in front of its black farm-sized double doors, which I was pretty sure once belonged to a horse stable but was probably sold for ten times as much, I couldn't deny Gordon his style sense. Or, perhaps his new wife. Either way, to walk up the modest poured concrete walkway sanded to appear years older than it was, one would never believe such a property belonged to an infamous crime king. A rock star perhaps, or an A-list celebrity wanting prime location but few paparazzi.

I was delaying. It was obvious, since my finger hovered near the doorbell but wouldn't press, my mind instead providing real estate critique that I probably siphoned from reruns of *Million Dollar Listing* that Verily loved watching.

It was better than what waited inside.

I would have loved to case the property, peek through windows and figure out where Theo was being held and Trace and their father held court. But cameras had already spied me, and it was no wonder, since such a fashionable home would be outfitted like a fortress.

After a breath, I pressed the bell.

No echoing ring was heard or annoying *ding-dong*. These walls, doors, and windows were soundproofed. Unconsciously, I squeezed the necklace. My only hope, the last weapon to bring the Saxons down. All of them.

No one would hear my screams.

The door swayed open, and a butler of sorts appeared. He was dressed in slacks and a polo and resembled more of a professional wrestler than a server. He held no tray, smiled no greeting, but made sure his holstered gun stuck in his belt was on full display.

He said nothing, merely waiting for me to step inside. Once I did, he *thunked* the door shut behind me. The bustling city outside disappeared. Emergency sirens couldn't break through the screen of silence engulfing this home.

"Stand still," he said.

Arms out, I allowed the frisk, front teeth clutching my lower lip as his calloused hands grazed the exposed skin of my forearms, my thighs. He paused at the denim between my legs, lingering much too long, but moved right when I was going to break his face with my knee.

When he untucked my shirt, I shoved away. "Don't you dare."

"Oh, I dare, honey. You're in Saxon territory now. Shirt up, or I'll tear it off you."

I tasted blood from my teeth cutting into the vulnerable tissue of my lip, the metal fear scoring across my tongue. "No."

"No?"

His hand snaked around my neck too quickly and I gulped air, fingernails scratching at the girth of his tattooed forearm.

"Then we're doing it the hard way." He said it with such ease, like he lifted weights with girls half his size on a daily basis. Using his other hand to lift up my shirt, he felt around, met my bulging stare, and squeezed a breast with a half-smile. If I'd had enough saliva, I would have spit in his eye.

I gasped when he suddenly dropped me and opened my windpipes. I doubled over, gagging.

"You're clean," he said, off-hand. "Follow me."

I steadied my gait as I followed him down the wide hallway with exposed ceiling beams and industrial lights. It wasn't the mansion I imagined. I pictured Gordon Saxon encased in velvet and antiques, a cigar dangling from his lips as he remained comfortably seated on a tufted red chair bordered by intricate wooden carvings. Maybe a Doberman on either side, ears pricked for the muttering of their master's "*attack*."

The butler/wrestler stepped aside to allow me entry into a main room, the dark paneled wood underneath my feet unchanging from the hallway to the room. Cream couches—the types with very stiff cushions and not much comfortability—were the focus, and on one, sat Gordon Saxon.

I hadn't seen him since one brief night at a charity event two years ago. Heard talk of him during my first days as a cocktail waitress, and certainly understood the threat of him years after. Gordon Saxon was a forewarning that greeted me before I entered other houses, sat at other tables. There wasn't a poker room that he didn't know and didn't know him. The Saxons ruled the underground, and ensuring I stayed away from his rooms wasn't enough. Standing here, I wondered when I ever thought it would be.

Gordon was incredibly good-looking. Not sallow or pot-bellied like I'd envisioned most mafia bosses to be. For someone who stayed out of the spotlight and relied on the murmuring of his name as enough threat, I'd pictured a goblinesque, short, chain-smoking old man with streaked white hair. A navy suit costing more than five years of cocktail waitressing narrowly disguised a soft gut, but otherwise, his frame was trim. Muscled. Tailored to a multi-millionaire.

"Scarlet Rhodes," Gordon said through carved, pale pink lips rimmed with salt-and-pepper stubble. Gordon's sandy hair, tinted with gray, was swept back in a singular wave, long enough to curl at the edges and give me the impression that this was how Theo would look if he grew out his hair. His cheekbones jutted out under addictive blue eyes, an exact match to Theo.

I hovered in the archway, unable to speak. My lungs had bunched up and settled behind my collarbone, shriveling the instant I locked stares with this man.

"I'm surprised you came," he said.

I rubbed at my throat. Images of Lauren's torture—Theo's previous girlfriend—centered themselves directly in front of my pupils. I hadn't been witness to it, but I'd heard enough.

"Please, take a seat. Would you like a drink?"

I shook my head.

He chuckled. "Of all the ways I pictured your arrival, I did not predict this. I'd heard your quips made even the most seasoned players speechless, that you could read a man through a glance and predict his cards in one sweep. Yet you stand before me a tired, scared young girl with nothing to say."

"Where's Theo?"

"Ah." He threw an arm across the top of the couch and crossed a leg at the ankle. "I'll add predictable to the list."

"Where is he?"

"Patience. Sit down and talk a while."

"You got what you wanted. Trace is here," I said through the cogs in my throat. My lungs offered very little breathing room. "Theo did as you asked."

"Yes, he certainly did."

"Why do you want to kill me?"

He cocked his head, his eyes just as startling on an angle as they were head-on. "You aren't so vacuous as to fail to understand why I want you out of the way."

"Theo and I aren't together anymore."

Tony tilted his head the other way. "No?"

"We're not," I said, firmer. "He needed me to…"

To what? Theo didn't require my services to locate his older brother. He was only using it as a pretense.

"He needed me to play in a few games." I made sure to sound strong. "To infiltrate ones Trace was known to put horses into or play himself."

"I assure you, Theodore has told me the same thing."

My relief was short-lived. Gordon smiled. "Your stories match, but I haven't enjoyed stories since I was a babe in my mother's arms."

"I haven't done anything wrong."

"You made a mistake the instant you stepped through the doors of my House a few years ago."

"Then I'll leave," I said. "Show me Theo, that he's all right, and you'll never have to see me again. I'll stop playing poker. I'll move out of the city."

Gordon rose, walked toward me with the ease of a predator. When he was close enough, he raised his hand to stroke the forming bruises on my neck. I swallowed, the action pressing his fingers deeper for a mere second, but it was enough to have me reeling back. I didn't break eye contact.

"You're responsible for Theodore's demise," he said, hand still raised in mid-air. "I want you to know that. It's because of you he's shirked his duties, discarded the Saxon name, and stayed away from my city for so long. In truth, you took Trace with you in the same action."

Gordon's handsome features morphed, a vulgar mask

warping what was a misleadingly kind face. It was like searching for an angel during a storm.

"You've ruined two of my sons. I have one who hates you and one who would do anything for you. In both situations, you are a distraction. Tracey must focus on what's important—this empire, this city—and Theodore needs to fall in line. Oh, and he will." Gordon's veneers glimmered in the industrial lighting. It was in that moment I realized why this house lacked plushness, fabric, carpeting. It was due to calculation. Crime scene clean-up was so much easier this way.

"I want to thank you," he said, the mask falling to the ground. Gordon came back, his lips, though deeply lined, mellowing into a relaxed downward curve.

"For what?" Shockingly, my tone remained steady.

"For bringing with you the realization that I should never have initiated a contract against you."

"If you want to be the one to personally kill me, then do it."

Gordon's brows jumped, deepening the lines on his forehead, but he slammed them down just as fast. "I'll be glad to."

When he'd raised his arm to touch me, I caught the holster under his arm, the gun nestled inside. I'd felt a gunshot before, and at the time, that pain was supposed to end me. By some luck of the draw, it didn't. I'd endure it again, but for one reason only.

"Shoot me," I said, chin up, teeth clenched. Trembles cascaded from my shoulders to my heels. "Go on. Do it."

I almost missed it. A flicker of respect. "You want the suffering to end that quickly, do you?"

He stepped forward, and this time, I didn't have the space to back away.

"You poor doe," he said, tutting as he ran one finger down my cheek. I refused to flinch. "First losing your sister, your twin no less. And your attempts to find solace in darkness, I admire that. Danger causes grief to all but disappear, doesn't it? Adrenaline.

Power. Nothing else matters. But here's the problem." He let his hand drop once he completed the path down my face. "I don't want suffering to ever end."

"Show me Theo," I all but whispered. "Let me see him, and you can do what you want."

Cool air hit my flushed cheeks when he backed up. "Be careful what you wish for."

When he turned, he sent a look to the doorway, one that caught the butler/wrestler's eye. The man who groped me came at me again, and this time I snarled. "Don't touch me."

"You asked to see Sax. Well, you're gonna." He latched onto my arm, dragging me out of the room.

"You're lucky," Gordon said over my struggles. "Most people don't have such excellent reception when they arrive." His gaze flickered to my shorts, then up again. "I give you credit for not pissing yourself."

"Where are you taking me?" I asked—dumbly, automatically, pointlessly.

"I don't believe in slaughtered lambs," Gordon said with disinterest. "So you'll wait out your time with my middle son. Butcher, you know what to do."

My shoes skidded against wood, but I was a toothpick compared to this man named Butcher. My heartbeats were stronger than my muscles, but I continued the fight, batting against tree-trunk arms and twisting.

I was good at this. Yet all my chances were trickling away the closer Butcher brought me to a door that led to captivity. He restrained me in a way that I couldn't reach the necklace or press it if I tried. It required an exact touch, a precise click, in order to activate.

There was only one thing left, and I had nothing to lose.

"The police!" I shouted at Gordon. "They know I'm here. The FBI. If anything happens to me—"

"Oh, those men?" Gordon regarded me with a droll expression. "I have no worries about them. Half are in my pocket. Does Peter Chenko mean anything to you?"

I screeched through his arrogance and would've clawed him if I could.

"She's like a fucking street cat," Butcher said over my head. "Calm down before I knock you the fuck out."

I believed him.

With his free hand, Butcher threw open a door leading to darkness. And without any further ado, he threw me down the stairs.

IN SELF-DEFENSE CLASSES, you were taught how to fall.

When thrown down steps, instead of tensing and bunching up muscles—automatic instinct—it was crucial to stay loose, to flop, while protecting the head.

I did what I could to practice what was preached, but nobody promised it would hurt any less.

Once at the bottom of the stairs, I groaned, the sound buried under the slam of the door at the top of the steps. For some reason, coughing followed, as if during the spiral, my lungs fused flat to my spine. Lifting to my forearms, I took stock of the new environment. Weak light allowed me to case the room while squinting through the dust I kicked up, noting the naked walls, the cracked concrete floor, the two wooden support beams near the center, a cluster of wooden barrels in the corner. Carefully, I moved to a sit, rubbing my elbows and knees, which had taken the brunt of the short fall down one ... two ... eleven steps.

Then, I rubbed at my neck, thankful I seemed to be in one piece.

Scraping caught my attention, broke my focus on the details of the basement. I jerked to the sound coming from a far corner, noted a bent leg moving at the ankle between the barrels, then falling flat to the floor. Another groan, not mine, came from the same area.

"Theo?" I whispered, because that gurgle of pain, the ache of inflicted wounds in that tone, was not Sax the mafia prince. It was my Theo.

When did he stop being Sax in my mind? I supposed it was in Rada's bathroom, his hands in my hair, guiding me back to my sister.

I wobbled to a stand, fell when my body recoiled, so adopted a crawling slide. "Theo? Can you hear me?"

The leg didn't move.

"*Theo.*" A fit of coughs got to me again, but I didn't stop sliding closer, nearer, to God knows what. "What have they done to you? Answer me, please answer. Don't be..."

Don't be dead.

At last, I made it to the tip of his shoe and jiggled it lightly. "I'm here," I said to him, scooting closer. "You're not alone."

He was so far into the darkness, there was no way to gauge his injuries properly when I couldn't see him. Gently, ever so carefully, I shifted him by the shoulders so his face would come into the light.

"Oh..." I said, thickness trickling into my throat.

Theo was bloody. Too red. One eye was swollen, the other fused closed, by stinging tears, saliva, who knew. His nostrils were black with clotted blood, his dried lips holding the streams that escaped. A quick scan, some light touches to his cheekbones, and my non-medical training told me perhaps nothing was fractured. The pieces of his face still made sense, nothing was crushed. And his skin was warm. Pushing back his hair on his forehead, I noticed a deep cut near the center, probably the reason for all the blood. Head wounds were terrible bleeders.

I prayed he hadn't lost too much.

It appeared to have clotted closed, all his wounds had,

meaning he hadn't taken any recent hits. He'd been left in this basement for a while, on his own, with nothing to look at except for scarred wooden beams by other victim's nails. If he'd been conscious at all, that is.

Now, the major worry was concussion and how long he'd been out.

"Theo, wake up." I patted his cheek, using my other hand to feel for a pulse in his neck. The movement hurt, but I was able to get up on my knees to do it. "It's me. Scarlet."

Did I see that? I peered closer. A twitch of eyelashes, perhaps a small brow furrow, usually a sign that he knew I was near.

"Can you hear me? Or"—I gave a light poke near his jaw, hoping he had no loose teeth—"Feel this?"

"Mmf." He moved his head away from my fingers.

"Thank God," I breathed, and continued to lightly poke. "You have to wake up. All the way. I know it's a bitch, but I'll be even bitchier if you die. Come on, open your eyes."

"Nuh..."

"Yes, you bastard. Open them before I pry them open with my broken fingernails."

Adrenaline retreated to the back of my throat, leaving room for fear and anger.

"How dare you leave with him?" I asked through Theo's grumbles. "What in the hell made you think that was a good idea? You knew what would happen, didn't you? That instead of you bringing Trace home, it would become the opposite. Trace was always your dad's favorite. He figured out that to get back in Gordon's good graces, he needed to predict your moves. And you were going to escape this life, weren't you, you jerk? After you found Trace, you were going to disappear again. Under the guise of keeping me safe. Speaking of which, *why* didn't you inform me that your father wanted me *dead*?"

Theo frowned. "Too ... much..."

"Too much what? Danger? Excuse me, but have I not shown you I laugh in the face of—"

"…talking."

I sat back on my haunches. "Oh. Sorry." I glanced around the room. "I was really on a roll there."

"…nervous."

Rolling my eyes back to him, I said, "Even half-conscious, you're obnoxious. I know I talk too much when I'm nervous. You don't need to throw it at me."

"Scared…"

I went quiet.

He coughed, and instead of my dusty, dry croaks, his were clogged with blood bubbles and mucous, and shook his entire, weakened form.

"God … here." I flew to protect his head, hold his neck steady, while the cascade overtook him. "Please be okay," I whispered, mostly to myself.

"Fine. I'm—fine."

"Yeah, you're a real trooper." But, in a fit of emotion, I laid my forehead against his temple while I still held him closer. "You scared the shit out of me."

"You do that to me … on a daily basis. Every minute."

Theo was sticky, but warm. His hand moved to find mine, and I met him halfway. "Then I guess we're meant for each other," I said.

"Where are we?"

"Your father's basement. Maybe one of many, I don't know."

"How did you get here?"

"Gordon invited me."

Theo stiffened, the action causing his cheek to wince under my skin. "And you came? Why?"

"Because he knew where I was, that I'd come back. If I wasn't going to come willingly, he'd take me. Forcibly. Possibly putting

Kai in danger. Or Verily. I'd rather do as your father wants than have my friends face the consequences."

"Interesting. If only you'd thought that way before re-entering poker rooms after getting shot by my brother."

"I see that the coughing fit helped clear your airways." I lifted off so I could glare at him better.

Theo's eyes were open, the clear, opulent blue at a severe contrast to the blood and shadow of this room. The blue moved closer.

"How long have I been down here?" he asked.

"I'm not sure. But it's taken me a day and a half to get back to New York. And I started the process immediately after I realized what you'd done."

His upper lip lifted into what maybe was a smile. "It was either you or me, sweetheart."

"Doesn't it always come down to that?" I asked. "Why can't we just be two people who found each other through a dating app?"

"Because you're you, and I'm me." He let out a low rumble in an attempt to clear his throat further.

I studied the length of his form, then back up again. "Why did they do this do you?"

"Exactly what you said during your nervous ramble. Father figured that once I located Trace, I'd send him back with Bo and make my own disappearance."

The mention of Bo had me licking my lips. Theo caught the hesitation.

"What happened to Bo?" he asked, but it was with very little inflection, like he already knew.

"Bo's the one who told me a lot of efficient men were going to be paid if I died." I massaged a residual ache at the back of my neck. "He decided to become one of them."

"Jesus. No." Theo attempted to lift of the wall, but fell back at the waste of energy. "Why did you go back there?"

"How could you think I wouldn't? You were gone. And the only place I could think to make sense of what happened was to find Drea. The one who gave us up in the first place."

"Yeah. I figured that one out, too."

"Instead it was just Bo there. And he was angry."

"Are you all right?"

"Aside from being trapped here in a dungeon with you?" I didn't want to tell him I killed Bo. "Sure. Dandy."

Theo's gaze on me didn't waver. I was conscious of him assessing my every tell. "It's my fault."

"No, it isn't. I have a knack for sticky situations."

This time when he lifted off his wall support, he was steady. "The contract was put on you because of me."

"I'd deduced that."

"What you didn't figure out was that as soon as Trace was returned, it would be lifted."

That caught my attention.

"It was what made me do my father's bidding in the first place," Theo continued. "If I didn't find my brother, you would die. And you would continue to be at risk of death until Trace came back."

"So I was used as a pawn. The entire reason you left me two years ago was to prevent that."

"He knew," Theo said. "Father knew what you meant to me well before you took a bullet. I thought I could redirect his attention and he'd forget about you if there was no more mention of you, not a whiff of your presence around our family. But..."

"I continued to play."

Theo sighed. "Yes."

I used the resulting silence to wonder if this was the time to tell Theo about the FBI and the deal they'd forced me to make while still lying prone in a hospital bed from said bullet. That I didn't play for profit, or to piss off the Saxons, as Gordon assumed, or maybe even Theo himself. It would be just like me to revel in the possibility that I was getting to Theo, that talk of me and my hands would reach his ears and piss him off enough to come back.

But for once, I hadn't been tossing my pride around.

"What are you thinking about?"

I lost my nerve. "How to get out of here."

Theo rested his elbows on his knees. "We wait."

"Seriously?"

"They cornered me. Now they have you. I know my family. We're about to see their final play."

"And when that happens?"

His eyes glimmered underneath his brows like a cat's reflecting in the dark. "You and I will be ready."

I avoided the instinct to scoff. "With what? Our bare hands?"

"Scarlet." He held me steady in his stare. "You and I don't get by with fists and weapons."

"You're right," I said, beginning the calculations. "We plan ahead."

Noises clamored much too soon.

Light cracked through the darkness, then blazed as someone at the top flicked the switch. With the instinctive sense of belonging to a pack, I glanced over at Theo, garishly wounded now that I could pinpoint every gash.

"Oh, my—"

"I'll be fine." He refocused his attention on the stairs, and with a grunt, pulled himself up despite my attempts to help.

It came as a surprise when my left thigh screamed as soon as I put weight on it. The fall down the stairs was making itself known in detail, especially when I demanded my battered muscles to move. But what was the alternative? I was hardened now, a woman who'd seen fingers broken and loose teeth on the ground. Being locked in a basement with a wounded Theo beside me and a psychopath father and son above shouldn't be so unnerving.

Yet ... they'd never been *my* fingers and teeth.

A set of designer shoes clomped down the stairs, groaning beneath his weight. It made me thankful they were wooden steps, not concrete, since I'd been tossed down them like scrap meat.

A form came to a stop in front of us, his chin lowered until the exact right moment, his walk lean and unhurried. Trace. When he raised his head, I was once again appalled at the beauty. A man so lethal shouldn't look that good. I felt sorry for all the women and men who fell for his outer grace and too late realized the inner demon.

A reflection of Theo, yet he couldn't come close to the man standing beside me, one shoulder more stooped than the other, the thin lines of his lips containing a grimace. He was their beauty, their grace, personified. He'd done horrible things but was pained by it and repentant.

He was a prince born into the wrong story.

I reached for his hand. If we got out of this alive, perhaps he could become a part of mine.

"Brother," Theo said.

"Ah, brother mine," Trace replied. "What a twisted web we're in."

"Aren't we always."

"Thank you for bringing me back."

"Yeah," Theo said, pointing to his face. "I got all the thanks I need."

"No worse than what we looked like as young children," Trace said. "Come on, bro, you still got your teeth."

Trace smiled, and for the first time I noticed how white they were, how perfectly straight. Veneers.

Trace cocked his head in a playful manner. "You know how Father is."

"So, was it all a ruse, then?" Theo asked. "Having me go overseas, using the family's funds, to find a son who was already located?"

"Actually, no," Trace said. "I had no intention of coming back here. I was having lots of fun where I was. Drea says hello, by the way."

Trace said the last part to me, and for a brief moment—one I wasn't proud of—I buckled beneath his pointed stare.

"I'm glad she's okay," I said dryly.

"Better than. She's upstairs."

"Oh good. Give her my regards."

"I sure will. *Letty*."

I looked away when I swallowed, unwilling to show any obvious weakness in front of this man.

"Why are we here, Trace?" Theo asked. "As far as I can see, you're back, Father has his favorite son at the helm, there's no need for Scarlet to be beside me right now."

"Father has his reasons."

"And is he going to come down here and explain them?" Theo asked.

"Eventually."

"I see." Ever so discreetly, Theo had been inching forward, so that most of his left shoulder and half his torso protected me. "To what do we owe the pleasure of your visit, then?"

"Simple. I want to know how you found me. Was it your little mistress?"

Trace's anger could be felt through Theo's suit, through his *body* and into me. Hot pinpricks, sharp needles, it was all directed at my old wound. Trace hadn't forgiven me for the drug botch years ago, and I hadn't expected him to. But what I feared was that he'd torture me for it.

Where was Gordon? I needed them both here.

"Don't do her any favors. You leave quite a trail, if one knows what to look for," Theo said. "Blood. Trauma. Beaten up females."

"I'm getting a sense of deja vu here. Aren't you?" Trace asked us both.

"You're not touching her." Theo growled the words, like

they'd been etched into his windpipe and he had to grind them out of the tissue.

"I thought Scarlet means nothing to you?" Trace asked.

"She doesn't. But I don't enjoy watching women suffer."

"Yes. Lauren. I remember. I'm so sad I wasn't a part of that."

Theo's muscles bunched under his torn, filthy suit. I laid a subtle, calming hand on his lower back.

Trace's attention slid over to me. "But I can be a part of *this*."

"Where's Papa Saxon in all of this?" I asked. Having Trace look at me like that ... he might as well have knives in his hand and start carving. "Isn't he overdue?"

As if I'd snapped an elastic at him, Trace blinked. "Do you remember, brother, how we used to play?"

The change of subject didn't throw Theo. "It's not easily forgotten."

"Do you ever watch MMA fighters?" Trace asked me. I shook my head in response.

"But you know what they are, I assume," he said. "That's what Father did with us. As children. He had us fight other kids, with he and his buddies placing bets on us. Orphans, street kids. Sometimes abducted ones. Remember all that, brother?"

"What are you getting at, Trace?"

While Theo sounded exasperated, a quick study of his eyes and they were sharp as a jaguar's.

"Ward got out of it. Because of you. Always the protector, my brother. Never the protected."

"No, he didn't. He still had you to contend with."

Trace shrugged with one shoulder. "Well, a boy needs to practice on something."

"You were beaten just as badly as me. Worse. Why you still enjoy imputing it to other, smaller, vulnerable people, is well beyond my understanding," Theo said. "But I've stopped trying to understand you."

"We stopped being brothers decades ago, haven't we, Theodore?"

For an instant, I watched Trace's lips fall, his cheeks sink, his eyes droop. Crestfallen. In the same second, his features cleared, but it was the biggest clue I'd ever noted inside this barbwired prison of a man. I was convinced it was a hallucination. There couldn't be any humanity left in a person like this.

"We went through the same things," Theo said, "yet turned out so different. For so long, we've enjoyed our separate paths. So why don't we go back to that? You go your way, I'll go mine. The only reason we're together again is because of Father. The only reason we're pitted against each other is because of Father. You said it yourself. He enjoys watching us fight. One day it will be to the death."

Theo stepped forward, away from me, toward Trace.

"How about we bring a stop to this?" he continued. "I'm tired of being Father's pawn. Aren't you?"

I monitored the war beneath Trace's features, the flashes of these brothers' pasts uniting with the present, Trace's conflict of deepening Theo's hurt versus letting him go.

My stomach sank. At the worst time—or the best, depending on your perspective—a door slammed from above and more foot-steps sounded.

Gordon was on his way.

The sound registered with Trace, shutting down any weaken-ing. His stare went to blue ice.

"Nice try, Theodore," Trace said, the corners of his mouth ticking up higher with each syllable. "But we both know only death will stop this competition."

Gordon, the same height as his sons, came to a stand beside Trace.

Theo said nothing. A fast study of him revealed how hard-ened he'd become, as if bracing for the next hit. But he wouldn't flinch—he'd take the bruise, the break, the further amputation from his family. He'd done it enough times.

"You don't have to, anymore," I said to him in a whisper.

With a flicker of surprise, he glanced over long enough to tell me he was listening, but focused his attention back on his father.

"Tracey," Gordon said, without looking away from Theo.

These two men, one the patriarch, the other the prodigal son who failed him, faced off with an intenseness that would heat this cave into an inferno if left unbanked.

"You brought Tracey back into the family," Gordon said without any inflection. "For that I thank you, boy. I'll concede you're the smartest, hence my request going first to you."

Trace's mask faltered for the barest of seconds before falling back into place.

Theo remained silent. I felt an infinitesimal brushing against my knuckles and I resisted the urge to glance down.

Theo was trying to tell me something ... warn me? But what? I frantically thought through any potential scenarios.

"I would hope wanting me to return to the Saxon dynasty was more than just your ego, Father," Trace said.

"My eldest, you must admit, you're not the brightest." Gordon turned his attention to me before continuing. "The escapade of years ago notwithstanding. I lost millions in that transaction, dear girl. You'll have to pay penance. You know that, don't you?"

"I've stayed away from the Saxons," I began, but Gordon was already back to speaking with Trace.

"And you absconding like that ... that is not how I raised my boys. And certainly not how I expect you to act in the future."

The silk in Gordon's voice took on a tautness, as if it were tearing, but slowly. Deliberately. Trace showed no outward turmoil—unless you were looking for it. I caught the lightest of flinches, of fingers twitching into a fist and then releasing, before he caught himself.

"There will also be consequences for *you*. Bring her down." Gordon didn't call behind him—he didn't have to. Whoever was listening had predicted his command, and a scuffle of feet, a garble of muffled fear, cascaded down the staircase.

The sounds of struggle became visible when Butcher stepped into the bare cone of light with his captive.

Drea.

Still so bruised, her legs pale sticks in a simple red romper. Crescents of cuts rained down her arms, and her neck was almost purple from previous pressure of someone's—Trace's—hands.

I couldn't see how her mouth was doing, her bandaged nose, because Butcher's meaty hand was across them.

"Why is she down here?" Trace asked.

He was terrified. If I could see it, Theo certainly could. And Gordon.

It was amazing to me that a known batterer and killer could have feelings for this girl. But it was right in front of me. Trace did not want his father to hurt her.

Oh, but he would.

Unconscious demand had me stepping back, as if hiding behind Theo could drown out what would happen.

Gordon caught my movements, however subtle they were.

"You're next."

Theo's hand gripped my forearm. "Go ahead and try, Father. I'm not the seventeen-year-old I once was."

Gordon turned to his eldest. "Trace, you understand what must happen."

"I do."

"That's a good boy. You fled when you shouldn't have. Stopped communications when the first thing you should've done was come to me. Made quite a few messes across the ocean that I'm left to clean up."

What made a man so cruel and crafty, oh so willing to inflict pain, bow entirely to a higher force was beyond my comprehension. Yet here Trace was, ceding to his father without a fight. It made me wonder—

"Why'd you run?" I asked him. The question was startling, and Trace raised his chin to me.

"If you were just going to let your father do what he wanted, anyway. Take from you, why did you give him a reason? Why meet Drea?"

At the mention of her name, Drea's Bambi eyes skittered back-and-forth in their sockets, finally resting on me.

"You've only given him more ammunition," I said to Trace.

"You wouldn't understand," Trace said. There wasn't a single crack to his guise as he regarded me, his father's words having their effect.

I gripped Theo's arm, praying Gordon's intimidation tactics would continue bouncing off his scarred exterior.

"Here's what you're missing, dear girl," Gordon said to me, his baritone burying deep into my blood cells. "Every time, my boys will come back to me. They. Are. *Me*. And as a result, they will never leave. Not fully. Not ever."

"You're not going down with them," I murmured to Theo.

I pulled a bobby pin out of my shorts' pocket. Because I'd practiced in mirrors—on Theo's charter plane, at Rada's, at Kai's—I was able to stick it in the hole at the back of the necklace without looking down.

Theo registered my movements, his neck moving, then the rest of his profile, until he faced me dead-on.

And his expression registered fear. "Scarlet ... *no!*"

Too late.

I pushed the button.

Theo lashed out, swiping my necklace and ripping it off my neck so hard and fast it burned, then stung as blood seeped through the rings of cuts the gold chain left behind. When it landed near a wooden barrel, Theo's eyes stretched wider.

My gasp was cut short when Theo grabbed my elbow, tossed me over his shoulder and sprinted to the staircase.

Confusion was in full swing as the necklace pooled silently in the far corner, tiny green light flashing in-out-in-out, Gordon's mouth opening and closing—he must be making sound, but I couldn't hear it due to the clang of adrenaline rushing my ears.

As Theo sprinted up the steps, I spotted Trace screaming after us and pulling out a gun to shoot—

"Oh, God, *Theo!*"

That was me, screaming at Theo that Trace was going to fire at us—

My vantage point erased when Theo took the last step, but the sound of a bullet, *another fucking* bullet from Trace, tore through the crush of blood swelling my ears and I swore it was headed for my back this time.

I couldn't breathe. There was a sting of impact in my thigh, my carotid artery hit, blood seeping down my legs, losing life the same way a fish loses water. I bucked against Theo, but it was useless, because he wouldn't stop. I was dying and he was running, unknowing of the hit, completely clueless that I was going to sag on top of him, dead weight since he hadn't known to save me.

He didn't know.

"Theo..."

But the name was hitched and swallowed back, Theo's shoulder digging into my stomach, pressurizing any sound that intended to escape. Including my last gasp of life.

"Th…"

Unhearing, he burst through the main entrance, broke the iron gate, and flew to the other side of the street.

"Sax … help…"

Then came the boom.

THE NECKLACE WAS A BOMB?

The asphalt shook beneath my body, Theo's weight on top of me driving the vibrations deeper into my stomach. I couldn't see the cause of such violent noise and feeling, Theo's arm over my downturned face blocking the view.

Wasn't sure if I *wanted* to see it.

"Did I just blow up a house?" I screamed through the fabric of Theo's sleeve.

Wait. I screamed.

I was alive.

Needed Theo to get off me so I could check my extremities, make sure I wasn't shot, bleeding out underneath him while he pointlessly tried to protect me when I was already dying.

Except ... he wasn't moving.

"Theo," I gritted out, testing his girth by heaving up on one forearm. I quickly collapsed. "Are you awake?"

Because that was what you asked an unconscious person seconds after something blows up in his face.

"God..." I puffed out air with the word.

Theo was barely standing before this. His stance in front of his family was all show.

Then I came into the picture with an unknown IUD and forced him into a sprint, carrying me on his shoulders up a flight of stairs and out of the house in order to escape the blowback.

"Theo, I need to get up," I said to him, needing to say, do, something, so I didn't think about the consequences.

Where were Trace and Gordon? Was their younger brother in there as well? Staff? What was the state of the mansion? Was Theo hurt? Mortally wounded? Was I?

The worry bubbled through my arteries, hissing as it hit veins. It gave me the strength I needed to roll to the side, my left hip grinding into the pavement and *twanging* as nerves scrambled underneath. My lungs compressed, one rib cage having to do the work of two in order to protect from cracking.

One breath, puff out. Two, heave ho. Heave. *Ho.*

I yelled out when I finally maneuvered Theo enough to slide out from under. Coughing, I made it to a sit. There was ash in the air. Squinting through the grit, I spotted the house, smoking at the edges, but otherwise standing.

Next, I looked down at myself, feeling for the wound I was sure was there, but what I registered on the back of my thigh was a large splinter, which I pulled out before thinking how much it would hurt.

Wood from the staircase? A jagged piece that broke off when a bullet tore by?

There wasn't time to ponder. Theo was next. I'd rolled him to an awkward side sleeping position, so pushed him the rest of the way, splayed open his blazer, and felt him down.

"Stay with me, baby," I whispered like a mantra, frantically checking for wounds, broken bones, wet, red blooming stains.

Nothing. Oh, thank God, nothing.

In the background, I registered the wail of sirens, coming closer. I looked up through my strands of hair in an attempt to spy

Trace or Gordon crawling through the iron gate, but couldn't spot a single hair belonging to them.

Wait—sirens. *Sirens.* Police. The FBI.

The *necklace.*

Kai.

Oh, *Kai.*

"What have you done, Kai?" I asked the empty space in front of me.

Theo and I couldn't be here to figure that out. I had to get him up and out of here before the emergency crusade found and cuffed us.

I glanced down at his face, perfect despite the mar of a difficult life criss-crossing in fresh cuts and cold scars. My fallen angel.

My fallen, *sleeping* angel.

Hopefully, he collapsed from fatigue and not a flying piece of debris that hit the back of his skull as he fled with me.

The wails ricocheted closer, firing up my synapses again, giving that spurt of adrenaline that was oh so familiar these past weeks.

The world spun in front of me from the effect. If I wasn't careful, I'd end up like Theo, too.

"I'm sorry," I said to his slack expression.

Then slapped him.

"I'm *sorry,*" I said, cringing, when his brows pushed together in pain.

I clutched his shoulders, my legs on either side of his torso. "Wake up. Sax, I mean it this time! I can't carry you. I can't ... well, I can try to drag you, but I won't be able to hide in time for the—"

"...Scarlet?"

"Yes. *Yes,* it's me. Open your eyes all the way. We gotta move."

"Are you ... hurt?"

"No. No, I'm not."

It could have been the effects of the adrenaline, the sheer nature of avoiding death for a third time, or, the limited chance of feeling true happiness. But I laughed, grabbed his cheeks, and kissed him.

"I'm alive. We're both breathing," I said as I came up for air, then spun left at the approaching blue-and-red lights. "And we need to keep it that way. Can you sit up? Quickly. We have to *go*."

He complied, his lopsided expression not registering much. He was my puppet to conduct as I forced him to an unbalanced stand, gasping and grunting at the full force of his weight on my spindly legs.

We didn't have a chance at outrunning the police, but possibly we could hide until Theo gathered enough energy to escape this neighborhood. There were plenty of hiding spots ... that the police would search as soon as it was deduced that a man-made explosion caused this fire.

"Okay, we can..." I mumbled as I thought, but a gentle clang of metal-against-metal cut through my thoughts. "Are those keys in your pocket?"

"What? Yes?" Theo shook his head sharply, dislodging as much dizziness as he could. "I'm back. I'm coming back. Just gimme a sec."

"I can't." I dug into the inside of his blazer with my free hand. "Which car?"

"The..."

I pressed down on the unlock button and an answering *beep-beep* sounded. My eyes flashed over to the abrupt blinking of red brake lights.

"Porsche. Shoulda known," I said, then dragged both Theo and I over to the midnight blue vehicle.

"This should be your lesson," I grunted as I pulled the passenger door open, then bent Theo down. "Low-riding vehicles are stupid for women in high heels and dresses, *and* wounded mafia men."

After one last growl of effort on both our parts, Theo was in.

"Something tells me this isn't your first rodeo with this bull-shit escape car," I said, then slammed the door shot.

I ran around to the other side, glancing over the hood to see the flashing lights coming. Manhattan tended to create sound tunnels, making horns and sirens sound much closer than they appeared, but spotting actual spinning lights wasn't a good sign.

"Shit," I said, and slid in with only a few minor winces.

I curled my fingers over the wheel after starting the engine, allowing a few precious seconds to say, "Oh, shit fucker."

Put me at a round felt table and I could run the other players like a professional gamer destroying their enemies one-by-one, but put me in a getaway vehicle and I'd tangle us up in a garden hose before getting us free and clear of any police chase.

"Gotta try." I nodded to myself. "Only choice."

"Drive back to the house, around back. There's a side road."

Theo's head was tipped back, his eyes at half-mast, but his voice sounded stronger.

"Okay," I said.

I tore out of the parking spot on the side of the road and speared through the gates, knocking one iron half to an awkward angle.

"Sorry," I said over the motor. "That's gonna scratch."

"I care so little right now."

Jaw clenched, I wrenched the car to the left, tossing Theo against me. He cursed, I apologized again, then pressed harder on the gas.

There. Side road entrance.

I gunned toward it, tires skidding, praying I didn't hit an

animal or—dear Lord—a human, because I wasn't in any position to slow down.

We hit gravel, stones spitting up and spattering against the chrome, spewing dust in our wake. If ever there was a person to leave an evidence trail, it was me.

"Trace? Dad?"

"I don't know," I said to Theo.

He sighed, despite being jostled around.

"We'll hit level road soon," I said. Hoped. Or a bridge. That would be nice.

"We should go to Kai's," he said. "They won't suspect..."

"Who? The police or your family?" Then I added, "We can't go there anyway."

"Why not?"

"Let me get us out of this, then we can talk, okay?" My butt bounced up and down in the bucket seat. Another fucking treat to low-riding cars, feeling every single goddamned pebble.

"You're avoiding the question."

"What if I am?" I said, then made a sharp right onto actual road. The gravel side-street had only been about a block and a half long. "I don't drive that much. I have to concentrate."

"You're doing a great job."

I risked a glance at him so I could spot the sarcasm. I couldn't.

"Thank you," he said.

"Consider us even," I said. "We keep saving each other's lives in one way or another."

"Wow," he said.

I risked another glance. "What?"

"I expected a rebuff to the thank you."

"Consider me a changed woman," I muttered as we bounced over a pothole. "One who is actually becoming tired of this crazy shitshow I call a career."

We made it another half a block when a figure sprinted out into the road, hands up, staggering to a halt at the same time I slammed the brakes.

Theo and I flipped forward, the seatbelts too tight on both our necks to allow for enough breath to curse. When the ricochet stopped and the back of my skull slammed into the headrest, I opened my eyes, praying I didn't hit the person.

A man who was still standing in front of our vehicle.

And it wasn't his hands he was holding up.

It was a gun.

"Trace," Theo mumbled. He blinked hard, rubbing at the back of his head and grimacing when he pulled back his hand and spotted the blood.

How many head wounds had he sustained today? The pessimistic part of me reasoned it didn't matter, since there was now a gun pointed at it.

Trace mouthed through the grit and ash lining his face, "Get out of the car."

His voice was muffled, barely heard through the cooling engine and my now heavy breaths. I didn't want to get out. Actually, I did, but I wanted out of this entirely. Gone with the wind. No more crime family nipping at my heels.

"Get," Trace mouthed a second time, "*Out*."

The windshield cracked with a gunshot and I screamed, covering my head and grabbing for Theo at the same time.

"I mean it!" Trace yelled, much clearer now. "Get out or I won't miss next time!"

"Come on," Theo said. He squeezed my hand, where my fingers were latched around his biceps, then moved to unclip his seatbelt. "He's not bluffing."

"We can't—"

"We have to, Scarlet."

"I can run him over."

"Not before he lets loose another shot."

"We can at least try—"

"Whether it goes wide or not, the chances of him hitting one of us are high. I'm not risking you anymore. Let's go."

"Get out of the fucking car!"

Trace rounded to my side, his face a mask of dirt and devil, the pink of his flesh only seen through carved out age-lines, the grime making him seem decades older. Perhaps, in his poisoned soul, he was.

He jiggled the locked door handle, and when that didn't work, slammed a palm against the window. I couldn't help it—I cried out and jerked back.

Trace raised the pistol and aimed for my face.

"I'm coming!" I yelled with raised hands. Slowly, I lowered one to press the unlock button.

Trace didn't wait for me to open the door myself. I was yanked out by the arm, my legs tangling, and I landed shoulder-first onto the road.

Self-defense kicked in and I shielded my face while lashing out with my legs. A lot of movement meant less chance of an accurate shot. During these years without the Saxon brothers in my life, I'd learned plenty about bullet trajectories and the odds of having one embedded in your body.

An unearthly roar followed, and the sound of shoes crushing loose stones, before Trace's shadow no longer loomed over me, bright sun taking its place before Theo eclipsed it with the span of his form.

Panting, Theo towered over his brother.

How much energy could Theo have left? I raised myself to my forearms, swiping tangled hair out of my face, and for the second time in my life, felt a different kind of fear.

It wasn't a fight or flight response, or even the surge of adrenaline. It was an anchor, sinking at the center of my gut, its chains wrapped around my heart. With each second ticking by, the chain grew heavier, heavier still, until my heart followed the anchor to the depths of despair.

This had only happened once before. The last time I was with Theo, the final seconds when he confronted Trace and denied his family calling. When he stood in front of a gun and told his brother to shoot him.

It's not fear you're feeling, Letty. It's love.

Love.

Gasping, gulping, I pulled myself to stand, one hand out as if I could stop Theo from taking it any further through psychic command.

Losing someone you knew was bad enough. Watching a person you loved die before your eyes, that was a different anchor entirely.

And I felt those chain links straining with effort.

"Theo, let's go," I said, and staggered toward him. I was weaker than I anticipated, but no matter. Once we got back into the car, metal and mechanics could be strong for me. "He's out cold."

"No he's not," Theo said through his teeth.

Before this moment, even with the new cuts, the fresh blood, I was able to spot the man beneath. No...

Now I couldn't find the man I'd come to understand again.

Theo reared and kicked his brother in the stomach. Trace spasmed, grunts spewing forth with saliva and blood.

"You goddamned *bastard*." Theo's voice ground against his vocal cords. "You escape this city, and still I can't escape you. I leave you alone, yet you and Father won't allow me to live my life. You manipulate, you mutilate, you *kill*, and still that's not enough. What *will* be enough, brother?" Theo laid out another kick. "When I'm dead? When it's me at your feet? Let me tell you this, you will *never* have me under your heel, do you understand?"

Trace mumbled incoherently, raised the gun he somehow still had in his hand, but Theo swatted it away with the toe of his shoe like it was nothing but a spatula Trace was attempting to fight with.

Then stood on his brother's throat, pressed just enough to elicit a choking cough.

"Hear this, *brother*. I have you under my heel, but no matter how far you push me, how many people I love you threaten, I will never kill you. I swear, on a Saxon oath, that I will never turn my back on my family. When you call, I come. When Father beckons, I do as bid. But not because you control me. Oh, no." Theo bent down further. "But because I'm patient. I've waited for this day. Your greatest punishment, Father's greatest fear, is to lose this kingdom. And he will." Theo pushed off Trace's throat, and Trace rolled to the side, sputtering. "You will. And I get to witness it all."

"You'll always be a Saxon," Trace coughed, cutting Theo a glance sideways. "You're here because you love it. The violence. The cruelty."

Theo lifted his lips. "You touch Scarlet again, you *look* at her again, so much as ask her directions, I'll have no trouble taking one of your limbs." Theo spat at the ground beside Trace's face. "I should've taken at least one of your fingers last time."

"Nice scar, brother," Trace said through the blood bubbling on his lips. "Where'd you get it?"

That earned him another kick to the gut.

"Where's Drea?" I asked Trace's shuddering form. I stepped up beside Theo.

"Wouldn't you like to know," Trace ground out. "She got to

you. I've forgotten to ask her how, considering the only person getting close to the zipper on your pants has been my brother."

I wasn't proud of it, the instant weakness as soon as I laid eyes on Drea, shrunken and beaten in a chair much too big for her body.

"You did that to her," I said. "I'm not ashamed I felt something for a frail woman beaten half to death."

"She wanted it."

"The poor girl wanted *you*," I said. "That I can forgive her for, considering she's not the only one drawn in by the Saxon lure. It's the betrayal I can't fathom. The idea that she ran to you as soon as she realized who Theo and I were."

"I learned from my father." Trace smiled weakly. "Always have people in the right places, and there will always be a right time."

"Where is she?" I asked again.

Theo moved deftly, readying for another round.

"She's safe," Trace said, eyeing his brother. For once, the flicker of pain I noticed flash through his features wasn't due to physical violence. "Butcher, however, is not."

"That's who the bullet was for," I surmised.

"I had to give her time to run," Trace murmured, so quietly I didn't think Theo caught it.

"You are one fucked up individual," I seethed. "To maim a girl you care about so badly."

At last, Trace met my stare. "She's no substitute for you."

Theo rumbled with a growl.

"Let's leave," I said. I grabbed Theo's elbow, tried to pull the tree-trunk that was my ex-boyfriend. "Trace is useless to us. We don't know where your father is. We've got to get out of here before the police find us, before *Gordon*—"

"Hands off my son, dear."

"Fuck," I whispered, a visceral sound in my throat.

Theo didn't flinch.

"Who are you right now?" I asked him quietly before I backed away, knowing without having to look that Gordon would be holding another bigger, badder weapon on us. A semi-automatic. An automatic handgun. One of those guns that shoots bullets that shatter on impact and eviscerate organs. All of the above.

"Don't become them, please." I was staring at him, but Theo wasn't paying any attention. His focus was on his brother, but he wasn't *seeing* him. It was a beast hovering over its prey. A dragon circling its kill.

It was not Theo Saxon.

Or was it? My hands clenched at my sides as I retreated. Was this the new man, the person Theo had been trying to hide from me since boarding the *Hatari*, pretending to be a prince in the darkness, when really, he was a demon in sunlight?

He was only showing me what had always been there, if I'd only thought to see clearly.

"Turn around. There's a good girl," Gordon said behind me.

Closing my eyes with a sigh, I did.

"Well, you came out of that house a lot better than me," Gordon said.

Although I didn't want to, I blinked Gordon into focus.

His face was red, burned, a few flakes of skin marring his cheeks, his hair askew, his suit ripped and dirtied. Gordon favored his right side, using his left hand to aim the gun instead of his dominant one.

"I had a head start," I replied.

Gordon inclined his head. It was like watching a vulture size up the nearby wounded to estimate who would die first. "I'll admit, the mini-bomb was unexpected."

"How did you get here?" I asked. Stalling. *Come back, Theo. Turn on that humanity switch. Come back to me.*

"Oh, my dear, think that one through." Gordon chuckled, coughed, then winced. His left arm came closer into his torso, and instinctual maneuver to protect and soothe.

"We have more than one way out of that basement," Trace supplied from the ground. "Several, actually."

"Get up," Theo said, and when Trace didn't, Theo hooked him under one arm and hurled him into a stand, then tossed him over, stumbling, to their father.

"You have him just like you wanted him," Theo said to Gordon. My heart broke over how deadened his gaze had become. "It's over. The FBI is around the corner. Give up, Father."

"You're involved in this crime, too," Gordon said, then eyed his middle son carefully. "But you know that."

"I'm ready to accept the consequences." Unexpectedly, Theo's shoulders sagged. "I'm so damned tired."

"No," I said, automatically moving toward him.

"Stay right there, sweetheart," Gordon said.

"Go," Theo said to me. "You can go. This isn't your world anymore."

"If she leaves," Gordon said, "I'll shoot you, Theodore."

"Then do it already."

"*No*," I said with emotion this time.

"Or what? You'll jump in front of him again? That's so two years ago, dear. Just stay where you are."

"Run, Scarlet," Theo said.

My gaze bounced back and forth between the two of them, unsteady on my feet.

"It's near impossible to shoot a running target with that gun," Theo said to me. "So go. Now."

I shook my head, vision brimming.

"*Now*," he barked.

Gordon laughed, followed by Trace's hollow chuckle.

A chill spiraled down my back, as if a ghost appeared in shadow behind me and ran a misted finger along my spine.

If you go, he will lose his life. He will not be arrested. Theo will die by his father first.

"I ... I can't," I said to him, the very pain of him dying in front of me lacing through my voice.

"Scarlet." Realization leeched through his expression, dried blood going stark against his pale skin. "Don't do this. Don't be stupid."

"Do you remember when you told me you weren't a hero?" I said to him, then stepped forward, grabbing his hand. "I don't claim to be, either, but I'm not going anywhere. I'm not running away from you, Theo."

"Good *God*," Trace scoffed, speaking through the blood in his mouth, one hand resting on his father's shoulder to balance his weight.

Gordon narrowed his eyes at me.

"You have no idea, do you, girl?" he asked.

At my pained expression, he continued. "The necklace. What have you made of it?"

Kai came into my head, but I clamped down at the thought. He couldn't have—wouldn't have—betrayed me. There had to be another reason, another cruel twist to this fate causing what was meant to be a safety net become a weapon—

I stared at Gordon with newfound clarity.

"You," I said.

"Indeed." To Gordon's credit, he did not roll his eyes at my deduction. "It wasn't easy, mind you, but it is crucial to find moles where you most need them."

Moments, locations, people, blew through my mind with the force of a stack of playing cards slipping through a dealer's hand.

"Rada?" I said the name as a question, a breath of air, while processing the possibility.

"You were correct, dear boy, she *is* a smart one," Gordon said to Theo. "It took Tracey at least an hour to figure that one out."

"But how...?" I asked Theo, Gordon, Trace, myself. "I never took the necklace off..."

"Oh, but you did," Tony said, the sound of his voice like a snake slithering through a dried out pond.

I stared at the ground as I thought, fingers tight around Theo's. Gordon was right ... there was one time I unclasped the necklace, one moment, in Rada's bathroom, when Theo and I were in the shower...

"By the way, Rada wants her pistol back," Gordon said.

"She replaced the necklace?" I looked up at Gordon. "It was a dupe?"

Gordon didn't bother to answer in the affirmative. "The effect of that replacement was always meant for you, Theodore being collateral damage if needed, but you were meant to have used it much sooner. Granted, it's a small device, meant only to kill the person wearing it—but in Theodore's attempt to save you, he threw it near a barrel of bourbon. Or maybe that was deliberate, an attempt to kill a brother and a father in one throw. But, my dear boy Theodore, Trace and I survived, so maybe you should turn your attention to Scarlet, and why she was wearing the original necklace in the first place."

"I never trusted Rada farther than I could speak to her," Theo said, then turned to me. He didn't acknowledge Gordon's accusation. "But I can't plan for what I don't know about. Why were you wearing that necklace?"

Gordon stared at us, a sneer escaping.

"Don't," I said to Gordon, but I knew it was useless.

Theo kept his attention on me. "Don't what?"

"She doesn't want me to tell you," Gordon said, smiling. "But I admit, I can't resist."

"Whatever he says," I started, "it means more than what he's making it out to be—"

"Scarlet was going to give you up to the cops, my son," Gordon said.

I clutched Theo's arm. "It's not that clear cut—"

But Theo's expression was clouding over, confusion, hurt, abject betrayal. If his eyes were ice before, they were frostbitten when he collected his thoughts enough to regard me with nothing but heavily banked rage.

"Scarlet made a deal with the FBI. Two years ago, with Peter Chenko. Remember him?" Gordon continued.

"Shut up," I said, then louder, "Just *shut up!* You have no *idea* what you're talking about."

"I know what Chenko said to you in that hospital room," Gordon cut in. "I'm the one who told him *what* to say."

"Theo." I spun to what was important. "I didn't have a choice. Any chance I had to spare you, I chose it. I didn't want to do this. I didn't make a deal with the goal of *betraying* you—" my voice broke.

"Nothing you do is spontaneous," Gordon said darkly. "No action you take is your choice. The minute you stepped into my son's life, you've been mine. And you are merely a doll on strings I can discard."

"So you admit it, then?" I asked, turning my rage on him. "You admit to wanting to punish me for interfering with your racketeering, your drug trade, for getting your son—the true heir —to fall in love with me? You wanted me out of the way—"

"Long ago," Gordon spat. "I wanted you dead long ago, but with my eldest disappearing and you making yourself so well-known in my circles, I couldn't just off you like you deserved. And so I cultivated, I waited patiently, and despite having that necklace blow up in front of *me* instead of just you and my son, here we are." He pointed his gun at me. "The devil's on my side."

"That's your weakness," I said softly.

Gordon squinted while Trace stilled beside him, looking past me. "Father..."

But Gordon wasn't budging. "What did you just say?"

"You think you can anticipate other people's moves flawlessly. But you can't. My not pressing that necklace earlier, when I had Trace and Theo in the same vicinity, should've given you your first clue. I do not act impulsively. Like you, I predict, I analyze, I plan. But unlike you, I've been taught a lesson. To keep in mind human variables."

"Yes?" Gordon closed one eye, aimed. Theo reacted by stepping in front of me, yelling at his father to put down the gun. "What variable am I missing besides adding Theodore to the mix. This bullet is strong enough to go through the two of you, my son. Choose wisely."

"Father, we need to go," Trace said. His eyes had gone wide, his gaze pinging among the homes we were in the middle of, the too-quiet nature of this city environment where there should be honks, sirens—at the very least, dogs barking. Babies crying.

"Always have a Plan Z," I said, loud enough to be heard behind Theo's large form.

Gordon quieted. I could only assume he was clicking off the safety.

"I'm sorry, Theo," I murmured. He cocked an ear to me, but had no time to do anything else, because I yelled, *"Now!"*

"Father!" Trace boomed.

He was too late. A blast came from behind us and Gordon's thigh bloomed red. He cried out, buckled to his knees, and dropped his gun. Theo acted first, rushing to his father and bending over him, but not to staunch the bleeding. It was to grab the weapon.

Trace collapsed over Gordon, crying out and grabbing whatever he could to stop his father from bleeding out.

I reached for Theo, to drag him out of the way, but he shook me off, and the look he gave me...

Oh, the *look*.

I wouldn't forget it for the rest of my life.

"Don't finish the job," I said, but wasn't sure if he could hear me. If I clawed at his back, he wouldn't react. If I slapped his face, his jaw wouldn't move. All Theo could see was his father, lying on his back in the middle of the road, and Trace, leaning over him, screaming in his face not to die.

"It's not worth it," I tried again. Gently, I laid my fingers on the crook of his elbow. "They're coming. You know that gunshot wasn't from—"

A swarm of black enveloped us, men and women in SWAT gear grabbing at our arms, our shoulders, slamming us to the ground facedown. Theo had his feet swiped out from under and he crashed down beside me, his cheekbone cracking against the concrete as they wrestled the gun out of his limp fingers.

Our hands were cuffed behind our backs at the same time.

"Theo, listen to me—" I tried.

He closed his eyes, acquiescing to everything else but me. My lips trembled, forming the words *please* and *only*, but not voicing them, since platitudes meant nothing to Theo.

Theodore Saxon was done with Scarlet Rhodes.

I HADN'T CHEWED on my cuticles since elementary school.

At a table like this, actually, with a powerful person oozing authority on the other side, elbows propped, glasses on, mouth screwed up in rebuke.

Last time it was the school principal. This time it was an FBI agent in an interrogation room.

"Let me tell you, you have quite the resume," this man said as he fanned through a file-folder. A peek at the margin and I saw my name in bold, black sharpie. *SCARLETT RHODES*.

They'd spelled my name wrong.

I focused on that wayward T like it was a lifeline. Anything to stop myself from traveling back, thinking of Theo and his expression before I was torn away from him. Right about the time cracks began to form in my heart, fissures opening, breaking, allowing the rest of the darkness to creep in.

"You gave us quite a few days' work," this man continued. At my blank expression, he added, "Quentin Sawyer. I'm head of the Metro Gang task force in charge of the Saxon case."

It was hard to think of the Saxon crime family as a *gang*, but I supposed that was what Congress had the budget to classify them as. Quentin Sawyer was one head over Chenko, not quite the boss, but close enough. I'd guess that having three Saxons in custody was a big boon, requiring his presence and therefore ensuring his name would be on all the paperwork going forward. And up.

"Your cooperation will be noted," Sawyer continued. His dark cap of hair was thickly waved back, with black-framed glasses, more hipster than nerd, resting on his straight, Roman nose. I pinned him in his forties. "Especially during this last day and your help leading us to the Saxon brothers. Gordon Saxon especially."

"Kai was integral to that," I said. It was the first time I'd spoken since my cheek scraped across pavement, and it sounded just as rough.

"Duly noted," Sawyer said with a half-smile. He was glad I'd spoken. "But his status in the FBI is none of your concern right now. What should concern you is how we're going to handle your current situation."

I inclined my head, arms crossed. "And?"

"And," he repeated, except with more syllables, "we're thankful for what you've done. Without you, I doubt we'd have any Saxon, never mind three."

"My importance to you is written out in marker right there." I pointed to my incorrectly spelled name on the folder, as much as I could while shackled. "So forgive me if I'm reluctant to trust what you say."

Sawyer frowned. "Your history doesn't show problems with authority figures. Not until—"

"College. I'm aware. Got ahold of my one-semester transcript, did you?"

"We have everything, Scarlet. I know more about you than your mother does."

Sad, but true.

He reached to his right, picking up a Sharpie, the sound of

the lid popping off the only noise in this small, concrete-lined room. In a big, pungent X, he crossed out the second T.

"Despite what this shows, you're very important to us. For a long time, you've been our only viable link within the Saxon crime family. You've accomplished more than a lot of our undercovers were able to."

"Because I broke the rules."

"Yes," he nodded. "You did have that advantage."

I lifted my hands, the clinks of the handcuffs ringing against the metal table I'd been attached to. "Is this your thanks? Because I'm ready to be booked, put in a holding cell. I'd like my lawyer now. I'll wait for them there."

Sawyer leaned back, nothing short of amused. "Time with the Saxons has really done wonders with your personality."

"You don't know me."

"You're a fugitive. You aided and abetted two of the most wanted men in New York City."

"I boarded that plane with Theo because your *team* gave up on this mission. The paperwork, the barriers, lack of warrants, the red tape. It was made near-impossible to wrangle Theo, never mind Trace, and bring them to your federal wishes when I couldn't step foot in a poker room without calculating tax deductions on a log sheet first."

"Oh, you mean the law?"

"Yes, that. It was a cockblock in the most literal sense."

"And so you became your own, unauthorized agent and entered into an international underworld where you had no experience, no backup, and not only could have ruined what was a years-long investigation acquiring plenty of useful information, despite your opinion otherwise, you could have also ended up dead."

"Haven't you figured that out? I'm dead inside already."

Sawyer widened his eyelids like he was preparing for a roll. "You're a bit old for teen angst."

"Don't belittle what you've now been given in a big, red bow. Not only do you have Trace and Theo"—my voice broke slightly on his name—"in custody, you also have Gordon Saxon."

"All thanks to you?" Sawyer arched a brow.

"You certainly wouldn't have gotten them by following the law to the goddamned letter."

Sawyer steepled his fingers over my file. "You've gotten yourself in quite a lot of trouble, and now you've just admitted to willingly breaking the law."

"I was given a tracker system made by the FBI that—turns out —was a pretty little IUD, made by an agent of yours who was likely a mole for Gordon Saxon. Not to mention, my *antics* have exposed not one, but at least two weaknesses in the FBI pointing to leaks and more than likely the reason why Gordon has been able to stay out of your radar and continue his illegal activities without you guys able to do shit about it. And if that isn't enough." I steepled my own fingers as much as I could, considering my barriers, "I've asked for a lawyer and you've continued to question me, meaning anything I say after that request is inadmissible."

One of Sawyer's cheeks ticked like he was grinding his molars together.

I narrowed my eyes at him. "I'm teen angsty and smart."

The metal door, painted a dull green, behind Sawyer opened with the *bang*, and a large figure overtook the doorway, his belt jangling when he moved into the light of the room.

Shit.

I fell back in my chair, hoping to dislodge the chill along my spine, that incessant numbness of fear that constantly occurred when his name was mentioned, never mind his presence.

"I see you're your usual pleasant self," Chenko said to me as he approached. He meandered over to Sawyer's chair and rested an arm on the back for balance. To his credit, Sawyer seemed displeased.

Staring Chenko down wasn't the greatest weapon, but it was all I possessed. One was never supposed to show fear when confronted by something bigger, badder, no matter how overweight and bulbous. Chenko made his hunt clear two years ago, and had been circling me ever since. If this was the moment he bit into my throat, so be it, but it didn't mean I'd go limp in his jaws.

"Being a gentleman to her doesn't work," Chenko said out the side of his lips. "She prefers the bad boys, don't you honey? The ones who like it rough."

I remained tight-lipped.

"Leave her to me," Chenko continued. "I'll get the information you need out of her."

"I don't believe that is wise," Sawyer replied, and for the barest moment my eyes cut to him in surprise.

"Not all of us are unseemly," Sawyer said to me. Chenko responded with a frown, but as he continued to stand and Sawyer remained seated, he seemed to take authority from physical position, because he said, "You wanted her here, I got her, boss. You wanted her arrested a week ago, and I convinced you to leave her long enough to lead us to our guys. And she did. I was right. I implore you not to forget that."

My eyelids flickered, the only sign I was thinking. Chenko was aware of my location the entire time I was in London—of *course* he was. He was Gordon's guy, meaning he was receiving information at the same time he funneled it. What game Gordon was playing remained unclear, but if Chenko knew my location, if he knew everything I was up to the minute I boarded a Saxon charter plane ... oh, God.

Chenko knew about Bo.

The gleam when he regarded me told me he knew *exactly* what went on in that London apartment.

"I won't forget your role in this," Sawyer said to Chenko. My attention flicked over to him, but for once, could not read what was going on in his features. Sawyer was schooled, professional, not an ounce of anger or competition on his face. As if he dealt with Chenko on a daily basis and was used to his puffery.

Could Sawyer be one of Gordon's men, too? No, he was much too professional, play-by-the-rules, kind of person. Unless this was duplicity at its finest. Be the person everyone expects you to be, and no one would suspect the devil's playground underneath.

I could trust no one.

"Then allow me to leave you with a piece of advice," Chenko said, bursting through my paranoia. "In order to get this girl to do anything, she requires incentive. Allow me to show you?"

Sawyer studied me, tapping his pen against my file. My stony silence must have given him the answer he needed, because he said, "By all means."

Chenko leaned on the table, his hands as anchoring fists to his meaty, stumpy arms. His balding head reflected the bulb of light above us. He was small, paunchy, more red-faced than flawless, but he was not to be ignored.

"Guess who we have in the interrogation room next door?" Chenko said. His teeth, just as stubby as the rest of them, were a sickly yellow. I remembered studying this exact grin while prone on a hospital gurney.

"Theo," I said, sounding throaty. "Theo Saxon. I know."

The grin widened. "Try again, sweetheart."

Concern peppered my brow, but I smoothed it immediately under Chenko's joyous study. Could it be Kai? Was he in as deep trouble as I was? Did he get himself—

My gaze screwed into Chenko's.

"That's right, sweetheart, think it through."

Remember the hospital room, he was saying, and his threat then. What it caused me to do. How it forced me to act in the interim. How it brought me to this very interrogation room, Theo cuffed and behind bars in another.

"Verily," I choked out. "You have Verily."

Chenko pumped the air with over-enthusiasm. "Brilliant deduction!"

"She has *nothing* to do with this. Any of this," I said, but pebbles clogged my voice. "Just as she didn't back then."

"Back then?" Sawyer asked but was ignored by Chenko.

"I beg to differ, Miss Rhodes. Verily was seen at Kai's apartment a mere hour before the whole hoopla that was this afternoon."

"To convince me to stay safe!" I cried. "Not to help with the Saxons. She has no idea—she's an innocent victim in all of this!"

"Not since she met you," Chenko purred. "Seems you have a knack for getting innocent people in trouble."

"Leave her out of this." I turned to Sawyer. "We're not even friends anymore. She heard I was back in town and was worried about me, wanted to try one more time to get me out of this ... what did you call it? Situation? I was in. Please, let her go. *Please.*"

Sawyer remained unexpressive. Instead, he reopened my file, reading through with his pen running down the page. "I believe there's enough probable cause to keep her."

I tried standing but was hampered by the cuffs. In doing so, I appeared weaker than I was, *wanted* to be, and plopped down hard, staring at nothing but this man in front of me, Sawyer, who followed the law more than his gut.

"Look at the facts," I said. "Verily hasn't been involved in *years*. I've made no contact with her, not for months. Not since I started working for the FBI. You don't have probable cause, you barely have reasonable doubt"—I was throwing out all the law terms I could think of—"you can't keep using her against me like this."

Sawyer raised eyes his from the paper. "We've used her against you before?"

"No matter what you think," Chenko cut in. "We are following the law here, and that is leading us to what Verily knows. Like I said, if I have to arrest her, I will."

...If I have to plant evidence against her, I will. You understand, Scarlet? If you don't do what I want, what I ask of you, I won't make your life hell, I'll make everyone you love's lives an utter fire pit. I'll start with Verily and end with your dad. I'll make them all complicit with the Saxon crime family. I'll fill their bank accounts with extorted funds, I'll leave a drug trail a mile long. Get it? I. Will. Win.

Chenko learned from Gordon Saxon, and the same way the patriarch exacted his demands, Chenko outsourced his. I'd been his pawn these years, giving him cuts of the money I won, providing information I knew wasn't going to the FBI in order to reign in Trace, undercutting police work and making Chenko richer. Kai didn't know, Theo had no idea, and nor, it would seem, did Chenko's superiors have any clue just how dirty their agent was.

But two years was exhausting. Living two lives was soul-depleting. I studied the table underneath my hands, scratches and scrapes in the metal from all the suspects, the innocents, the arrested before me, and I couldn't handle it anymore.

I looked first to Sawyer, silently begging him to see Chenko for what he was, then held Chenko's stare when I said, "I want my lawyer. Now."

The FBI didn't press charges.

I employed the services of Louise Cognomi, a shark bite of an attorney that demanded I call her "Lou" whom I retained about a year ago, when my poker rooms were getting sketchy and Chenko was demanding more and more money.

She was half the height of Sawyer and argued on my behalf, stating in detail the amount of assistance I'd given the FBI (ever since signing her retainer, she'd kept thorough logs of my activities I provided her), and given the amount of danger I'd put myself in to get to the FBI's main goal—capturing the Saxons—which was completed, therefore there was no point to charging me as a fugitive, considering I'd done their bidding, kept none of the cash I won in boatloads for them (that they knew of), and wasn't paid anything for my services. Besides that, there were bigger fish to focus on, primarily, Gordon Saxon, and what charges could stick.

When it was clear he was going to get no further information out of me, Sawyer cut me loose, a steaming Chenko beside him.

I'd pay for this, I knew, as my cuffs were unlocked and I stepped out of the Federal Plaza building and into a small, stone courtyard until I reached Broadway to hail a cab. Worse, Verily might. Theo would.

Lou used her services and also argued Verily out of the interrogation room, who wasn't a suspect, wasn't under arrest, and was free to leave despite the cops' intimation otherwise. Verily was home safe, protected from the reach of the law, but not from the arms of Chenko.

I had to figure out some sort of protection for her. Needed to find out what was happening with Theo. I'd asked Lou to represent Theo, since she had famously represented Charlotte Miller a few years ago, and many others since. Surely, she could do something for Theo who was in just as dire straits.

But he had his own representation, she said with a cool, classic, eyes-to-the-ceiling approach. "These mafia types, they have honchos on retainers. This isn't Sax's first rodeo and it won't be his last. Better to leave it to the stiffs who know him best."

Still, I chewed on the inside of my cheek all the way to Kai's apartment. Picked my cuticles until they were bloody. I may be out of the woods—for now—but Theo wasn't. And in the end, he had nothing to do with the drug bust years ago, the exact reason the police pursued Trace. Yes, he conducted underground game rooms, took illegal cuts from gambling, was associated with the Saxon name, but his takes under the table couldn't be proven, his game rooms clean to any cop who searched it.

Too much. You've taken on too much, Letty.

I shook my head at the voice. If anything, this was the time to take on everything, because too many lives were on the line.

It's all because of you.

No. "No," I said again, aloud, drawing the attention of the driver.

I clamped my mouth shut, thinking maybe the cab I'd hailed was employed by the Saxons, too, and was in the middle of taking me to my final, bloody destination.

But, if the cabbie were doing as I asked, first thing to do was get Kai. Safety in numbers. Smartness in more than one head. Then, I wanted to see Verily, but knew that carried too much risk. She was better served without my presence anywhere near her, but perhaps Kai could help figure out a way to keep her safe.

At any moment, I expected sirens behind me, to be swarmed by multiple cop cars as Chenko blasted over the speakers that I was a killer.

Better sense took over and reminded me as to why I was so bull-headed in the interrogation room. Bo died on English soil. If Chenko were to admit what he knew, I'd be flown out of his jurisdiction and given over to the Scotland Yard. Completely out of reach. I'd gambled that he still needed me for something, or at the very least, didn't want me mouthing off that he was dirty to his superiors, whether or not they believed me.

And so, my mind clicked over to the idea that I was being tailed.

Paranoia isn't going to help you right now.

"Neither is your fucking lecture."

The cabbie glanced at me in the rearview again, and I snapped, "As if I'm the only crazy you've chauffered around in New York City today."

He kept his mouth shut.

When he turned onto Kai's street, I sifted through the clear ziplock bag the Bureau had given back to me, containing what they'd collected off my body, and I was pleased to note my cash was still there.

I was focused on counting the bills to ensure Chenko hadn't skimmed a few hundreds for himself when a sudden **CRACK** fissured across the side of my skull, black spiderwebs coating the backs of my eyes.

"*What—*"

The rest of my sentence was cut off by squealing breaks, a

screaming driver, and a high-pitched ringing in my ears with a sudden, immense spike of pain on the side of my head.

Seatbelt. I hadn't been wearing it.

And we'd crashed.

Crashed?

Holding one side of my head, I rose from my crumpled position in the backseat, facing smoke seeping through the vents and an unconscious cabbie.

"Sir?" I asked, reaching for him but wincing when I moved too suddenly.

No response.

I scanned the interior, then the exterior, to find the source of the accident. A biker, pedestrian, other car? NYC was full of random—

It's not random.

I counted one, two, three men approaching the vehicle. Not to help, which my scrambled brain initially thought, because they were walking too calmly—swaggering—and when they came close enough, I spotted dark, gleeful expressions.

"*Shit,*" I whisper-screeched, then made to shove open the car door closest to me.

It was slammed back with such force I nearly lost fingers.

"Not so fast, princess."

Chenko stood on the other side, his grin a macabre sneer against a clean-shaven face. "Allow me," he said through the window.

I'd scrambled to the other side, but there was another man blocking the door. Chenko lifted the lever and was inside, grabbing for me, in less than a second.

I yelped, kicked, ignored the spears of pain in my skull and the suspicious wetness seeping into the collar of my shirt.

"You fucked up my life," he said between swipes at my ankle.

His smile had turned feral, a sneer of a psychotic off drugs. "It's time to fuck up yours."

"Get *off*!"

His thick fingers clamped around my foot and pulled. The slippery leather of the seats did nothing to hinder my propulsion into his arms. When he wrestled me out, I scratched, bit and swiped, but his anger gave him fuel that was immune to a screaming victim.

"You really thought I was gonna let you go?" He said into my ear when he got me into a headlock. His forearm pressed against my throat dangerously. Spit hit the sensitive skin around my temple. "Leaving you to the law would've been pointless."

He dragged me to his waiting car, angled in the cut-off position he'd used to derail my cab.

"You know how it works at this point," he growled, then kicked my legs from under me, growing tired of my efforts. "Days, months of processing. You already knew I was dirty. So, now you know I exact black revenge. Fucking Quentin Sawyer doesn't know half the shit that goes on to collar gangsters. Or who needs to die."

"Let—me—" I gagged when his arm tightened.

"You won't be missed."

I crashed against his car when he threw me, the road tilting and growing frequency waves. I blinked, desperate to stay conscious.

"No one's here to save you now, stupid girl." He hooked my elbow, hard enough to leave bruises, and tossed me into the back of his car. "Your Romeo's incarcerated."

"No!" I cried instinctually, even though it would do no good. Chenko could *not* take me to the second location. Everyone knew once that happened, chances of surviving were ridiculously low.

When Chenko's back flew into the passenger side window so

hard it should've cracked, I'd been busy calculating my odds of crawling over the console and taking control of the car.

But the roar that sounded, the effervescent bubbling along the surface of my skin, paused everything going on in my mind.

I lifted off the cushions, pressing my hands to the glass to see better, because Chenko had regained balance and charged at whoever smacked him into the car. Punches sounded, grunts, then more men came—the other two who surrounded my cab— and dwarfed the person who'd taken on Chenko.

I grappled for the door, realizing it was on child lock, then crawled to the drivers' seat to get out. It happened so fast—the bodily *thwacks* of fighting, the shouts of war—that by the time I got out, I was worried I wouldn't have a chance to escape. That whoever came to my rescue would be outnumbered and Chenko would be back to trying to kill me.

The men with Chenko, they had to be Gordon's. No cops would be party to this...

Get out get out get out.

I shoved open the door into cool air, shivering at the sudden cold. The car rocked when another body was flung into it. My palms skidded over the side of the car as I launched myself away, but then—

"You *fucking* coward!" came the voice.

A sound I knew so well.

I whirled. "Theo?"

There he was, in the roadway with Chenko and his goons, fighting for his life through punches and flipping bodies, a man given incredible strength through rage.

Wondering *how did he get here* gave me no advantage. Instead, I ran toward the fight, scouring the asphalt for any dropped weapons, any objects I could use to help Theo.

There. By Chenko's ankle. A crowbar.

That must've been the reason for the showering of glass I felt in the cab. These were the things I thought of as I raced over, latched onto it, and raised it over my head in an arc.

My aim was true.

I hit Chenko in the center of his skull.

He crumpled at my feet and the crowbar dropped beside him soon after, *clanging* in the deserted street.

My chest heaved as if I'd run five blocks to Theo, and I looked from Chenko to the crowbar to Theo.

He stared back, two unconscious bodies on either side of him.

Now, I thought. Now was the time to ask. "How did you get here?"

He blinked, a beast-switch going off, and stepped around Chenko to me. "Take off your clothes."

I blinked. "What?"

"Take them off. Now."

His expression was pure hysteria—or, as hysterical as Theo could get. His mouth solid granite, the skin on his cheeks flushed pink, sweat dotting his temples. And that scar, flashing lightning in the middle of his face.

"You need to explain—"

"There's no *time*." He strode toward me and lifted my shirt. It wasn't in anger, or with jerky movements. Inexplicably, I considered it gentle during such confusing pandemonium. And in response, I complied, helping him peel off my shirt, help unbutton my shorts.

"Underwear, too."

"Theo, we're in the middle of the street."

"You're covered by the car. Quick." He stomped over to a crumpled form, peeling off the black clothing of the man who, while skinny, was still a man.

I tried to focus on covering my naked self and not on predicting Theo's moves and that it was more than likely he was going to use a body to seem like me in order to buy us time.

When Theo came back over, his arms heavy with clothing, I said, "We can't *kill* anyone."

"We don't have to." He helped pull a black t-shirt over my head. When what felt like cold paint hit my chest, I knew before Theo had to say, "He's already dead."

"Did you—"

"No. Chenko. In an effort to escape."

I glanced down at Chenko. "Did I...?"

"No." In a fervor, he grasped the sides of my face and laid a heavy, emotion-laden kiss on my lips. "You don't have to do that anymore."

The answer was in his gaze. "Theo, *no*. You can't keep killing."

"I'll do what I have to to get you out of this."

His attention tore over my shoulder. "Take her. Now."

I spun, denial already on my lips, but the determination stuck when I saw who it was.

"Kai," I said. A phantom necklace weighed heavy against my collarbone and the repercussions it caused. While Kai wasn't responsible, he was a conduit, but in this moment I couldn't reconcile the two—it was too confusing. I swayed on my feet.

"You're a cat's incarnate, Scar. You really are. Come on."

"I can't—"

"You *can*," Theo said at the same time Kai yelled, "Let's go!"

I turned back to Theo, feeling like I was being ripped away from something crucial, like I was leaving behind an appendage I'd have a horrific time living without.

"Go," Theo said, then again as Kai pulled me, "*Go*."

It killed me, but I went with Kai.

The two of us raced to the next block, then up a side street until we reached Kai's apartment. He ushered me in and scanned the immediate surroundings before shutting us both in.

When we'd reached his apartment and Kai double-locked

that door, I allowed myself the imaginative pleasure of leaping into Theo, my arms a vice against his neck, before we had to say what felt like our final good-bye.

"What will he do?" I asked Kai while standing in the middle of his living room. The shirt that wasn't mine fell heavy and wet against my chest.

Kai ran into his bedroom without answering, though he didn't have to. I heard the opening and shutting of doors, the sounds of efficiency, of continuing movement, while I remained bolted to the floor.

Gas, probably. Theo was going to light the car on fire, with all bodies in it, and make it appear like one of those bodies—the smaller one—was mine. DNA would eventually figure out it wasn't me, but that could be weeks, *months*, from now. Plenty of time to get me out of here and keep me away. For good.

My parents. Verily.

Theo.

Kai appeared with fresh clothing, a hoodie and basketball shorts, and he motioned for me to strip. "Shower first, honey, then put these on."

"I ... is there time?"

"I can't exactly transfer you anywhere with blood on your chest, so there will have to be. Hurry."

"Am I going into witness protection?" My voice sounded shrill.

"Of a sort," Kai replied, then pleaded with me to move. To keep going.

This was the end result of all my actions. Being ripped from my family for their safety, cutting off all contact with Theo and never seeing him, any of them, again. It wasn't a stranger's clothing making me feel heavy now. It was consequence.

And terror.

"Gordon isn't going to stop, is he?" I asked Kai when I

reached his open-air bathroom. "He's going to keep coming after me, even while in jail."

"He has people everywhere," Kai agreed. "Even my department isn't safe. No one can know where you are."

"Ever again?" My lower lip trembled.

Kai slumped, for mere moments his hurriedness disappearing. He came before me, his hands warm on my bare shoulders. "Let's take this one step at a time, okay? I know you're scared. But all everyone who loves you wants is for you to be safe. And we're gonna do that."

"I can't vanish," I said. "Please don't let me disappear like my sister."

"I won't," he said. His hands slid off my arms and I stepped in the shower.

Robotically, I cleaned while my mind spiraled. That moment on the roadway, with bloody bodies and broken cars in a silent street, was the last time I had with Theo. My last words were ... *I can't*, when really, all Theo did was *can*.

I couldn't be weak. After all I'd been through, now wasn't the time to fall apart. I'd leave to keep my family out of trouble, to keep attention away from Verily. If I were considered dead, Gordon would have no reason to come after them. Maybe Theo's reach went to DNA tampering, possibly Kai would be involved.

But then, Mom and Dad would have to think me dead. Verily would have to be at peace with the fact that she could never save me.

Could I do that to them? What was the alternative—have Gordon exact revenge through their torture?

There was no right choice.

Just as there was no rhyme or reason for me to still be in love with Theo.

Life had no treasure map.

A strange calm washed over me when I turned off the tap.

My movements were lithe and smooth as I combed my hair into a ponytail and pulled on Kai's clothing. I'd been appearing as someone else for years. Wearing others' clothing, donning opposite personalities, multiple hair colors, walking like a dame and hiding the true peasant underneath. It all started with the car crash and my sister, and it wasn't about to end here and now.

I desperately wished time would stop moving forward, so I could have time to process, to mourn. I blew out a long, drawn out breath, staring at myself in the mirror for a few precious seconds, allowing myself to say good-bye, for the last time, to Scarlet Rhodes.

Maybe she'd been gone for a long time before this.

Sifting through Kai's bathroom cabinet, I found what I needed. Kai was the type to play Sudoku while on the can, or do crosswords, or brainstorm active cases. With the small notepad and pen, I scribbled out a note, smearing the tears that stained the page with the palm of my right hand.

The squeak of the shower taps must have clued Kai in that I was done, because he was standing in the living room when I exited the bathroom, a full duffel bag at his feet, and—

And—

Theo at his side.

"Theo, I..."

"Don't," he said, then turned and paced the apartment.

"I'm gonna get some ice for your head, Scar," Kai said quietly.

I lifted my fingers to my temple. They came back sticky and red. "I'm fine."

"You're definitely not. Sit down before I slide a pillow near you in case you fall," Kai replied.

I rolled my eyes, then covered the dizziness that caused by jutting out a hip. "I'm not a damsel in dis—"

"Sit down, Scarlet."

Theo's snap drew both Kai's and my attention.

"You're hurt," he continued. Theo was a looming presence in the middle of the small main room, the windows behind him putting his form in blurred shadow. But I didn't need to see him in high definition to know his hands were burned, he was covered in ash. "And all your posturing will make it worse. We're already narrowly alive. Don't lessen our chances by becoming weaker."

"*Weak?*" I asked, shock turning my body rigid. "You think I'm some kind of liability?"

A finger twitch. That was all I received in answer.

I stalked over to the couch and sat, and hell if I was going to show any sort of pain by doing so.

"If you're mad at me, just say so," I seethed at him. "But don't cover it by tossing out lies, or statements that would make me so angry I'd forget the purpose of your smoke screen. That's right, Sax. I know you better than you think. Even after all this time."

Kai came around the side, gently laying ice covered in a dish-towel on my head until I took over.

Theo remained in stony silence.

"Fine," I said, leaning back with the ice pack. "I'll just go ahead and get to the point. How are you here? How'd you get out of custody?"

"It doesn't matter."

"It sure as fuck does," I said. "Considering how your unex-pected freedom just saved my life."

Of all the statements, I doubt he was expecting such frankness.

"You saved my life, Theo," I repeated. "You—those men back there..." I couldn't finish, so changed tactics. "Despite the very real fact that I betrayed you."

There. A brief flick of emotion, a line forming near his lips then disappearing. The most I could expect.

"I turned you in," I continued. "Your family, your brother and father. And I walked out of that precinct without a scratch. So, what made you chase me down and protect me?"

Come on, Theo, get *angry*.

"I didn't deserve it," I said. "Yet you helped me anyway. Why?"

"Scarlet..." Kai warned.

"*Why*, Theo?"

"You need to rest," Theo said carefully. "Once we move you—"

"I'll rest when you do."

"Then you'll sleep in your grave," Theo replied.

Like a time bomb that ticked to 0:00, I clued in. "That's how you got out of custody. You made a deal with them, too."

Theo startled, then said, "I had to, in order to be released."

"No," I said, all the while gathering my thoughts. "Before. You made a deal with them long before reaching out to me again. That's the only thing that makes sense. You ... you..." I stared at the floor, then back up to him when clarity hit. "What did they promise you? What did *Kai* promise you?"

"Scarlet," Kai said, "You've just been through some pretty epic events. Perhaps it's better if we regroup, then—"

"Don't treat me with kid gloves," I snapped. "Both of you, tell me the truth. Tell me what the hell that was out there. Why Chenko wanted me dead. Why *Gordon Saxon* put a hit on me."

When neither of them said anything, I stood, dropping the sack of ice to the floor. "One of you better speak."

"I love you."

Theo's words stilled the room. My chest wouldn't even dare rise and fall in such resulting, sweeping silence.

"I love you," he repeated, his eyes anchoring mine. "Which is why I felt like someone was removing my organs, one by one, when I realized what you'd done. Who you made a deal with, what you were willing to do."

Speechless, I stepped toward him, hand raised ... beseechingly. Terribly. Uselessly.

He used his own hand to halt any further steps. He said, "Which is why, despite all that, I understand the *why* in everything you'd done."

My lips parted, and while my vision pooled, blurred, I couldn't summon the strength to blink tears onto my cheeks.

"If I remember anything about my cocktail waitress, my girl, it's her loyalty. To those she cares for, she'd do anything to protect."

"You can't do this," I whispered through the thickness. "You can't treat me like this, knowing what I've done to you."

"And you should remember I do whatever the fuck I like," he replied, but it was with softness, a satin he'd only reserved for us, in dreary mornings, during dusky nights. "I'm not going to pretend I'm not angry, that I wouldn't want to pull one of these wooden beams off the ceiling and use it to stake something. Someone."

"That's been your entire life," I said. "Punishment. Solutions through beatings, rage."

"Yes," he said. "And it took whatever soul was left in me to walk away from you instead of stay and fight for you that night."

I shook my head. "Stupid. That's the word I come up with if you'd stayed. But it took me a really long time, this moment, to realize that."

"And yet I've put you in the same position you were two years ago. With your life at risk."

"Because I'm so innocent," I snapped. "I know the part I've played in this. But you still haven't told me how you're involved."

I love you. The words stayed near but were just far enough that they were difficult to grasp. With the time between us, the deaths, the torture, a *gun* in my hand mere days ago, pressed against a man's head. Love couldn't be forged within trauma like that. It shouldn't. I should be reeling, puddled in a corner, tremoring out the brutal realization that somebody died at my bidding, another man was betting on my death, and all the danger, all the reasons for my motives and the workings of my current fucked-up inner circle came back to...

Him.

"I'm telling you the truth," Theo continued. "I made a deal. I'd testify against my father, Trace, and I'd work on my younger brother to do the same, in exchange for immunity."

"Immunity?" I asked.

"Yes. I'm out because I swore I'd be a key witness."

"Wait, you came out of custody the *legal* way?"

Theo nailed me with a wry, chastising look. "Not everything I do has to be through questionable channels."

"But this puts you in incredible danger," I said. "Your father will be..."

"Rage-fueled. I know. But he's behind bars at the moment."

"You could die for this," I whispered.

"You were going to die for me. A second time. I couldn't simply let that go."

"But the whole Saxon crime syndicate..."

"Is falling apart at the seams," Kai chimed in. I'd forgotten he was there, so immersed was I in Theo's aura. "There was a hit on you for a reason. The fact that a *girl* could pick apart the Saxon dynasty, despite making deals with dirty agents, despite being watched thoroughly. You pissed Gordon Saxon off so badly he made mistakes. Starting with the assumption that you'd tap on that necklace the instant you saw the chance."

"He doesn't know me. He never will," I said.

"We're going to make sure of that," Kai said. "You feel okay? Can you start moving again?"

"Yes," I said, then with more firmness, "Yes. I can."

"Okay. Let's go," Theo said.

He offered his hand, and after slight hesitation, I took it.

The three of us made our way out of Kai's apartment and behind the building, where a nondescript black car idled. I supposed they'd give me verbal directions to tell me where to go. The first few hours of being dead would be through roadways, over bridges, a drive into the unknown and perhaps permanent.

My throat swelled.

"Here," I said to Kai and pressed the crumpled note I'd scrambled to write in the bathroom. "Give this to Verily to give to my parents."

Kai's mouth went grim.

"Please," I insisted. "Read it. It doesn't say much. Just that I love them and—and..." I collected myself, aware of Theo's intense scrutiny a few feet away. "And to never blame themselves. They have to know *something*, Kai. I can't leave them after everything they've been through—"

"All right," Kai said, tucking the note into his pocket. "I'll do it."

"Promise me."

"Yes. I promise."

"I'm coming back," I said, holding his stare steady as he passed me the duffel bag. Kai didn't answer, but there was no need for him to. *Forever* wasn't a term to be thought about right now. Only the present and getting out of here before Gordon Saxon blanketed his rage over NYC and upped the price on my head. To utilize the time Theo gifted by having me presumed dead.

In a fit of emotion, I threw my arms around Kai and pulled

him close. "This isn't goodbye." I buried my face in his neck. "This is thank you."

"I know," he said, rubbing my back with light swipes. It was clear he was holding it in as much as he could—the outburst, the need to come along, the desperation that this was our last shot at safety. "I love you, too. And I'll buy you as much time as I can."

I nodded, then let go.

Theo's presence was like a magnet, a hot pull against my skin, goosebumps prickling the flesh where he was closest. But in order to survive, I had to avoid it. If I leapt into his arms, if I held onto him, I wouldn't let go. I'd scream and cry and beg to stay with him. Just one more night. A few more moments with him and it'd be over.

I loved him, too.

Avoiding eye contact, I opened the drivers' door, but jerked back when it met resistance.

The source of the door not opening all the way was Theo, standing steady, his hand gripping the top.

His emotion was entirely in his voice when he said, "You're on the passenger side."

"What?" I looked to Kai like he'd have answers, but he seemed as confused as I was.

"Scarlet," Theo said, drawing my attention back. "Have you not figured it out yet?"

"I..." The duffel bag was a heavy weight at my feet. "No. I don't think so."

"I'm coming with you."

My heart flew sky-high at the same time I said, "No, you're not."

Theo cocked a brow. "I am."

"No," I said again, then pointed in the direction of Kai. "You have immunity, you need to testify to keep your father behind bars, to get Trace life in prison. You have things to do here, important matters."

"Do you really think I'm going to wait in some city apartment for my moment to testify? I'll be killed just for stepping out for some coffee."

I pursed my lips.

"It's the best cover," he said. "You presumed dead. Me in the wind. My father's syndicate will never die. He has people, even now, crafting a list to make witnesses disappear, to destroy any evidence, to essentially make it so he's the cleanest businessman there ever was to be dragged to the precinct."

"But..."

Theo grabbed my hand, his dry callouses like rubbing velvet the wrong way against my skin. "Perhaps the trial will be successful, or my father and brother will take a plea. But I am not about to bet my odds against something so unsure. Not when it comes to your life. So, I'm going with you. I'll stay with you. Return when I have to testify. Then leave again."

I shook my head, dumbfounded over the probability that I was no longer in this alone. That Theo Saxon, a man I'd pushed out of my mind for so long, was waltzing back in to drive me off into the sunset.

I shoved at his shoulders, and he fell back, shocked.

"You do *not* get to do this!" I shouted at him. "After all we've been through, after the years you spent giving me *no* hope for us, you do not get step in at the last minute and promise me everything."

My voice rose and fell, hitched, broke, and I blinked crazily, catching tears in my lashes but most falling onto my cheeks. "I have no hope left," I breathed out roughly. "You're not allowed to give me that kind of flame again. You can't. You *can't—*"

"Scarlet."

Theo rounded the open door and pulled me to his broad

chest, the smell of him all-consuming and *melting*, but I pushed away. Then pushed again. But he wouldn't let go. So I pounded with closed fists, but they opened, went limp, as he murmured in my ear and I sobbed.

"I'm not making the same mistake again," I heard him say. "I'm with you. You understand? You are my hope, Scarlet. *You.* And I'm not letting you lose anymore."

"Theo," I cried into the skin of his neck. "There's no chance..."

"There is." He stroked back my hair, the ponytail mussed from my fight. "And goddamn it, we're going to find it."

It was almost physical, the way my lungs expanded yet it was my heart that filled. A stitch falling off, no longer needed, because that section—the broken, jagged piece left by my sister and clotted by Theo's departure—was healing. And with compelling clarity, I didn't search for ways to reopen it. I folded into his embrace instead. And dared to believe.

"Guys," Kai said. "You have to go. *Now.*"

Kai eyed Theo as we parted, and he squeezed my hand when I passed him to get into the car. "You sure about this?" he asked Theo over the car's hood.

"Never been more so," Theo said, then folded into the vehicle and started the engine.

I glanced through the window at my friend, a man who'd become my partner in more aspects of my life than I thought possible. I pressed a hand to the glass, and he lifted his.

Until we meet again, I mouthed to him.

Kai sniffed, then swiped under his nose. It was the only sign of upset he gave before he smacked the side of the car, giving Theo the go ahead. Theo made a three-point-turn, and we drove out of the alley-way, through the avenues, and over the Brooklyn Bridge, Manhattan glittering its morning dew over the river.

I covered Theo's hand over the stick shift. He flipped his over and held tight.

Whatever happened next, whoever I had to become, it wasn't going to be alone this time. We were in it.

Together.

THE OCEAN WAS the deepest azure I'd ever seen, a close second to the color of Theo's eyes.

Clad in his button-down shirt, I turned away from our tiki hut's small patio and into the bamboo styled room, where Theo was just finishing up our breakfast. His scar was tamed today with a light application of my foundation, the closest we came to disguising his distinguishing mark from curious—or shrewd—stares.

"We should see the ruins today," I said to him as I resumed my position, curling my legs under me on the couch beside him.

"Have you not gotten your fill of the Mayan temples yet?" Theo asked, gliding his finger down the opening of my shirt. "Because I can think of a few other things we could do."

"We already did that," I said, laughing as I pulled in the collar, dislodging Theo's hand. The sound felt brilliant in my throat, a musical instrument that had been occurring more and more lately.

"And?" He pushed aside his empty plate, his grin sexy and mischievous. "Let's do it again. And again."

"We *can't*." I laughed again and pushed him away. "I have an appointment, remember."

"Cancel it."

"I already have. Twice."

He nuzzled my neck. "Third time's a charm."

"Mister *Channing*," I managed to say within my moan. "If I don't go to this one, they'll never allow me to book there again. And I need to."

He growled but lifted his head. "Fine, Mrs. Channing."

Theo's cell rang, and he grumbled as he rose to get it. "Seems you're not the only one," he said.

I smiled at his back, those delectable muscles between his shoulder blades rippling as he walked to the other side of our small suite to retrieve his cell.

I picked at a cluster of grapes as he answered.

"Yeah?" he said.

Silence.

I looked up, primed for what had been eight months of waiting. After leaving New York City, we boarded a flight with new passports, provided by Kai, to the Philippines and have been bouncing around ever since. When news of the workings of the Saxon trial reached us—plea deals were still being negotiated, if taken at all—we'd unobtrusively moved closer and were now in Tulum, Mexico, the nearest we'd ever been.

Initially charged with murder, Gordon Saxon faced eleven felony charges, the worst being the killing of me, Scarlet Rhodes. But once the dental records came back as not a match to my supposed body, that charge would likely be dropped and news of the possibility I was still alive would reach his ears. But he still had those other bodies to contend with, and kidnapping, false imprisonment, conspiracy to commit murder.

Trace faced multiple counts of assault with a deadly weapon along with conspiracy to commit murder. Drea, his latest victim, refused to testify, but that didn't prevent the evidence from mounting against them both.

Would Trace and Gordon get off with the minimum felony charges? That was a large possibility, hence my new moniker of Madison Channing, with my husband, Darren Channing, currently enjoying our "honeymoon." But with the small chance of their being jailed, I could come back to city and see my parents face-to-face, rather than secret notes and coded postcards passed to them hinting that I was okay.

I'd come to accept that I'd likely never return as Scarlet Rhodes, at least not officially. I'd made an enemy of the Saxons—that domino falling years ago—and they held grudges. But with Theo by my side, it didn't feel as brutal an axe. As these months went by and he stayed, I spent less time jerking away at night, searching for his form beside me, and more curling up in the bends and folds of him as he slept, tucking his arm around my waist.

Trust wasn't something given freely, and it was taking time to know each other's habits, to get used to the fact that we were together and weren't parting any time soon ... an upgrade to our relationship I'd never expected. Were we perfect? Of course not. We fought about ludicrous things like who used the last of the toothpaste and what the chances were of a Saxon assassin finding me and exacting Gordon's revenge. Usually things not reserved for normal, average, happy couples.

The Theo I'd known and crafted in my head during those missing years was constantly planning, organizing, betting and on the move. This guy, however, spent all his time with me, relaxed and easy save for calls like these that flipped him back to the man he was.

But, we were healing together. Or trying to.

"Okay. Thanks," Theo said, then clicked off.

"Well?" I asked as he approached, the phone hanging loose in his hand.

"There's likely a plea deal with my father. Ten years."

"That's *it?*" I rubbed my hands on my knees, expelling nervous energy.

"More than I thought," Theo said. "As for Trace ... I'm sure he'll also work out a deal."

"Damn," I muttered.

"We can do this," Theo said, massaging my neck. "Whatever happens, I'll keep you out of danger."

"Now that I've honed my abilities to *avoiding* villainous situations rather than running to them, I'm doing pretty good on that, too," I said.

He smiled. "I do appreciate the foresight you had in creating your own account in the Cayman's."

I popped a grape into my mouth and savored the juice popping over my tongue. "The government didn't deserve *all* my winnings. Still, it's a pittance compared to yours."

Theo kept that ingenue grin on his face. "We're comfortable."

I used that moment to glance at his watch. "Shit," I said and jumped up. "We're going to be late."

"I don't think this place operates like the city you're used to," Theo called behind me, but I ignored him, pulled on a light sundress, finger-combed my hair, then grabbed his hand and pulled him out of the hut.

When we got to the hospital, my pulse was noticeably pounding against my wrists. Theo rubbed at the sensitive spot underneath one of my palms, providing tickling reassurance.

"It'll be fine," he said.

"I'm not sure what the definition of *fine* should be anymore," I said as we walked into the entrance, the tropical breeze lifting my hair and heating my neck. "Like, should it be hey, we're alive, so we're fine. Or hey, we can live out the rest of our lives under fake IDs, so we're fine. Or hey, we can still—*oh!* Do you have the postcard I meant to mail? I can't believe I forgot it—"

"I have it," Theo said, rubbing my back. "I dropped it into the post box half a mile back. You must not have noticed. Your parents should get it in a few days."

"Good." I added, as we strode into air conditioning.

"And Verily's. I got that one, too."

I deflated, grabbed his hand. "Thank you."

He kissed the top of my head in answer.

We got to the waiting room, gave my—new—name, and much to my chagrin, were seen immediately.

When I was shown into an examination room, Theo came with me. It was painted pale green with a pot of local flowers on a shelf below a nondescript abstract painting of different colored brush strokes. It was a room meant to be as calming as a doctor could make it, considering why most people came to a doctor in the first place. I focused on the white roses peppered throughout the vase, taking it as further motivation to calm down. Those were Cassie's favorite blooms. If she was here, then I'd be okay.

I was asked to get into a hospital gown, which Theo had to help me do since my fingers were shaking too much.

"I hate hospitals," I muttered pointlessly.

Theo lifted my chin as I bent down to pull off my shoes and kissed me. "It'll be over soon."

"Yeah."

I slid onto the table, legs dangling. In moments, the doctor came through.

"Hello," he said while flipping through a clipboard. "I'm Dr. Gonzales. I'm told you'd like an IUD inserted today?"

I nodded. When he didn't look up, I cleared my throat and said, "Yes."

He set the clipboard near the sink and went to wash his

hands. "We have to do a urine sample first. To rule out pregnancy."

"Yes, I gave it to the nurse already," I said. "It's just been difficult being on time with my birth control pills, you know? I'd rather have a better solution. Th—my husband and I, Darren, move around a lot, so this seems the best thing to do for ourselves."

Theo squeezed my thigh. I told myself to shut up. Stupid nerves.

"We're on our honeymoon," Theo added. "As you can imagine..."

Dr. Gonzales laughed. "Yes, yes. All right, let me see if the nurse has your results. The IUD will start working immediately upon insertion, so you won't have to worry about that. I'll be just a minute."

When Dr. Gonzales disappeared, I loosed a breath.

"You're doing great," Theo said in the chair beside me.

"How hilarious would it be if I'm pregnant," I guffawed. Theo cut a look at me saying, *don't you dare put that out into the universe.*

"I'm kidding," I said, taking my turn and rubbing his shoulder.

Dr. Gonzales returned, and the nurse who did my admittance tests was with him, pushing some contraption on wheels into the room with us.

"Mind if we do a quick ultrasound?" he asked. It was in the same tone he greeted us with, which meant normal people wouldn't take issue with it. I, however, went on high alert.

"Why? Is there something wrong?"

"Not exactly." Dr. Gonzales continued his chipperness. The nurse smiled kindly. "We may not be able to do the procedure. The urine analysis says you might be pregnant."

My jaw dropped.

Theo popped off his chair like he'd popped off a gun. "Excuse me?"

"Indeed." Dr. Gonzales clapped his hands. "Let's take a look and confirm, shall we?"

I turned to Theo like he could somehow snap his fingers and *poof* us out of there, but he returned my stare with just as useless a look. For two people who got themselves into and out of sticky situations with the flair of the lucky, in this moment we were buffoons.

Before I knew it, my legs were splayed, a white sheet draping over my thighs. What looked like a dildo with warm goo smeared over it was gently inserted into my hoo-ha. The nurse dimmed the lights and I automatically went in search for Theo. He spotted my flailing hand and grabbed it, keeping close to my side and squinting at the small monitor in front of us.

"Mmk," Dr. Gonzales muttered. "Here we ... this won't take a minute. My silence doesn't mean anything's wrong, it just means I'm taking a look and assessing."

"Okay," I said, but it was more of a question. Was I meant to be worried at his silence? Which was more anxiety-inducing, finding a fetus or finding something else?

"Uh-huh, there we go. See?" Dr. Gonzales pointed to the screen, his glasses flashing against the light as he looked from it to us. "A heartbeat."

"Holy motherfucking Jesus Christ," Theo said.

Both the doctor and nurse jolted, and I didn't bother to smooth out the situation. I was just as gobsmacked as him.

"Yep and let me see ... oh yes." The doctor moved his hand to show another part of my womb. "Both of their heartbeats are going strong."

I froze. "I'm sorry. *Both?*"

"Sure as sugar, dear," the nurse chimed in. "You're having twins."

"They're about seven weeks along," the doctor added. Two tiny lima beans were showcased in black and white on the screen, what seemed like lights inside them flickering in-and-out in a rapid-fire rhythm. Heartbeats.

I looked at Theo. It was unclear if I still had the capacity to blink. Theo looked like a hornet had stung him between his eyes.

"Darren..." I said.

He closed his mouth. Then opened it. Then closed it. His Adam's apple bobbed. "We're having twins," he repeated. Much slower.

"We're having twins," I seconded. "Identical?"

"I'm seeing only one placenta, so yes. Identical twins. We can't discern the gender via ultrasound until about twenty weeks, however, unless you want to do a blood test in a few weeks to find that out. Congratulations!" Dr. Gonzales smiled broadly, made more garish when the nurse switched the lights back on.

The spotlight was on me, but instead of flinching back, I found myself tracing my stomach, picturing a rounded curve and the tiny fireflies fluttering around inside.

Theo bent and laid his lips on my forehead, murmuring, "we're fine."

"Fine," I echoed and met his eyes. "As in, our family will be fine."

There were no windows in the examination room, no natural wind or puffs of air. Yet, a single rose petal fell from the bouquet and landed on the spot on top of my heart.

Start over with these new sisters, Letty. I'll love you forever.

I sincerely hope you enjoyed Scarlet and Theo's journey through the New York City underworld. They are two characters who have stayed with me long after I finished their story, and if they impacted you in any way as well (good or bad!) I would love if you could leave a review. Those little golden stars are what motivate me to keep writing!

As a special thank you for being such a valued reader, flip the page for a sneak peek at the first book in a new, romantic suspense series, *From This Day Forward*.

Happy reading! xoxo Ket.

I made a big mistake.

It was too tempting to fall into old habits and accept the email request to explain his version of events, even though it was super obvious what Trevor's side of the story was. But, in typical Trev fashion, his plaintive tone won out and he managed to morph and spin our conversation until somehow I agreed to dinner.

Damn it, this would be the final time.

Trev and I were done, and if he needed a few minutes to unload and plead and reminisce about our past, fine, but his chances of success were about as likely as my customers expressing gratitude through gratuity.

I adjusted my black tank top as I poured another draft for another dude who thought his incredible come-ons would be a sufficient substitute for a tip, but you'd think I'd just flashed him my breasts, the way he was gobbling up the show. Between the constant text buzzes against my butt and the dapper compliments of college boys wanting me to lubricate their throats and their dicks, my evening shift couldn't get any better.

Trev: Babe.

"I'll take a Jack and Ginger, sweetie."

Trev: You're the love of my life.

"Just a draft, darlin'. Is it fresh? No wait, are you fresh? Haaaa."

Trev: You have me feeling like a bastard right now.

"Twelve bucks," I said to the newest patron, then cocked my head. "But my tits are worth at least a hundy."

College Boy Number 25 lost his concentration on my chest. "Wait, what? *Twelve* bucks for a beer?"

I added the sweetest smile. "Welcome to New York City craft beer college life. Cash only."

"Son of a...." But he handed over a twenty and I fished his change out of the register behind me. When I plopped it down in front of him, he left nothing behind on the varnished bar but a grease stain before he went back to his group of friends and hollered at the football game on the mounted TV.

Sighing, I moved onto the next guy, and then to the next round, as Saturday night filled up the small, off-campus dive bar called Oliver Blue, affectionately and originally called Oliver's by the regulars and staff. We played no blues music. On rare, good nights I could bring back two-fifty in tips, and after working here for two years I could run these boys just fine. Normally their hooting and wasted come-hithers didn't bother me and I truly admired their belief that drunken slurs of "you're fuckin' hot. You give me beer whenever I want it" would have me humping them on the bar. But today didn't have the usual beginning, and thus I wasn't in the mood to call anyone out on their habitual sleaze.

Underneath the bar in a tiny cubby hole I called my "locker" sat my tote bag, and within that tote bag curled my recent essay from my writing class on medieval culture, and more specifically, Dante. Yep, the man who described the nine circles of Hell was the main focus of this spring semester's class. I thought it'd be a bird to pass, as most idiots do when it comes to writing courses.

Wrong, Beauregard. Oh so *wrong*.

The professor was a nut. A smart one who dug up his jollies by soaking his class with his favorite color: Red. My paper had flesh wounds all over the place, bleeding points of *where is the continuity of Western tradition here?* And *how is this applicable?* And, my favorite part, a glaring, bold, gash of a **C minus** in the top corner.

As I strode past the locker, I gave it a kick with my heel.

My grades were slipping, and with that downward spiral would go my summer internship at Madison PR, a position I'd been gunning for ever since I entered these city streets as a freshman. I *couldn't* go back to Wyoming jobless and prospect-less, otherwise my parents would employ me at their grocery market and Emme Beauregard, the girl who shot out of her small town with cannonball accuracy and wowed all her relatives by saying she was going to make it in the big city, would spend her life bagging groceries, marrying her high school sweetheart and finagling six kids.

That storyline didn't contain enough fervor to complete the future that I'd been fighting for for years. It might not look like I was, standing here in a dank bar which I was pretty sure housed asbestos in the wooden beams above and *definitely* human excretions on the floor. But this was mine: I moved here, took control, and made this chunky soup-like part of New York City my own.

However, I would be remiss if I didn't account for the high school sweetheart that followed me.

Trev: Em, talk to me!!!!

I shoved my phone back into my jeans' pocket, finding renewed focus in mixing drinks and pouring drafts. I loved Trev very much, but it turned out he didn't love me. For how could you truly care for a person when you're busy banging her coworker?

I discovered this doozie when I picked up the wrong cell

phone at work two weeks ago. We tended to leave them lying near the cash register so we could tap in quick texts, check Instagram, Snapchat, the usual, as we pretended to spend extra time counting out change. Laurie and I had a similar gold case and neither of us bothered with passcodes or fingerprints due to the necessity of being quick part. So, without really concentrating and therefore not noticing the kittens-in-a-basket background, I swiped open the phone, opened messages, found Trevor and—

Totally recognized it. Was very familiar with it, actually, right down to the pinkish tone and silky feel to the tiniest of bumps near the tip.

My boyfriend's penis.

All well and good, except he never sent me cock shots, because honestly, what was the point when I could just be home in an hour and see it in person?

It took me a second to understand that while odd, it wasn't completely off-putting, because I liked his penis, enjoyed it really, and maybe he was trying something new in our six year relationship. But then the gasp came beside me and a tanned forearm flew into my vision and yanked the thought right out of my hands.

"That's my phone!" Laurie said, and tucked it into the back of her denim skirt.

I froze for a moment, empty hand dangling in midair, as a horrible dawning smoothed out every single one of my features. "I'm sorry, your phone?"

"Yeah," she said, then pointed to the other gold-cased phone beside the cash register. "There's yours."

"My bad," I said, and she wheeled away, blond waves arcing gracefully, her perky butt now my focal point. I added, "But do you mind finishing off that text I was writing to Trev asking him if he's bringing home any syphilis by sticking his dick in you?"

That got the attention of the people hanging by the bar, as

well as Laurie's. And infuriating tartlet that she is, she didn't bother to deny it. "How can I, when it feels *so good?*"

I wish I could say I latched onto her hair extensions and spun her into the bottles lined up behind us, shattering both their glass and her stupid face, but I needed this job. So instead I replied, chin up, "He's yours. Enjoy listening to him sucking on his teeth at night," and followed that up with a simple text to Trevor.

We're done.

Fast forward two weeks, one hundred and fifty text messages and eighteen emails from Trev later and here I was, working side by side with Laurie, hiding a C average for this semester and possessing B-cup boobs that while apparently nice to look at, weren't gaining me any currency.

"Hey, mind if I order?"

...and add six more hours with drunk college sophomores and their bottomless beer bellies to that list.

I drew on the brightest smile I could and met my new customer's eye. "What'll it be?"

"Just a beer. Yuengling, I guess."

I grabbed a glass but glanced back at the guy a couple of times as I poured. He seemed different. Way too sober for one, and a little bit older than what usually babooned through this place. Scruffy, sandy hair, light eyes, angular jaw. I topped off his draft and slid it in front of him. He left fifteen dollars on the wood and then proceeded to knock my pants off.

Clear green eyes that punched right through me and a tiny chin cleft I wanted to press my thumb into, all paired with a head tilt and a gentle lift of fingers as thanks. As such, I inched away from him as soon as I professionally could.

I greatly disliked anything charming enough to bemuse me, because that kind of talent only came from those who knew how to use it.

He said, "Do I know you from somewhere?"

Never mind. "I don't think so."

"No, I mean it." He eased closer. "You're familiar, not simply a lady I'm tipping a whole three dollars to talk to me."

My lips twitched.

"We have a class together, I think. Dante in Modern Times with Professor Harper. Right?" he asked.

Blegh. "Yeah, I suppose we do."

Though now that he mentioned it, he did look familiar. I had the sneaking suspicion he was the tousled head of hair three rows and two seats in front of me that I played imaginary lasers with, also known as a one-player game where I pretended my eyes were lethal red beams that shot into his skull every time he flashed a paper with **A :)** in the top right corner.

"I'm Spencer. Spence," he said, holding out his hand, which against my better judgment, I took. It was calloused, warm, completely dry and unlike the usual bar hands I shook that were damp and freezing.

"Emme, like the awards statue," I said, and followed up with, "Except with an E at the end instead of a Y."

Then cringed.

"How'd you do on the paper?" he asked.

"You mean, that whole 'how are Dante's literary conclusions related to the social development of Western civilization' thing?" I waved him off. "Totally aced it."

"Wow." Spence rested his forearms on the bar. "I never knew staring at a phone for entire lectures would be the secret sauce of success."

I zeroed in on him with squinty eyes. "I'm very busy looking stuff up."

"Uh-huh. And when your head falls back, are you drooling out the answers to Dante's universe?"

I bent to his level, our elbows almost touching. "You are a fairly presumptuous asshole, you know that?"

He grinned, and it was even better close up. "Harper's a tough one. You basically have to tape your eyelids open and record his lectures ten times over to score any kind of A in his class. There's an idea. Maybe that's what you can do with your phone. In between nap time, of course."

I pushed off the bar and answered someone's yell for another pitcher by grabbing an empty jug, but had the time to retort, "Is that what you do to maintain your coveted position near Harper's ass?"

Spence followed me to the draft station. "You noticed, huh?"

"You detected my drool. It's only fair I catch the A-plus-pluses Harper lays out on your desk before you purse your lips."

His brows furrowed with emphasized contrition. "Don't hate me because it works."

"Hey, kiss ass proudly. You said it yourself, his classes are the first circle of hell."

"Let me help you."

Spence seemed as surprised to have said it as I was to have heard it. I fumbled the pitcher, foam spilling over the sides. "What makes you think I need any?"

"Your face."

I barked out a laugh. "Excuse me?"

"As soon as I mentioned the D-name this whole bar came under a storm cloud, and you know where the eye of that looming hurricane was? Right there." He pointed toward my nose. "Big ol' frowny face."

This time my laugh was coupled with a shake of my head. "Believe me, buddy, this squall has been forming for weeks now."

"Then let me at least lighten it up a bit," he said, kindly. Jesus Christ—*endearingly* was the better word.

I set the pitcher on the bar. Phantom hands went for it, green bills were left after it, but I barely noticed. "Are you offering to tutor me?"

Spence shrugged. "Yeah, I guess I am."

Where was the catch, I wondered, because rarely was anything offered so guilelessly. I glanced down at my breasts, wondering if they had more power than I gave them credit for. "I can't accept and give nothing in return. I'll pay you."

Spence dragged his teeth across his lower lip, hiding a smirk. "There's no way I'd tutor for free."

I snorted, readying for another eye roll. "Of course not."

"I do it part time, especially for Harper's class," he said, then winked. "Unfortunately, you're not my first."

"But I'm unique enough for you to notice me two rows behind you scrolling through my phone."

"No, that would be your ringing entrance a few weeks ago," he said, and I winced at the memory of rushing in late and my metal water canteen rolling under the seats. "But apparently I am, for you to know what row I'm in."

Damn it. I covered his win by tucking my long hair back and fishing for ice.

Laurie picked that time to bump into me, scattering cubes everywhere. She snarled, "Some of us are working here."

I ignored her, but Spence sent a wry glance her way as she passed. "She seems nice."

"Feel free to forget to tip my boyfriend's mistress often," I said.

His eyebrows shot up.

"So tomorrow afternoon then?" I asked, and dumped ice into three glasses.

"Uh. Sure," Spencer said, and backed away from the bar as I busied myself. "Library at three?"

"Great. Make sure you bring all your work to date. I want to see if you're as good as advertised," I said and turned around to find the vodka, but tossed over my shoulder, "I ain't paying until you prove your worth."

"Emme, believe me, I am *that* good," he said to my back, but I sensed the confidence, the utter sexiness of his conviction, in those words.

I stifled my amusement though he couldn't see and didn't respond. By the time I finished mixing and plopped the vodka-sodas in front of their new owner, Spence was long gone.

"Thank you. But one's for you," someone said in front of me.

I blinked a few times, focusing on the present and the guy standing across the bar. "I'm sorry?"

"I got one vodka-soda for you," he said, and gently pushed one back toward me. He seemed to redden under my silence. "I mean...that's what girls drink, right? Vodka-soda? Because of the low calories?"

While his voice was soft, almost high, the guy was very tall, lanky even, with carefully slicked-back dark brown hair, huge almond eyes of the same color, and a smile that was somehow made awkward with his cosmetically straight, bleached teeth. His stare wouldn't leave my face as he waited for my answer, and mine wouldn't leave his. There was an intense earnestness emitting from him and the oddest sensation came over me, almost as if I were a white mouse caught in a snake's cage.

Which was ridiculous. Many people, drunk and sober alike, offered to buy me drinks and this guy was no different. I added a wink. "Honey, I'm a straight whisky kinda gal."

"Oh." Flustered, he cupped both drinks, his large hands dwarfing the glasses. His knuckles went white. "Let me get you that, then."

I capped off my wink with a smile. "I don't drink on the job, but thank you."

There was no time for him to respond because someone else wanted a rye-and-ginger, and then another three pints of beer, and so it went. Throughout my service, the guy didn't move, despite the many elbows and snide comments encouraging him to do so.

And during the entirety of my shift, I felt his eyes on my back.

Corrupt Empire Duet

Underground Prince

Paper Doll

Vows Duet

To Have and to Hold

From This Day Forward

Ketley Allison has always been a romantic at heart. That passion ignited when she realized she could put those dreams into words and her soul into characters. Ketley was born in Canada, moved to Australia when she was thirteen, to California when she was twenty, and finally to New York to attend law school, but most of that time was spent sitting in coffee shops and wine bars thinking of her next book.

Her other passions include coffee, wine, Big Macs, her cat, and her husband, possibly in that order.

<u>Sign up</u> for Ketley's newsletter to receive a FREE full-length book by her!

And join her new readers' group, Ketley's Crew, on Facebook! She'd love to meet you there!